Lazarus

Lazarus

A CHRISTIAN HISTORICAL NOVEL

DAVID G. FISCHER

Cover & Interior Design by Colleen Sheehan

ISBN (paperback): 979-8-9860843-0-5

Library of Congress Control Number: 2022906375

First printing edition 2022.

This book is dedicated to my wife, Laura, who has given me more love and support than I could ever imagine or deserve. She is a faith-filled Christian with whom I look forward to spending the rest of my life, both here on earth and throughout eternity in heaven.

This book is also written in memory of the late Pastor Eldon Weisheit, a true servant of God, brilliant author, and someone I considered a dear friend.

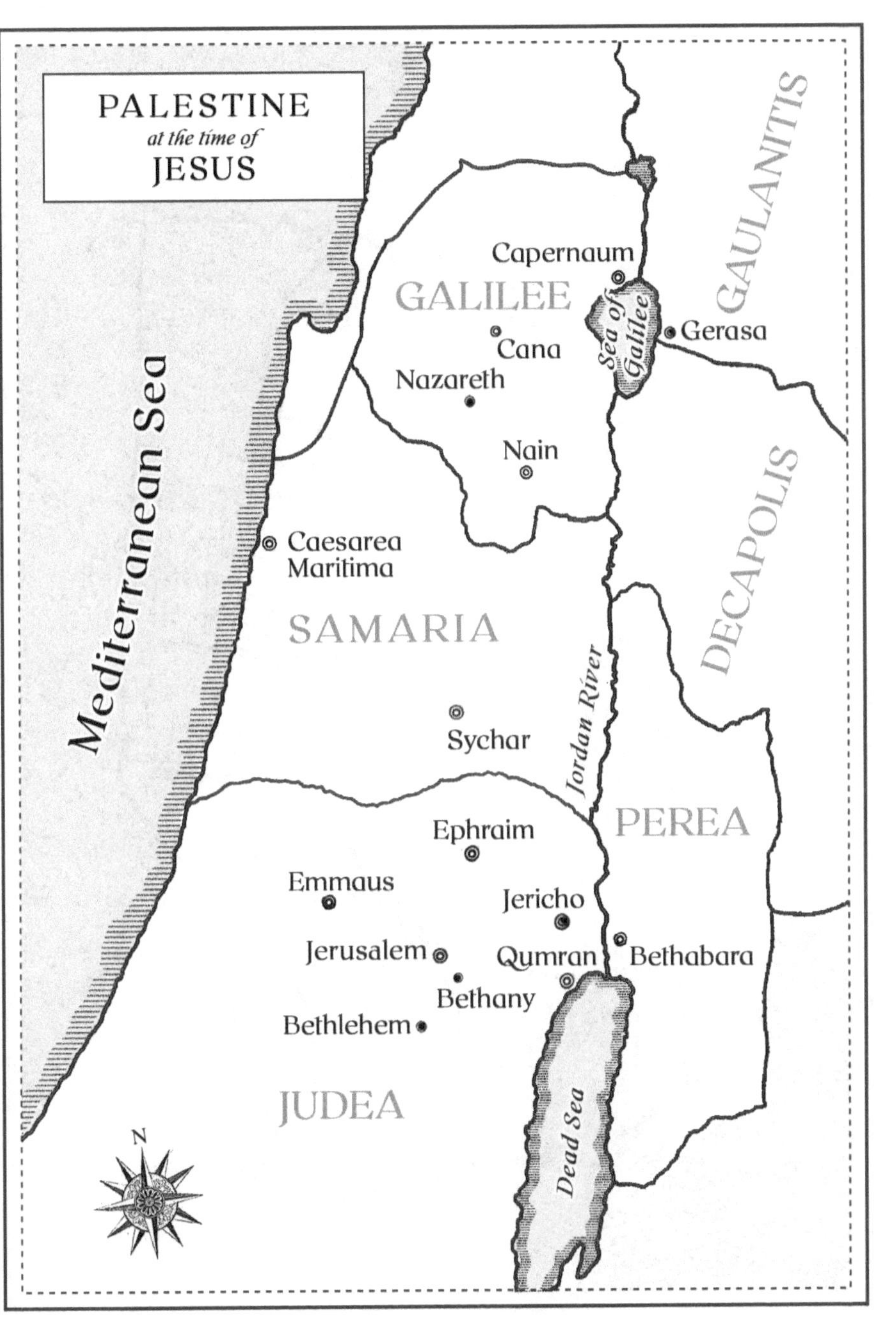

PALESTINE
at the time of
JESUS
Mediterranean Sea
GALILEE
Capernaum
Sea of Galilee
Cana
Nazareth
Nain
Gerasa
GAULANITIS
DECAPOLIS
Caesarea Maritima
SAMARIA
Jordan River
Sychar
Ephraim
PEREA
Emmaus
Jericho
Jerusalem
Qumran
Bethabara
Bethany
Bethlehem
JUDEA
Dead Sea
N

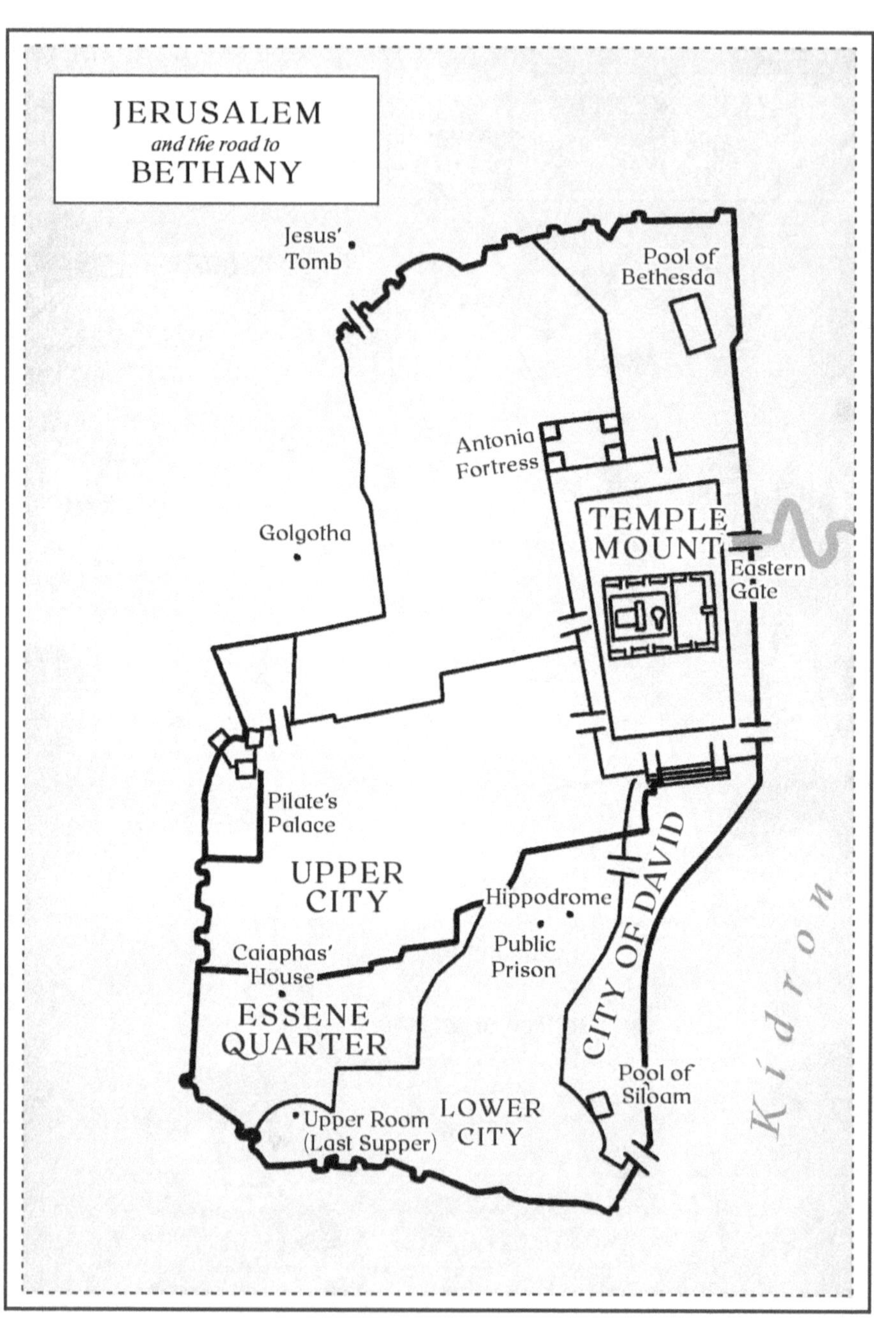

JERUSALEM
and the road to
BETHANY

Jesus' Tomb
Pool of Bethesda
Antonia Fortress
Golgotha
TEMPLE MOUNT
Eastern Gate
Pilate's Palace
UPPER CITY
Hippodrome
CITY OF DAVID
Caiaphas' House
Public Prison
ESSENE QUARTER
Pool of Siloam
Upper Room (Last Supper)
LOWER CITY
Kidron

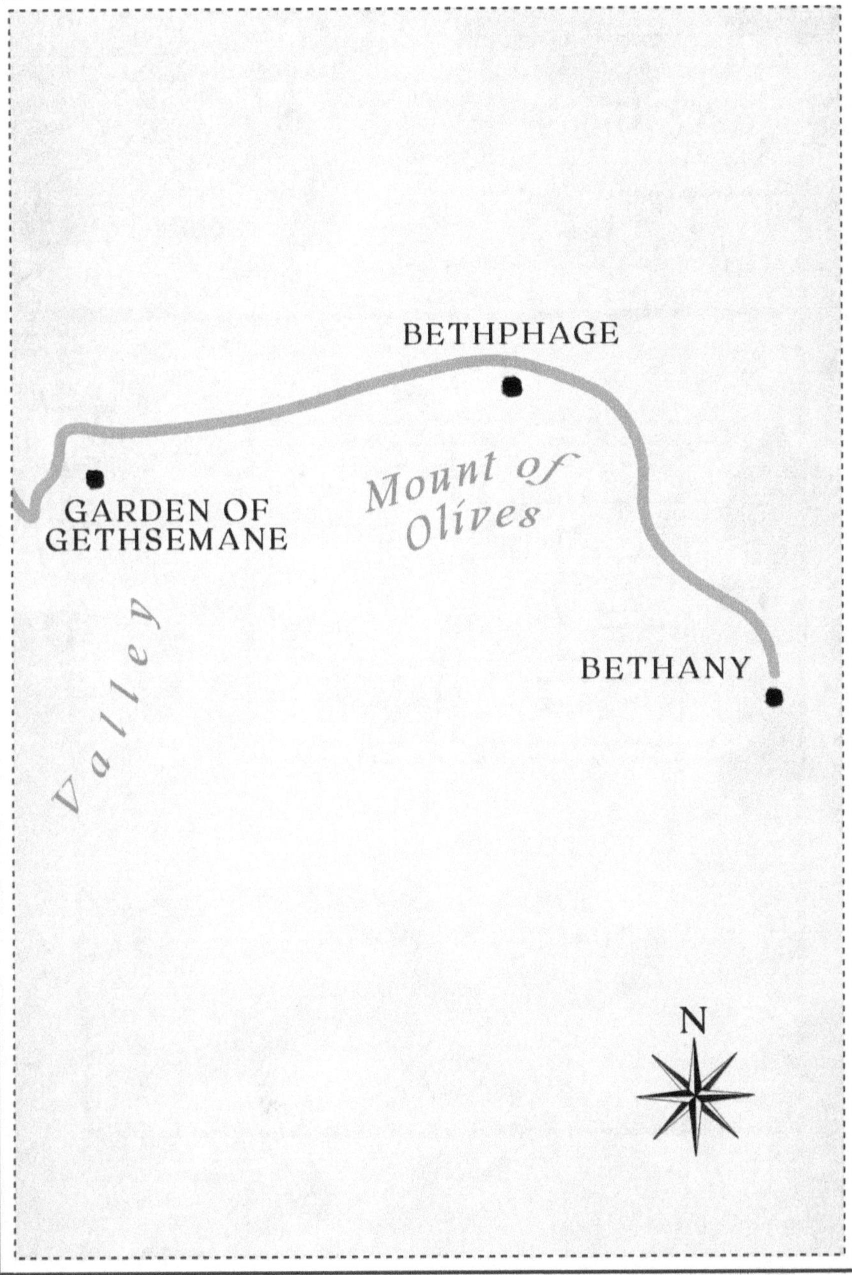

BETHPHAGE
GARDEN OF GETHSEMANE
Mount of Olives
Valley
BETHANY
N

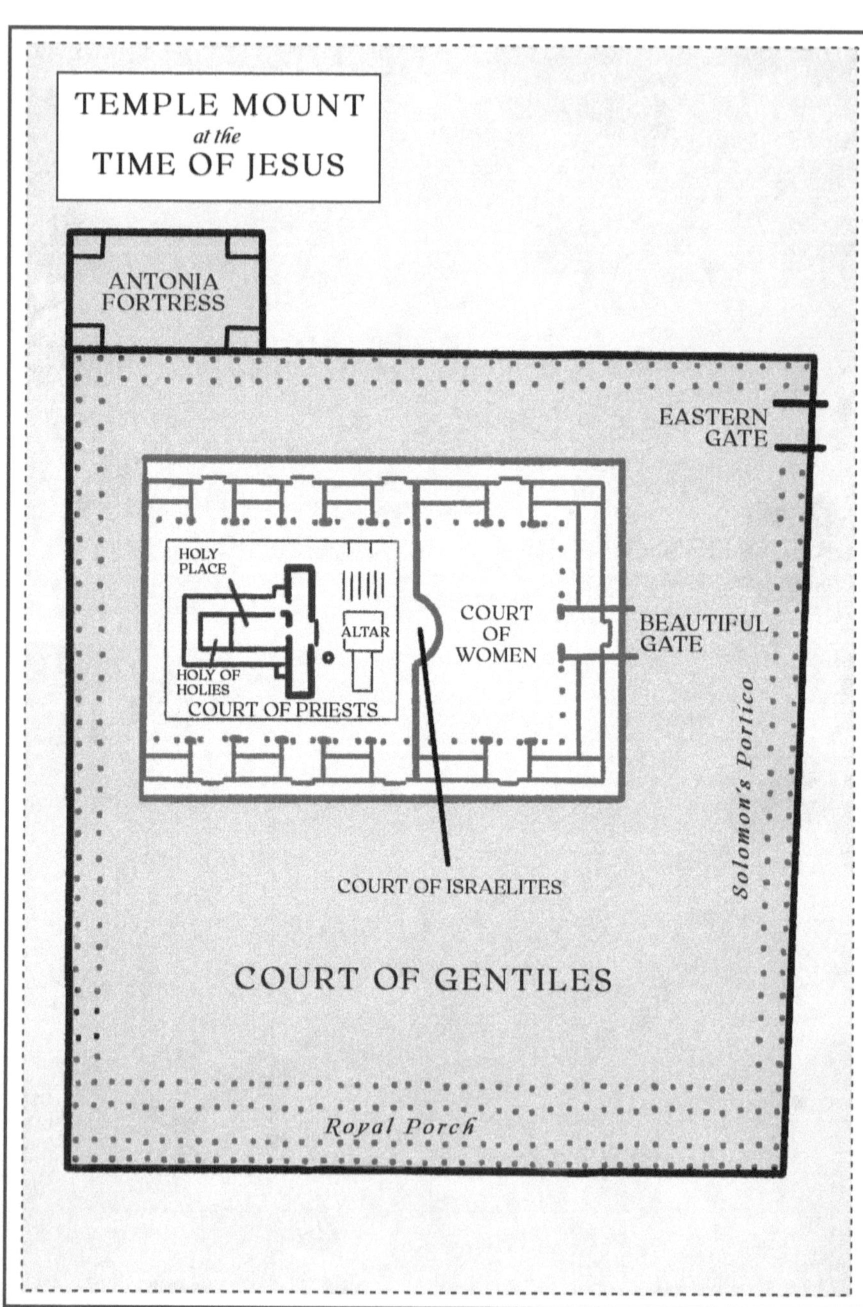

TEMPLE MOUNT
at the
TIME OF JESUS
ANTONIA FORTRESS
EASTERN GATE
HOLY PLACE
HOLY OF HOLIES
COURT OF PRIESTS
ALTAR
COURT OF WOMEN
BEAUTIFUL GATE
Solomon's Portico
COURT OF ISRAELITES
COURT OF GENTILES
Royal Porch

CONTENTS

When Martha heard that Jesus was coming, she went out to meet him, but Mary stayed at home.

"Lord," Martha said to Jesus, "if you had been here, my brother would not have died. But I know that even now God will give you whatever you ask."

Jesus said to her, "Your brother will rise again."

Martha answered, "I know he will rise again in the resurrection at the last day."

Jesus said to her, "I am the resurrection and the life. The one who believes in me will live, even though they die; and whoever lives by believing in me will never die. Do you believe this?"

"Yes, Lord," she replied, "I believe that you are the Messiah, the Son of God, who is to come into the world."

JOHN 11:20-27 (NIV)

Introduction

It is feared... it is inescapable... it is irreversible... it can strike without warning.

ALL OF THESE terms describe death. We can't escape occasional reminders of our own mortality. Reports of senseless school shootings touch our lives tangentially. The death of friends or family members hit much closer to home.

Yet physical death is often not the primary cause for concern. Instead, much of the anxiety stems from uncertainty regarding what happens after we die. Do we exist only from conception to our last brain wave? Or is there life after death?

How can we determine what to expect after we die? Chapter 11 of the Gospel of John tells the story of a man named Lazarus. He died after a short illness, and his body was placed in a tomb to decay. Jesus commanded him to come out of the grave alive... and he did!

What does this Bible story prove? It shows that Jesus has power over death. The raising of Lazarus from the dead was a preview of Jesus' resurrection. It is also a preview of our resurrection. Jesus promised eternal life in heaven to all who believe in him as their Savior. His promise takes the guess-work out of dying.

Chapter One

BEGINNINGS

The newborn squirmed as he struggled to take his first breath. Labor had ended quickly. A longer delivery would have cleared his lungs of the fluid that filled them before birth. The remaining fluid had to be expelled immediately in order for him to breathe. Deprived of oxygen, he had only minutes remaining before permanent brain damage or death would result.

To the relief of his parents, the newborn child began crying on his own. Crying forced fluid out of the lungs allowing air into the vacated space. His breathing was shallow and uneven at first, but soon it became stronger and more regular. His skin color turned from pale blue to pink. Unaware of how close he had come to death, the baby boy opened his eyes for the first time. He blinked twice, reacting to the orange glow from an oil lamp flickering nearby.

The boy's mother shed tears of relief and joy as her husband lifted the newborn to her chest. Rebecca held her baby close as Benjamin cut the umbilical cord. They had not anticipated the way events unfolded. Although the birth had been successful and their new son appeared healthy, he had arrived without much warning. The couple's other two children had been born after hours of contractions and pain. This birth was over in a few minutes. There had been no time to summon the midwife who had helped deliver their daughters.

Benjamin poured some water onto a towel and gently washed the baby. A white cheese-like coating that partially covered the newborn was easily removed. Once the skin was dry, Benjamin wrapped strips of cloth around the baby's body, a traditional practice intended to mimic the comfort of the womb.

Within an hour, the baby was nursing at his mother's breast. As Benjamin gazed at his wife and their new son, his eyes began to moisten. He bowed his head and prayed, "God of our fathers, you have richly blessed our family with the gift of a son. For this we give thanks. We dedicate him to your service and ask that you keep him in your care all of his life."

Although Benjamin could not know it at the time, the birth of another baby nine years earlier in the town of Bethlehem would have a tremendous impact on his son's life. But on this day Benjamin was making his own plans for the boy's future. Benjamin had established a successful pottery business in Bethany that he hoped to pass on to a son. His two beautiful daughters meant the world to him, but now that Benjamin had a male heir, the family unit was complete.

In a matter of minutes, the ceremony would be over. Rebecca sat on a wooden stool in the living room of their home. The baby boy, only eight days old, lay sleeping in his mother's arms wrapped snugly in a goat hair blanket. Benjamin stood next to a small table in the middle of the room. A bowl of water, soap, a cloth, and a knife had been placed on the table. Benjamin beckoned to his wife, "Rebecca, please bring the child to me. It is time to dedicate him to God."

Rebecca rose from her stool and walked to the table. She leaned forward and placed the baby down onto his back. She opened the blanket exposing his tiny naked body for all to see. A small commotion ensued as the relatives and invited guests jockeyed for a closer look. The baby's eyelids opened for a moment and then closed again.

While Rebecca stabilized the baby's shoulders and feet, Benjamin stood over his son and washed the area around the child's foreskin with soap and the dampened cloth. The baby squirmed for a moment but was quickly calmed by his mother's soothing voice. Benjamin replaced the cloth on the table and reached for the knife lying nearby.

Grasping the tip of the foreskin between his thumb and index finger, Benjamin could feel the excess foreskin extending beyond the head of the glans. In a series of precise motions, the knife sliced around the circumference of the foreskin just below his fingers. As the thin ring of foreskin fell away, the tip of the glans came into view. The main portion of the foreskin remained in place in accordance with age-old practice.

The baby began to scream and struggle as soon as he recognized the pain. A few drops of blood oozed from the incision. Benjamin dabbed the wound with the cloth. Rebecca pulled the blanket back over the baby, lifted him in her arms, and rocked him gently. His crying gradually subsided. Those in attendance voiced their approval of the successful circumcision.

"He will be called Lazarus," Benjamin announced in a voice tinged with both pride and thanksgiving, "because God will be his helper." The covenant made between Abraham and God two thousand years earlier had been renewed once again. At ninety-nine years of age, a childless Abraham pledged to obey God throughout his life. In turn, God promised Abraham he would become the father of many nations. Circumcision was a sign of that covenant. Benjamin's firstborn son, Lazarus, was now one of the chosen people, set apart from those who did not worship the true God.

As soon as the donkey came to a halt, four-year-old Lazarus jumped from the back of the wooden cart it was pulling. Like most children his age, he seemed to have boundless energy. That morning his entire family had traveled twelve miles east from Bethany to this isolated spot near the Jordan River. The purpose of the trip was to collect some choice clay for Benjamin's pottery business. The Jordan River basin had some of the richest clay deposits in all of Judea. Benjamin's pottery was in demand by residents of Bethany as well as travelers on their way to and from Jerusalem.

Benjamin unhitched the donkey from its harness. The animal needed water and shade after five hours of hauling the wagon. Rebecca laid out a blanket beneath one of the shade trees that flourished along the river. With one eye on her children, Rebecca began removing food from the cart in preparation for the afternoon meal.

Martha was the oldest child, two years older than her sister, Mary, and four years older than Lazarus. She was under strict orders to watch her younger brother and sister closely, particularly near the rapidly flowing river. Springtime flooding had ended a few months earlier, but it would be another month before the flow would slow to its normal leisurely pace. From shore to shore the river was about a quarter mile wide. The water was a greenish brown color from the mud, clay, and debris that had accumulated during the journey from the Sea of Galilee toward the Dead Sea.

As the three siblings ventured closer to the river, Martha took hold of her little brother's hand. Lazarus squirmed and tried to pull away, but Martha increased her grip and pulled him close. Lazarus continued to struggle, determined to break free and run to the river's edge. The undulating movement of the swiftly flowing water was hypnotic. The young boy had never seen so much water in a single place.

Just behind them, Mary cried out in pain. A sharp rock had penetrated her sandal and cut her foot. Blood oozed from the gash. Instinctively, Martha released her brother's hand and went to help her sister. Finally free from restraint, Lazarus' eyes widened with excitement. This was his chance to explore.

Lazarus hurried to the edge of the river, kicked off his sandals, and tested the water. It was cold but refreshing on his bare feet. He took three steps into the river and stopped abruptly. Lazarus realized he had made a mistake. He was standing ankle deep in mud, unable to pull his feet from the river bottom. The water, which once seemed so inviting, was now a threat from which to escape.

Panicking, Lazarus tried to turn back to the shore, but his feet remained mired. With each movement he sank a little deeper. He struggled to keep his balance, but the current continued tugging at his lower legs. With nothing to steady him, his knees buckled, and he fell backward into the river. As Lazarus plunged into the water, his feet and ankles became unstuck from the mud. Before he could right himself, the rushing water caught his clothes and propelled him downstream farther and farther from the shore.

After tending to her sister, Martha turned around expecting to see her brother standing there. Instead, she saw a set of footprints leading to the water and her brother's sandals lying on the shore. Her eyes shifted their focus downstream where she saw her brother's head and shoulders bobbing up and down in the river. Martha screamed at the top of her lungs, "Lazarus!"

Rebecca heard Martha's cry and looked toward the river. Seeing her daughters but not her son, she assumed the worst and shouted to her husband that Lazarus might have fallen into the river. Benjamin dropped the shovel he was using to load clay into the cart and sprinted toward the river. As he ran, he tore off his outer cloak and kicked off his leather sandals. Upon reaching the water's edge, he saw his son being swept downstream struggling to stay afloat.

When Lazarus fell into the river, the shock of the cold water prevented him from crying out for help. He gasped for air in staccato bursts, but none reached his lungs. Panic enveloped him like a dense fog. Lazarus inhaled deeply just as his head slipped below the surface of the river. His throat closed reflexively, but water had already entered his lungs and he began choking.

Deprived of oxygen, Lazarus had no energy left to fight the current. His heart, which had been beating mightily to keep his body warm, started to slow. His arm and leg muscles relaxed, and Lazarus settled into a state of calm acceptance. His mind, which had been racing aimlessly, now focused on a series of fluctuating images from his past. He saw himself as a baby in the arms of his smiling parents, a toddler trying to stand and promptly falling, and a young boy gazing in awe at a star-filled sky. These and hundreds of other positive memories flashed before his eyes. He felt weightless, almost like a puff of air. An indescribable mixture of peace and contentment filled his entire being like nothing he had ever experienced before.

Then Lazarus heard a voice. The sound reverberated like distant thunder yet was as soothing as water rippling over rocks in a stream. The voice said, "My son, it is not yet time for you to die." The moment he heard those words, every nerve in his body fired at once.

Moments earlier, Benjamin had risked his own life to rescue his son. While Lazarus was being swept down the river, his father raced along the shore. His best chance to reach the boy was to stay on land as long as possible. Fortunately, the shoreline was firm and clear of debris.

Benjamin pulled even with his son about a hundred yards downstream from where Lazarus had entered the water. He plunged into the water and swam toward his son. After reaching him, he treaded water while trying to keep Lazarus' face above the surface. Although the river was only chest deep, the swift current continued to sweep them downstream.

With great difficulty, Benjamin worked his way toward the shore until he could stand without falling. He slogged forward struggling with each step to release his feet from the suction of the muddy river bottom. Finally, exhausted and breathing heavily, he lunged onto the shore. As he fell forward, he propelled Lazarus forward to avoid collapsing on top of him.

Lazarus landed on his upper back between his shoulder blades. The jolt of the fall compressed his lungs with enough force to expel a combination of air and water. Benjamin crawled to his son and held his limp body tightly in his arms. He lifted Lazarus skyward and prayed in desperation, "Please, God, show mercy to your servant, and keep my son alive!"

Struggling to his feet, Benjamin carried the boy to a shady spot near the shore. He gently laid his son on a patch of grass and began sobbing uncontrollably. Through eyes full of tears,

Benjamin thought he saw the boy's chest move almost imperceptibly. "Is it my imagination? Or could it be that God has answered my prayer?"

As Benjamin watched in amazement, Lazarus' mouth opened slightly as if trying to take a breath. He bent down and picked up his son, holding the boy's chest to his own. Benjamin tightened his embrace. Lazarus coughed up some of the water he had inhaled and began breathing. The skin that had been pale and cold began to recover its color and warmth. Benjamin sobbed tears of joy and kissed Lazarus over and over again. Feeding off his father's emotion, Lazarus began to cry as well.

After regaining consciousness, Lazarus tried to recall what had just happened. He remembered falling into the river, but nearly everything that happened afterward was a blur—everything, that is, except the kaleidoscope of memories that had raced through his mind and the voice that told him it was not his time to die. But for now, all that mattered to Lazarus was the comfort and security of being in his father's arms. Benjamin whispered softly to his son, "Don't ever do anything like that again. I came close to losing you. It is fitting that we named you Lazarus. God was certainly your help today."

Chapter Two

PREPARATION

LAZARUS DID HIS best to match the pace set by Benjamin's longer stride. He was now five years old, the age at which Jewish boys started their formal education. He and his father were walking from their home in Bethany to the local synagogue where Lazarus would attend his first day of school. The synagogue, where Sabbath worship was conducted, also doubled as a year-round school. There, if all went as expected, Lazarus would spend most mornings of his next ten years gaining knowledge to become a devout and successful Jewish man.

Bethany was a small village located a little less than two miles from Jerusalem on the southeastern slope of the Mount of Olives. The early morning air was cool and dry. A light breeze carried the scent of wildflowers growing next to the dirt road. First traces of the rising sun appeared in the eastern sky announcing the start of another hot summer day.

Halfway to their destination, Benjamin slowed his step. He stopped, turned, and stood facing the young boy. Lazarus was taken by surprise. He had been lost in thought about the coming day. His father, looming above him, spoke in a solemn voice, "Son, today you are on your way to becoming a man. What you learn in synagogue school will guide you the rest of your life. Listen well and learn what God expects of you. God will bless you richly as long as you obey him."

Lazarus sensed the importance of this moment. Without fully understanding what Benjamin meant, he replied in agreement, "Yes, Father. I will." Lazarus tried his best to remain calm in front of his father, but his heart was beating rapidly with a mixture of excitement and anxiety.

As they continued their walk up the road, the synagogue came into view. It was the largest building in Bethany and sat on the highest point of the village's hilly terrain. The one-story rectangular structure had a flat roof. Its twelve-foot-high outer walls were made of white limestone cut from a local quarry. The synagogue was positioned so that worshippers entering the front door faced northwest toward Jerusalem.

At the entrance, Lazarus and Benjamin were greeted by a slender, bearded man dressed in a white robe. "Shalom. God's peace be with you, Benjamin," said Tobias. "I see that our newest student has arrived. Welcome to synagogue school,

Lazarus. I'm sure you will enjoy your time here. We will be seeing a lot of each other in the days to come."

Lazarus looked up at a man who was even taller than his father. His hair and beard were speckled with gray. Lazarus had seen his new teacher regularly at Sabbath worship but had not paid particular attention to him. Tobias now seemed much more intimidating than he recalled.

Tobias held the position of ruler in the Bethany synagogue. In larger synagogues, like those in Jerusalem, the ruler of the synagogue was an administrator with a number of staff people under him. Because the membership of the Bethany synagogue was small, fewer than a hundred men and women, Tobias had sole responsibility for virtually everything that happened there. Among other duties, he taught synagogue school, organized worship services, safekept the sacred scrolls, and maintained the premises.

After exchanging a few pleasantries with Tobias, Benjamin looked down at his son. "I have to go to work now. I know you're going to be a good boy and obey your teacher." Lazarus hugged Benjamin's legs tightly, wrapping his arms around his father's robe as far as he could reach. Benjamin bent down to give his son a kiss on the forehead before walking away. Lazarus' lips quivered as he fought back tears. Although school would last only half a day, he wished it was already over so he could be back home in familiar surroundings.

Tobias took Lazarus' hand. Lazarus felt the urge to pull his hand away, but he remembered his father's admonition to be a good boy and obey his teacher. The two of them walked toward the open door of the synagogue. Inside the entrance, a set of stairs led down to a large, rectangular, tiled floor. Eight wooden columns that supported the roof ringed the perimeter of the tile floor. On the right and left sides of the floor, a series of terraced stone benches extended to the outer walls. The design provided a clear line of sight from nearly every location within the synagogue. Light filtered into the building from small clerestory windows that ringed the upper walls.

Near the back wall stood a large wooden chest containing the Torah and other sacred scrolls that were read at Sabbath worship. To the left of the chest stood the menorah, a tall ornate lampstand holding seven candles that burned all day. Keeping the candles lit was one of Tobias' many tasks.

On the tile floor near the chest and menorah stood several chairs reserved for leaders of the synagogue and for honored guests. Located several feet in front of the chairs was a slightly elevated wooden platform approximately ten feet square on which stood a lectern. This space was reserved for the reader of the Sabbath scrolls.

The synagogue was empty except for Lazarus and his teacher. Instead of feeling alone, Lazarus took comfort in the quiet and calm, which he expected would soon change. Until now Lazarus had been tutored at home by his father and didn't have to deal with the stress of socializing with other children. He wondered whether his classmates would like him. Would they be smarter than him? Would they make fun of him if he made mistakes? All these thoughts raced through Lazarus' mind as he prepared for the worst and hoped for the best.

Rebecca heard a noise coming from the front of the house. It sounded like the door latch opening and closing. "Did you hear that?" Rebecca said to Martha. "Would you see if anyone is at the door? I wasn't expecting visitors this morning."

Martha left the room and returned shortly. "No one was there, Mother. Maybe the door was open a bit, and the wind blew it shut."

Rebecca was weaving cloth from linen threads that she had spun and dyed a few days earlier. The loom was located in a room at the back of the house. Mary and Martha watched intently as their mother wove the threads horizontally and vertically on the loom. In a few years Rebecca's daughters would be the ones making clothes for the family.

Several minutes later Rebecca responded to a knock at the front door. A young man, perhaps thirteen years old, was standing there, bent over at the waist, hands on his knees, and gasping for air.

"How can I help you?" Rebecca asked. "Are you all right?"

The boy caught his breath and stood up straight. "Rabbi Tobias sent me here from the synagogue. I ran all the way. He wanted me to tell you that Lazarus disappeared from school, and he couldn't find him anywhere. He's still searching the area around the school but hoped that Lazarus might have walked home."

In contrast to the young man's agitation, Rebecca remained calm. "No, I haven't seen him since he left for school with his father. But I have an idea where he might be."

From the hiding place behind his bed, Lazarus had heard everything. He knew it was only matter of time before he would be found, but he was too afraid and ashamed to emerge from his temporary refuge. He listened with increasing anxiety as his mother's footsteps approached until they stopped at the bedroom door. His body quivered as he struggled to stay silent. Finally, the anticipation was too much for him to bear. "I'm sorry, Mother," he sobbed as he crawled out from behind the bed. "Please don't tell Father. I'm sure he'll punish me for this if he finds out."

Rebecca cradled Lazarus in her arms. "I'm so happy you're safe. But you need to tell me why you ran away from school. You've been going there for a few weeks now, and I thought you were doing well."

Tears were still streaming down Lazarus' cheeks. "It wasn't my fault. A bunch of us were outside playing. Some of us pretended to be Roman soldiers. I was one of the Jewish fighters. One of the bigger kids, I think his name was Simon, wrestled me to the ground. Some other Roman soldiers piled on top of us. I was at the bottom and couldn't breathe. I tried to push them off, but they were too heavy. I was so scared that I started crying. They finally got off of me. Simon and the rest of the boys laughed when they saw me crying. I jumped up and ran home."

Rebecca ran her fingers through her son's hair. "It's going to be just fine. I understand why you did what you did. Your father won't punish you. You didn't do anything wrong." She led Lazarus to the front door where the young man was still standing. "As you can see, we found him. Please go back to the school and tell Rabbi Tobias that Lazarus is safe at home and will be back at school tomorrow morning."

Later that afternoon after Benjamin had returned from work in the pottery shop, he and Rebecca discussed what had happened at school that morning. They spoke in hushed tones so that Lazarus couldn't make out what they were saying. To his relief, neither of his parents appeared upset. After they had finished talking, Benjamin motioned for his son to join him. He led Lazarus into the backyard, where they sat together on a stone bench. The sun was beginning to set on the horizon turning the clouds into a brilliant display of color, but Lazarus was too preoccupied to notice.

"Lazarus," his father began, "your mother told me what happened at school today. I'm sorry you had a bad experience, and I want you to know that I'm not angry that you ran home. From what I heard from your mother, you were pinned under a bunch of your classmates and felt like you couldn't breathe. It's no wonder you were afraid and cried. Less than a year ago you went through a similar experience at the Jordan River. I wouldn't be surprised if that memory doesn't stay with you the rest of your life."

Lazarus had to agree with what his father was saying. The panic resulting from an inability to breathe had been similar in both instances, but this time the outcome was much worse. He had embarrassed himself by crying in front of his classmates. As a result, they treated him like a scared weakling who couldn't handle a little roughhousing. It wasn't fair. They didn't understand the reason he had reacted the way he did.

Benjamin continued, "Son, today might be a blessing in disguise. Your unpleasant experience might be something that makes you stronger. I remember when I was a boy, my father told me how to get through difficult times in life. Whenever I was afraid of what might happen, I needed to go to God for help. I needed to ask him to guide me in the right path. I've done that my entire life since then, and look how God has blessed me. I have a thriving business, a beautiful family, and the respect of everyone in the community."

"But I'm only five years old. Why would God listen if I asked for help?"

"Age isn't important. What is important is that you always obey God. In synagogue school you will learn what God requires of you. If you do what he wants, you can go to God any time and he will answer your prayers. Whenever you are worried or afraid, just remember the meaning of your name. Your mother and I named you Lazarus because it means 'God is my helper.'"

That evening as he lay in bed, Lazarus had plenty to think about as he prepared to face his classmates the next morning. In spite of his father's encouraging words, he hesitated to pray. What if God wasn't happy with him for running away from school? What if he had done something else to disobey him? If so, would God still answer his prayer for help? Lazarus closed his eyes and fell asleep. It had been a long day.

"Lazarus, what animals does God's law allow Jews to eat?" Tobias questioned. Lazarus sat up straight when he heard his name. His teacher and classmates were looking at him. Lazarus hoped that no one had noticed him daydreaming. After an initial rush of adrenalin, his body returned to a state of calm. Lazarus had heard enough of the question to respond. Fortunately, he knew the answer.

Lazarus was now nine years old and a four-year veteran of synagogue school. The same question had been asked of him and his classmates many times before. "The Lord told Moses and Aaron to say to the community of Israel: You may eat any animal that has divided hoofs and chews the cud,"[1] Lazarus answered, quoting verbatim from the book of Leviticus.

Lazarus knew what question was coming next. Tobias addressed him again. "Correct. Now tell me what animals the law has forbidden us to eat."

Lazarus answered confidently, "You must not eat animals such as camels, rock badgers, and rabbits that chew the cud but don't have divided hoofs. And you must not eat pigs— they have divided hoofs, but they don't chew the cud. All of these animals are unclean, and you are forbidden even to touch their dead bodies."[2] Once again he was commended.

Lazarus breathed a sigh of relief as Tobias moved on to quiz another student. He began daydreaming again. Other than the day he had run away from school in embarrassment, now a distant but sometimes recurring memory, his

---

1   Leviticus 11:3 (NIV)

2   Leviticus 11:4–8 (NIV)

last four years of schooling had been enjoyable. Lazarus was now in his last year of elementary at the Bethany synagogue school. Next year he would graduate and spend the following five years in secondary. Lazarus had mastered most of the elementary curriculum including basic skills such as reading and writing and more advanced studies such as mathematics. However, his favorite subject was religion.

Lazarus' interest in religion originated from his father's lecture on the day he ran away from school. He could still hear his father's voice. "In synagogue school you will learn what God requires of you. If you do what he wants, you can go to God any time and he will answer your prayers."

Just as his father predicted, synagogue school provided Lazarus with ample opportunity to learn what God wanted him to do. God's requirements, known as the Mosaic law, were taught from the Torah, a five-volume set of books written by Moses fourteen hundred years earlier. The process of learning the law, Lazarus discovered, was not easy.

In order for Lazarus to study the Torah, he had to learn Hebrew, the original language of the Jews. Most Jews in Bethany and throughout Israel spoke Aramaic at home and in public. Aramaic had replaced Hebrew during Jewish captivity in Assyria and in Babylonia. But in keeping with tradition, the Jews created copies of the Torah only in Hebrew. During Sabbath worship the reader of the sacred scroll spoke in Hebrew.

In addition to dealing with a new language, Lazarus had to memorize what he learned. Copies of the Torah were laboriously and meticulously handwritten on parchment or papyrus by scribes. As a result, copies were not readily accessible outside of synagogues or the temple. After four years of synagogue school, Lazarus had already committed to memory virtually every word of the entire five books of Moses.

Once he was able to memorize the Torah and know what God required, Lazarus assumed he would be able to comply with those requirements. In that case, according to his father, he could ask for and receive help from God at any time. However, to his dismay, Lazarus faced what seemed to be an unachievable goal. How could he obey, or even keep track of, all six hundred and thirteen laws in the Torah?

Faced with the seeming impossibility of keeping all of God's requirements perfectly, Lazarus wondered if God might be willing to give him credit if he were able to obey at least the most important ones. One day, just before school was dismissed, Tobias asked if any of the boys had questions. Lazarus raised his hand. "Do we have to obey all of God's laws in the Torah for him to answer our prayers?"

Tobias paused for a moment. "God expects us to keep all of his laws. Otherwise, he wouldn't have given them to us. On the other hand, I don't know anyone who has ever kept all of the law perfectly. That is why sin offerings are made at the temple. The death of the animal sacrificed covers our sins, and its blood sprinkled on the altar washes the sin away. In this way our past sins are forgiven. However, God still judges each of us by what we do each day. He expects us to do his will without fail now and in the future. The more we obey, the more he will bless us. If we fail to obey, we lose his favor and will suffer for it."

Lazarus thought about what his teacher had just said. It was comforting to know that no one kept every one of God's commands and that sin offerings would result in forgiveness. But Tobias hadn't really addressed his main concern: "How obedient do I need to be for God to answer my prayers for help? Conversely, how disobedient can I be before God refuses to hear me?"

Lazarus cringed when he saw the group of boys approaching. He was walking home from synagogue school a half hour after the other students had been dismissed. Lazarus had stayed behind to help Tobias clean the synagogue before Sabbath worship the next day.

Lazarus preferred to walk home alone. During the school day he got along well with the other students. His routine was structured, and he felt comfortable in his academic skills. However, outside the classroom, associating with other boys was not appealing to him. Lazarus had convinced himself that making friends and maintaining friendships would be more work than it was worth.

What Lazarus failed to admit to himself was an underlying fear of being rejected, or even worse, being laughed at. That fear had haunted him ever since the day when his classmates ridiculed him for crying after being nearly suffocated. Six years later, at age eleven, he still felt the sting of that earlier humiliation.

Lazarus' attempts to avoid socialization did not come without consequences. His withdrawn manner made him a target for bullies. Lazarus knew that the boys walking toward him considered him a weakling. He also sensed that they were envious of his academic prowess. Simon, the young man who had wrestled him to the ground years ago, was at the front of the pack.

Lazarus tried to avoid eye contact with the boys as they got closer to him. He hoped that they would simply walk by without incident. Instead, Simon placed himself directly in front of Lazarus, forcing him to stop. Lazarus tried to go around him, but Simon blocked his way. The other boys formed a circle around them.

"Where do you think you're going?" asked Simon gruffly.

Lazarus didn't answer right away and kept his gaze on the ground. "I'm going home," he finally replied.

"Why were you so late leaving school? Was the rabbi punishing you for something?"

"I stayed to help him clean the synagogue."

"Hey, everybody," Simon addressed his friends. "Lazarus is trying to be the teacher's favorite. You know what we do to people like that."

"Yeah," answered one of the boys in the circle. "We teach them not to show the rest of us up."

Before Simon or his friends could react, Lazarus bolted though the ring of boys and ran toward home. The boys laughed as he ran away down the road. Lazarus could hear them calling him a crybaby and a coward. After sprinting until exhausted, he turned and saw they weren't chasing him. He sighed and slowed his pace to a walk.

The rest of the way home, Lazarus realized he had failed to ask God for courage as the boys approached him. Everything had happened so fast. That night he decided to ask God for help. He thought about asking his father what to do but didn't want him to think his son couldn't take care of himself. In any case, his father had already told him to go to God when he was afraid.

"Mighty God," Lazarus prayed, "I realize that I have not obeyed you in everything I do. But I have tried to do your will. If I have somehow found approval in your eyes, I need your help. Some of the boys at school are bullying me. One of them named Simon is particularly mean. Please show me what I should do to make them stop." Lazarus fell asleep, hoping that his prayer would be answered.

The next morning Lazarus attended Sabbath worship with his family. He recalled helping Tobias clean the synagogue the previous day. "I hope God considers that an act of obedience," Lazarus thought. Simon and some of the other boys were sitting with their parents. They appeared to be on their best behavior. None of them seemed to pay any attention to him during the service.

The next day, to the surprise of everyone, Tobias required his secondary students to sit in assigned seats. This had happened only a few times before, usually after certain individuals were inattentive or caused trouble. Normally the students were free to sit where they wanted. The change to assigned seating was usually brief, but the message it conveyed to the students lasted a long time.

To his dismay, Lazarus found himself seated next to Simon. The two boys glanced at each other and then looked away. The secondary students sat on the stone benches used for Sabbath worship. The elementary class sat on benches on the other side of the tile floor, facing them. Tobias moved back and forth across the floor in order to teach each of the classes.

The morning progressed uneventfully. Neither boy spoke to the other. Toward the end of the school day, Tobias called on Lazarus. "Before Moses and the Israelites entered the Promised Land of Canaan and just before Moses' brother Aaron died, the people complained about the lack of water and the quality of food. What did God do to punish them?"

Lazarus knew the story from the book of Numbers. "The Lord sent venomous snakes among them; they bit the people and many Israelites died."[3]

"What did Moses do?"

"Moses prayed for the people."[4]

"What did God tell Moses to do in answer to his prayer?"

"Moses made a bronze snake and put it up on a pole. Then when anyone was bitten by a snake and looked at the bronze snake, they lived."[5]

"Very good, Lazarus. Those were all correct answers," Tobias affirmed. "But I have a more difficult question that

---

3   Numbers 21:6 (NIV)

4   Numbers 21:7 (NIV)

5   Numbers 21:9 (NIV)

you might not be able to answer. What happened to the snake on the pole after the Israelites went into Canaan?"

Lazarus had to think a moment. He knew this topic wasn't covered in the Torah, so it must be in one of the other books of the kings or prophets. Then he remembered a brief reference to the snake in the second book of Kings and answered, "Over five hundred years after the Israelites went into Canaan, King Hezekiah showed his obedience to the Lord. Scripture says, 'He removed the high places, smashed the sacred stones and cut down the Asherah poles. He broke into pieces the bronze snake Moses had made, for up to that time the Israelites had been burning incense to it.'"[6]

"That was excellent, Lazarus," Tobias exclaimed. "For that correct answer, I am going to allow you to stay home from school tomorrow. After class today, I will walk home with you to tell your parents what a good student you are."

Lazarus blushed with embarrassment. Embarrassment quickly turned into apprehension. Although he was pleased to be recognized, Lazarus realized he was sitting next to a bully who had recently accused him of being a teacher's favorite. Getting a day off from school, Lazarus feared, might send Simon over the edge with resentment.

Tobias interrupted Lazarus' train of thought. "I now have an even more difficult question to ask the entire class, with the exception of Lazarus. If anyone can answer it correctly, I will excuse you from school tomorrow as well. Is everyone ready to participate?" The class all nodded their heads.

---

6   2 Kings 18:4 (NIV)

"Lazarus was correct in saying that King Hezekiah destroyed the bronze snake because it had become an object of worship," Tobias began. "What name did the people of Judah give to the snake as they offered sacrifices to it?"

Lazarus saw smiles of hope turn to frowns of disappointment. No one in the class would know the answer. No one, that is, except him. The same Scripture he quoted from the second book of Kings also disclosed the name the Israelites had called the snake.

Lazarus glanced at Simon who was staring into space without any hope of answering the question. For a reason even he couldn't explain, Lazarus began writing on his papyrus tablet: N-E-H-U-S-H-T-A-N. After making sure that Tobias wasn't watching, he nudged Simon's arm. Simon's gaze shifted to Lazarus. Lazarus looked down at the tablet. Simon's eyes followed Lazarus' downward glance.

"Do any of you have the answer?" Tobias asked. "If not, I withdraw my offer and we will move on."

Simon raised his hand and all eyes turned to him. "Sir, I seem to remember that the name of the snake was Nehushtan. I'm not sure that's how you pronounce it. Could that be the correct answer?"

Tobias appeared stunned. His jaw dropped and his eyebrows elevated. "I'm amazed. You are correct." Tobias took another moment to compose himself. "How in the world did you know the name of that snake? It is only mentioned once in all of Scripture."

"Sir, it seemed to come to me out of thin air. Sometimes that happens to me when I least expect it."

"Well, then. Both you and Lazarus will have the day off from school tomorrow. I will visit your parents this afternoon and let them know you are excused from class. I will also let them know how well versed both of you are in the Scriptures."

The next day Rebecca let Lazarus sleep later than usual. When he awoke, it took a few seconds to realize he didn't have to go to school that day. Shortly after getting out of bed, Lazarus began reaping other benefits of his academic success. His mother's good morning hug was tighter than usual, and his morning meal included extra portions of bread, cheese, dates, and figs.

The prior afternoon, Lazarus' parents had beamed with pride as Tobias praised their son for his scholarship. Mary and Martha, however, did not seem impressed. Lazarus was tempted to flaunt the accolades in front of his sisters but decided against it. He understood they were both as intelligent as he was, perhaps even more so. But because they were girls, they weren't allowed to attend synagogue school.

Lazarus spent the balance of the morning lounging around the house and playing with his sisters. It was a relaxing time, but by noon he was bored. Since school was over for the day, Lazarus decided to thank Tobias personally for excusing him from class. After letting his mother know where he was going, he set off up the road to the synagogue.

Halfway to his destination, Lazarus stopped short. He couldn't believe his eyes. Coming toward him from the other direction was the same group of boys who had harassed him just days earlier. These bullies would not pass by without incident. His mind told him to turn and run home, but his body was too paralyzed with fear.

As the boys drew closer, he saw that Simon was not leading the group. In fact, he wasn't with them at all. "That makes sense," thought Lazarus. "Simon had the day off from school too. Maybe the rest of them won't bother me." His hopes were dashed when the boys once again formed a circle around him.

"You got away last time," one of them sneered, "but you won't this time. You showed us up in class by answering those questions. If you were really smart, you wouldn't have done that. I bet you didn't even know the answer to the question Simon got right."

The circle began tightening. Lazarus couldn't see any gaps through which he might escape. The boy directly in front of him made a fist and raised it as if to throw a punch. Lazarus covered his head with his arms waiting for the blow to fall. Seconds passed but nothing happened.

Lazarus peered out from between his arms. The boys had all turned to look at something outside the circle. "What's going on?" said a voice coming from that direction. "What do you think you are doing?"

The boy who had threatened Lazarus replied, "Simon, we were just finishing up some unfinished business. We looked for you earlier but figured you must have gone somewhere on your day off of school."

"I asked what you were doing," Simon repeated impatiently.

"We saw Lazarus walking up the road just now," another one of the boys explained. "We figured he must be going to the synagogue to butter up the teacher some more. You remember how he stayed after school to help the rabbi. Then yesterday he made us look stupid by answering all those questions. But I've got to admit, you really showed him up when you answered the hardest question. Today we're going to give him a reason not to look so good in front of the teacher."

Simon shoved his way through the circle and stood next to Lazarus. Lazarus expected him to land the first blow. Instead, Simon looked around at each of the boys and said in a menacing tone, "If any of you lay a hand on him or even look at him cross-eyed, you will answer to me. Do you understand?"

One of the boys spoke up. "We hear you, but we don't understand. Why are you siding with him now when only days ago you were going to give him a beating?"

"I have my reasons. Let's just say I had a change of heart."

Lazarus lowered his arms. He wasn't sure what to do next. Simon stepped out of the circle and motioned for Lazarus to follow. The two of them walked a short distance away, out of earshot from the rest of the group.

"Thanks for what you did yesterday. After all I did to make your life miserable, I didn't expect you to pay me back that way. I owe you. None of these guys will bother you anymore. From now on if anyone gives you any trouble, let me know and I'll take care of it."

Lazarus was speechless. He hadn't had time to process what had just happened, but it was clearly a good time to get away from there. Without a word or a glance back, he returned to the road and resumed his walk to the synagogue.

That night Lazarus replayed the day's events in his mind. He recalled a jumble of emotions, from feeling rewarded and relaxed in the morning to experiencing fear followed by relief in the afternoon. In spite of all the ups and downs, the final result had been exactly what he had prayed for. His prayer had been answered in a way that only God could have accomplished. Before he fell asleep Lazarus prayed, "Lord, thank you for finding me obedient enough to answer my prayer. Help me to do your will and continue to receive your blessings."

Benjamin's workshop was located behind the family home. Lazarus stood in the doorway after recently returning home from school. His father looked up from the potter's wheel. His foot kicked the flywheel that turned the platform on which the clay rotated. "Come in, Son. I could use your help today. I just got a large order from one of our best customers."

Thirteen-year-old Lazarus was now considered to be a man in the eyes of his fellow Jews. Two years of his formal education remained, but it was already time for him to learn a trade. In Lazarus' case, this meant learning how to make pottery. Just as Benjamin had done with his own father, Lazarus would become an apprentice in his father's pottery shop.

The clay gave the room an earthy but pleasant odor. Built into the back wall of the workshop was the brick kiln used to fire the clay. The bottom of the kiln consisted of a large fire box. Above the fire box was a hollow chamber in which the pottery baked. The entire structure was topped by a chimney stack that extended through the roof. Thick black smoke rising from the chimney could be seen and smelled throughout the neighborhood.

Near the kiln, pieces of formed clay were drying in preparation for firing. Nearly all the moisture had to be removed before baking or the piece could explode in the heat. An inventory of finished product was stored near the front of the workshop. Some of the completed pieces had been ordered by local residents. Others would be sold in Bethany's business district, where Benjamin owned a small outlet store.

Lazarus had visited the workshop many times throughout his childhood. As a youngster, making pottery was an intriguing operation. Shaping a pot or bowl out of a block of clay seemed almost miraculous. But by the time Lazarus began his apprenticeship, he looked at making pottery from a different perspective. He now understood the amount of effort required to convert raw clay into a useful and attractive piece of pottery.

"Lazarus," Benjamin said to his son, "I need more clay for the new job. I'd like you to go outside and prepare as many bricks of clay as you can today."

Lazarus groaned to himself. This was the part of making pottery that he disliked the most. Piles of raw clay, which had been dug out of the shore of the Jordan River, sat outside the workshop. Lazarus placed chunks of the dry clay into a large stone mortar, and in a physically draining process, he pulverized the chunks into dust using a stone pestle. He sifted the clay dust through a sieve into a metal tub in order to remove any stones or other impurities.

Lazarus then poured a jar filled with water drawn from the community well into the metal tub. He removed his sandals, stepped into the tub, and began kneading the clay with his feet. As the clay absorbed the water, the mixture became more and more pliable. Kneading also helped to remove any air bubbles and excess moisture.

Lazarus worked the clay until it was the right consistency, stopping periodically to add a few handfuls of crushed pottery that had already been fired. This additional material, called "grog," helped keep the shaped clay from expanding too much in the kiln during firing. After kneading for what seemed an eternity, Lazarus removed the moist clay from the tub and laid it out onto a wooden platform. The clay was then flattened and cut into blocks, which he then carried into the workshop.

"You did a great job this afternoon," said Benjamin. "This will give us a good start toward filling the order." Lazarus didn't reply. He was beginning to question whether making pottery was something he wanted to do for the rest of his life.

Lazarus took his foot off of the flywheel. The bowl he had been forming was now a limp lump of clay on the spinning platform. It was his third failed attempt at shaping the clay, and he was ready to give up.

Benjamin sensed his son's frustration. "I hate to say this, but perhaps you weren't meant to be a potter. You are very good at your studies, but you don't seem to have a knack for forming clay. I've always hoped that you would take over the business someday, but it seems like you might not have the interest or the skill to do so. What do you think?"

His father's comments hurt Lazarus to the core even though he knew they were true. Lazarus had just turned fifteen years old and recently graduated from synagogue school. At this age he was expected to become proficient in a trade that would support him and his future family. Lazarus did not want to disappoint his father, but he knew that he disliked making pottery. During the previous two years of his part-time apprenticeship, Lazarus had discovered that working with clay required extreme patience, an abundance of creativity, and a good measure of manual dexterity. He possessed none of these qualities in the necessary quantity.

"Father, as much as I know you want me to be a potter like you, I don't think it's something I would be good at. It seems to me that the pottery business requires someone who enjoys working with their hands and has a natural ability to do so. No matter how many times I've tried, my efforts have come up short of your expectations."

This discussion was long overdue. Benjamin had not wanted his son to feel like a failure, and Lazarus hadn't wanted to dash the dreams of his father. Now that they had broached the topic, both of them were relieved and anxious to move forward.

"Son, I've always been proud of you. My hope is that you will live a happy and fulfilling life. For you to follow in my footsteps was my dream, not yours. I wouldn't be a good father if I made your life miserable in order to achieve my own goals. Now that we've cleared the air a bit, I need to ask you a question. Since you don't seem to want a career in the pottery trade, what do you want to do for a living?"

"I've been thinking about that since I began having doubts about being a potter. I think I want to become a scribe. We have only one in Bethany right now. You know him. His name is Levi. He's over sixty years old and has no sons or other relatives to take over his business. I've talked to Levi, and what he told me about his career as a scribe seems to fit my interests and personality. I believe he would take me on as an apprentice, similar to what I've been doing with you for the last two years. Now that I've completed synagogue school, I can work with Levi on a full-time basis."

Benjamin thought for a moment. "Son, I can see how you would fit nicely into that role. As I understand it, one of the duties of a scribe is to teach and interpret the Mosaic law. Tobias has often told your mother and me that you are an excellent student of the law. I also understand that scribes often arbitrate legal disputes. That requires good judgement, which you have. Scribes also prepare official documents for the government and the general public. A scribe prepared the contract that my father-in-law and I signed before your mother and I were married. With a bit of training, you should be able to do that as well."

"I was hoping you would be supportive," replied Lazarus, grateful for his father's positive comments.

Benjamin added, "Don't scribes do copy work too? Wouldn't that become boring?"

"A number of scribes specialize in copying and recopying the Scriptures onto scrolls. This has been done ever since the days of Moses. Today most copy work is done by scribes who are specialists in that field. They work together in Jerusalem so they can carefully check each other's work for any errors. That type of work doesn't appeal to me. I want to do something that requires thought rather than rote."

"If your plan works out, it could provide you with wealth and prestige well beyond what an ordinary potter like me would ever achieve. Scribes make up a significant percentage of the Jewish aristocracy. A number of them are even members of the Sanhedrin."

His father was clearly warming to the possibility of an alternate career path. "I didn't consider wealth or prestige when deciding on a profession," Lazarus stated. "I was looking for something I would be good at and enjoy doing. My real reward would be the satisfaction of helping people understand God's law and apply it to their lives."

The wet clay slid smoothly through Martha's moistened fingers. The shape of a pot began to emerge as she pulled the clay upward from the rotating platform. Her foot turned the flywheel at a comfortable pace. In a few minutes the lump of clay was formed into a vessel ready to be dried and fired. Benjamin smiled as he watched his oldest daughter remove the pot from the platform and carry it to the back of the room near the kiln. She placed it on a shelf to dry with other items she had made.

Shortly after Benjamin agreed to Lazarus' plans to become a scribe, Martha informed him that she had always wanted to make pottery. During her visits to the workshop, she had fallen in love with the entire process. Now that Lazarus had turned down his opportunity, Martha asked her father for a chance to become his apprentice.

Martha was now nineteen years old and lived at home with her parents. Unlike most Jewish women her age, she had never married. Although her parents and other relatives encouraged her to marry and have a family, Martha showed no interest. Several potential suitors attempted to attract her attention, but she would have none of it.

When Martha first communicated her interest in the pottery trade, Benjamin reacted predictably; it was a man's occupation, and she should rethink her view on marriage. Martha decided to recruit her brother to help change their father's mind. Lazarus had always admired Martha's confidence and independent spirit. He knew that she could operate the business as well as any man. Lazarus agreed to her request and waited for the right opportunity to speak with their father.

"Father, I need to talk to you when you have a chance."

"Now is a good time, Son. What is it you want to talk about?"

"It's about Martha. She asked me to speak with you about an apprenticeship. She is very serious about it, and I believe she would be an excellent potter. Earlier you and I talked about the qualifications needed to make pottery. Patience was one of those. Martha has shown patience toward Mary and me when we would have driven anyone else crazy. Another quality we discussed was creativity. You probably don't know this, but Martha is a very good sculptress. She didn't want you to know, but she has been taking some of your clay to form figures of animals and people that are almost lifelike. She was too humble to show anyone else but Mary and me."

"All of that is good," Benjamin said, "but I need someone who can do more than fashion the clay. As you know, the job requires excellent physical conditioning. The clay has to be dug out of the riverbank and brought back to the workshop. It has to be mixed and kneaded before shaping. Wood for the kiln needs to be cut and transported here. Pieces of pottery need to be lifted in and out of the kiln. There's also a business component. Supplies need to be purchased, the finished product sold, and financial records kept. All of these things require a man to do them, wouldn't you agree?"

"You just described all of the reasons I didn't want to be a potter," replied Lazarus. "It wasn't because I couldn't do all of those things if required. I simply had no interest in doing them. You have a daughter who can perform every one of those tasks as well as any man and who would love to be given a chance to do them. What do you have to lose? If she doesn't work out, you can hire a man. But you should show your daughter enough respect to let her try. Even if she fails, which I don't think she will, Martha will never forget that you gave her a chance. If she succeeds, then the business that you and your father established will continue as a family operation even after you're gone."

"You've almost convinced me," admitted Benjamin. "Let me think about this for a while. Tell your sister that I will let her know my decision shortly."

After his talk with Lazarus, Benjamin did give Martha a chance. Following a brief probation period, Martha proved that she had the ability and motivation to operate her father's pottery business.

Lazarus was accepted as Levi's apprentice and began an extended training period to become a scribe. Similar to the occupations of priest and rabbi, Lazarus would not be recognized as a full-fledged scribe until he reached thirty years of age, at which time he would be considered qualified to do the work without supervision. Lazarus hoped to take over Levi's practice someday.

Chapter Three

ROMANCE

THE WEDDING FEAST celebrating the marriage of Mary and Caleb was in full swing. Food and wine were plentiful. Music and conversation filled the air. Everyone seemed to be enjoying themselves—everyone, that is, except Lazarus. He stood by himself near the door of the banquet hall, looking as if he was about to exit the building. Although delighted for his sister, Lazarus had a difficult time matching the enthusiasm of the other guests. From an early age he had always felt uncomfortable in large gatherings, particularly with people he didn't know.

The wedding banquet took place in a large hall adjacent to the only inn in Bethany. Caleb's father owned the inn, and Caleb worked for him. The buildings and property had been passed down from generation to generation. Caleb was an only child and would someday inherit it all.

Their courtship began innocuously. One afternoon Benjamin delivered a supply of bowls and pots to the inn and took Mary along. Caleb had seen Mary and her family at synagogue worship over the years but paid little attention to the scrawny little girl. At this point Mary was sixteen, and Caleb was twenty. His impression of her changed that day. Mary had blossomed into a beautiful young woman.

Over the next few months, Benjamin received a sizeable increase in pottery orders from the inn. The reason became apparent after Caleb began calling on his daughter. Benjamin approved of the match, especially since Martha, his older daughter, showed no interest in marriage. Three years later, after a long courtship and engagement period, Mary and Caleb were married.

Lazarus felt a tap on his shoulder. It was his new brother-in-law, Caleb. "Lazarus, I'd like you to meet my cousin Lydia. She came all the way from Jericho with my uncle's family to be at our wedding. They're staying here at the inn. I thought the two of you might like to get to know each other."

At the age of seventeen, Lazarus felt pressured by his parents and his libido to find a bride and start a family. Unfortunately, Bethany was a rather small town and didn't offer a wide array of potential candidates. The majority of women in Bethany who were his age or younger didn't appeal to Lazarus' selective tastes. The one or two girls who caught his eye were already spoken for by other eligible suitors.

Lydia stepped out from behind her cousin. Lazarus gulped. He had never seen a girl as beautiful as the one standing in front of him. His heart raced, his face flushed bright red, and his legs felt numb. "Hello, Lydia," he stammered. "I'm pleased to meet you." The moment he uttered those words, Lazarus regretted it. Why couldn't he have said something intelligent?

"I'm pleased to meet you too." The sound of Lydia's voice made his entire body tingle. "Caleb has told me some good things about you. I understand you are studying to be a scribe. That is a noble profession. Jericho has several scribes who are all prominent men in the community."

Lazarus' mind was spinning wildly as he struggled to form a reply. He desperately wanted to stay and make a good impression, but at the same time he felt the urge to escape. The impulse to flee prevailed. "I'm sorry, Lydia, but I don't feel well right now. I must have eaten something that didn't agree with my stomach. I hope to see you later. If not, have a safe trip back to Jericho." With those words Lazarus darted out of the wedding hall.

On his way home an initial feeling of relief washed over him. Relief was followed by a wave of regret. "Why can't I be more self-confident? Why do I worry so much about what people think of me? I'm pitiful. This has to change."

That evening Lazarus prayed for guidance, "God, you know my weaknesses. I need your help to overcome them. When I'm afraid, give me courage. When I feel inadequate, give me confidence. Help me to follow your commands and live a life pleasing to you. And, Lord, if I find favor in your sight, bless me with a God-fearing wife who will be a helpmate to me and a loving mother to our children."

A year following his sister's wedding, Levi arranged for a prominent scribe in Jerusalem named Nicodemus to work with Lazarus for a few days. Lazarus looked forward to the training session. He had always enjoyed learning, particularly when it came to the Mosaic law. In addition, the journey to Jerusalem was pleasant, and the quicker pace of the city was always stimulating.

After a week of training with Nicodemus, Lazarus decided to visit the temple before returning home. He entered the Temple Mount through a set of double gates that led to the Court of Gentiles, a large open area that encircled the temple. Both Jews and non-Jews could congregate in the Court of Gentiles, but only Jews were allowed to enter the temple itself. He purchased a young goat along with some grain from vendors who made a living servicing the needs of Jewish worshippers.

Lazarus entered the temple and walked through the Court of Women to the adjoining Court of the Israelites. One of the priests stationed there blessed Lazarus and took his offerings into the Court of Priests, where the goat was ritually killed and prepared for sacrifice. Its blood was collected and sprinkled on the altar. Another priest carried the meat and grain up the altar steps and placed them on the fire burning there.

Lazarus prayed that the aroma from his offering would rise to heaven and be pleasing to God.

After leaving the Court of the Israelites, Lazarus retraced his steps through the Court of Women. He planned to return to Bethany immediately after leaving the temple. The large crowd assembled there slowed his progress.

Suddenly, without warning, Lazarus was pushed forcefully from behind. He lurched forward into a young woman walking in front of him. Both of them tumbled to the hard mosaic floor, his body falling on top of hers. "Are you hurt?" Lazarus asked apologetically.

"No, I'm all right," the young woman replied timidly. Lazarus helped her to her feet. As she stood up, she clutched her right ankle. Her face contorted in pain and her eyes filled with tears. The crowd pressed around them, threatening to knock them to the floor again. Lazarus lifted the girl into his arms and carried her away from the surge of worshippers.

Her ankle was discolored and swollen badly. "Let me help you," pleaded Lazarus. "It was entirely my fault. You can't walk on that ankle. It might be broken."

"You are more than kind, but I'll be fine. My father is a Levite musician on duty today. I was leaving the temple after visiting with him when you and I collided. He should still be in the Court of Priests. His name is Asaph, named after King David's court musician. He will help me home."

"You need to rest that ankle. I'll find your father and bring him here. By the way, my name is Lazarus. I'm sorry we had to meet under these circumstances."

"My name is Rachel. I appreciate your concern. Most men would have walked away without a word of apology."

Lazarus helped Rachel to a nearby bench and went to find her father. He tracked down Asaph, explained what had happened, and apologized profusely. After locating a litter, the two men carried Rachel home where she lived with her parents. Rachel's mother determined that her ankle was badly sprained and wrapped it. Asaph thanked Lazarus and asked him to stay for dinner. Even though he had planned to return to Bethany without delay, Lazarus accepted the offer. He had a premonition that this young woman might be the answer to his prayer.

Lazarus sat across the table from Asaph. They both knew what would come next. For the last six months, Lazarus had been a frequent visitor at the home of Rachel's father. As he got to know her better, Lazarus became more and more smitten. He wanted to spend every minute with Rachel and thought about her nearly every moment they were apart. There was no question in his mind that the course of action he was about to take was the correct one.

"Sir, I would like your permission to marry your daughter. I have prepared the *ketubah* for you to sign. As a scribe with spotless credentials, I assure you that it is in good order. If you agree to the terms of this marriage contract, then I will be legally bound to your daughter. I pledge to love, support, and protect her all of my days."

Asaph unrolled the scroll that Lazarus handed him. He carefully scanned the specifics of the agreement, which were written in Aramaic. The substance of the contract appeared similar to the one that Asaph had presented to his father-in-law nearly two decades before.

One of the sections to which Asaph paid particular attention was the *mohar*, a type of insurance policy to be paid to the wife out of the husband's estate in case of his death, or out of his personal funds if he demanded a divorce. Lazarus contractually pledged two hundred *denarii* if either event happened. Jewish custom did not require a groom to fund the *mohar* prior to the marriage, but Lazarus promised to do so.

Another section of importance to Asaph was his daughter's dowry. This was the currency or property that Rachel would bring into the marriage. In most cases the amount wasn't much since most young women didn't work outside the home. Funds from the *dowry*, like those from the *mohar*, belonged to the wife in case she was widowed or divorced by her husband. Rachel's dowry was listed as twenty *denarii*, an amount that Lazarus knew she could easily provide.

Asaph finished reviewing the document and put it down on the table. "You did an excellent job preparing the contract. Your training as a scribe has served you well. However, there is one change I would like to make with your consent. I wish to add fifty *denarii* to my daughter's dowry."

This token of generosity surprised Lazarus. The bride's portion was rarely supplemented with additional amounts provided by her father, and Asaph was not a wealthy man.

Upon completion of the addendum, Asaph and Lazarus signed the *ketubah.*

In keeping with tradition, Lazarus announced, "It is finished." Asaph broke into a smile and embraced his future son-in-law. Even though the marriage ceremony would take place much later, Lazarus and Rachel were now bound to each other for life in the eyes of God and the Jewish people.

Caleb's voice broke the silence of the cool autumn evening. "Behold, the bridegroom comes!" The piercing tone of a shofar reinforced the announcement that Rachel's groom was waiting outside. A torch-lit parade through the streets of Jerusalem preceded the arrival of Lazarus and the rest of the wedding party.

Rachel had looked forward to this moment for some time. During the year since their betrothal, Lazarus purchased and furnished the house in Bethany where he and Rachel would live. Lazarus had saved enough money to fund the *mohar* and take care of any unexpected expenditures that might occur early in the marriage. It was finally time for the couple to begin their life together and raise a family.

The bridesmaids, alerted that the groom had appeared, joined Rachel to help pack the items she would take to her new home. Sarah, her best friend and maid of honor, helped Rachel into her wedding garments and covered her head with a veil.

Rachel's father and mother beamed as they gazed at their daughter. Asaph took his daughter in his arms and told her he loved her. Rachel's mother, tears streaming down her face, held Rachel in a long and loving embrace. Her family would travel to Bethany the next morning to join the celebration.

Lazarus and his wedding party waited patiently outside. After what seemed like an eternity, the front door opened. Lazarus shivered with excitement as Rachel emerged. Her face was barely visible through the veil, but he could still make out her gorgeous smile. Lazarus and Caleb loaded Rachel's belongings onto the back of a donkey and secured them with ropes. Rachel stepped into an elegant litter that four pole-bearers would carry on the journey to Bethany.

After arriving at the Bethany inn later that evening, the bride and groom were met by Benjamin and Rebecca, who gave their parental blessing on the marriage. Caleb and Sarah then escorted the bride and groom to the bridal chamber. Smiling broadly, Rachel and Lazarus entered the room and closed the door behind them.

The next morning, Lazarus emerged from the wedding chamber grinning from ear to ear. He announced to Caleb and Sarah that the marriage had been consummated and that his bride had, indeed, been a virgin. The two men went to the inn's banquet hall, where Lazarus made the same announcement to the wedding guests who had gathered there. A huge cheer went up when the crowd heard the news, and shouts of congratulations filled the air. Singing and dancing began almost immediately. Wine flowed freely and mountains of food began to quickly disappear. The five days of wedding festivities had begun in earnest.

Meanwhile, Sarah entered the marriage chamber to attend to the bride. Rachel motioned for Sarah to sit next to her on the bed. "I never knew that I could love someone so much," Rachel said with a sigh. "I hope someday you will experience the same happiness that I'm feeling right now."

"I don't know if I will ever meet a man as kind and thoughtful as Lazarus," replied Sarah. "I wonder if any of his friends are looking for a wife."

Several minutes later, Lazarus knocked on the door and entered before Rachel could respond. "Excuse me," he apologized, "I didn't know Sarah was still here."

"Don't mind me. I was just leaving. By the way, do you have any single friends here at the wedding?"

"I'll make sure to introduce you to as many eligible bachelors as I can. I'm sure you'll generate a lot of interest."

"Enjoy your next few days of celebration," Sarah declared as she left the room. "Caleb and I will provide you with anything you need. Make sure to get some rest when you can. You will need it when you return to reality after the wedding feast is over."

Chapter Four

DEATH & TAXES

THE BUSINESSMEN OF Bethany were gathered in the synagogue. Their purpose was not worship. Instead, they were there to discuss politics and economics. More specifically, the topic at hand was taxation.

The Romans had conquered Judea nearly ninety years earlier. Two decades later, Herod I, also known as Herod the Great, was named king of Judea by the Roman Senate. Herod was not born in Judea, but he had been raised as a Jew. During his reign, he attempted to appease both his Roman superiors and the Jewish people while leaving his own mark on the country. The result was a series of lavish building projects, which became his claim to fame.

While the colossal construction projects provided jobs for many of the citizens of Judea, the taxes imposed on the populous to finance them put an enormous strain on the pocketbooks of Herod's Jewish subjects. In addition to levies for local construction, additional taxes were assessed to support the government in Rome.

During the years after Herod's death, the pace of new construction slowed considerably. Businesses failed, and jobs related to construction were lost. Ancillary businesses also felt the impact of the economic slowdown. Fewer construction projects should have resulted in lower taxes. However, to the dismay of businessmen throughout Judea, the same exorbitant tax assessments continued.

In reaction to the ongoing heavy tax burden, Benjamin and the other businessmen in Bethany formed an alliance dedicated to reducing their taxes. Lazarus, now twenty years old and a seasoned scribe, was hired as a legal consultant. Their efforts began with a face-to-face meeting in Jericho with the chief collector of the tax district that included Bethany. His name was Zacchaeus.

Like many of his colleagues, Zacchaeus was a Jew who worked in duplicity with Rome. Decades earlier after the subjugation of Judea, the Romans appointed Jews to collect taxes in an attempt to lessen ill will toward Rome. These third-party collectors, also known as publicans, were compensated by a markup on the taxes remitted to the Roman government. The chief collector of each tax district also received a cut of the excess charged to the taxpayers. While a few tax collectors were relatively honest and assessed a reasonable markup, most of them used this unlimited authority to gouge their constituents and become wealthy as a result.

Unfortunately for the villagers of Bethany, the tax collector assigned to Bethany took greed and extortion to levels that exceeded those of any of his peers. His name was Jokim, and his appearance matched both his occupation and his personality. Relatively tall but painfully thin, Jokim always appeared to be in poor health. His spotty, graying beard partially covered a narrow face filled with pockmarks from a severe case of adolescent acne. A long, hooked nose was set between a pair of squinting, beady eyes. When he opened his mouth to speak, a broken line of yellow crooked teeth added to his repulsive look. But in spite of his physical shortcomings, Jokim was indisputably the most prolific money maker in the tax district.

The initial meeting with Zacchaeus in Jericho did not go well for Benjamin and his fellow petitioners. The chief tax collector, a rich man because of the efforts of his subordinates, was unsympathetic to the request of his visitors. He was not about to replace one of the most successful collectors in his employ. "I am under tremendous pressure from the Romans," Zacchaeus stated. "I'm just doing my job to the best of my ability."

Benjamin spoke up. "The citizens of Bethany are being treated unfairly. We would not be here talking to you if we were charged the same tax rate that similar businesses are paying in most other towns in Judea. We are simply requesting that you discipline your current collector, Jokim. If he won't comply with your orders, we ask that you replace him. He has threatened us with even higher assessments if we complain about his tactics. Further, he charges unreasonable penalties for payments made only a few days late."

Zacchaeus' response was clearly dishonest. "I have no control over what amounts are collected. The same is true of my collectors. We are simply following orders. I suggest you take your appeal to the Romans, who are the real oppressors in this situation."

Seeing they were making no progress, Benjamin and his contingent left Jericho and set out for Jerusalem. The alliance decided to pay an unannounced visit to the office of Governor Valerius Gratus before going home to Bethany. Ever since Herod Archelaus, the son of Herod the Great, was deemed by Rome to be an incompetent leader, Judea had been ruled by a series of Roman governors.

Unable to secure a meeting with the governor, the group met briefly with one of his representatives. As they had done earlier, the group expressed displeasure over the inequitable amount of taxes being assessed and the unfair treatment received from their assigned collector.

"I'm truly sorry," the representative responded with a tone of hollow empathy, "but it isn't feasible for the governor to grant your request. You must pay the taxes due or deal with the consequences. If you are given any level of forbearance, it would set a precedent that could spread throughout Judea. The governor is accountable to Caesar, who in his wisdom determines the amount of taxes each province should pay.

Here in Judea, collection of taxes has been delegated to your own people, the Jews. You will need to present any complaints you have to them. In my opinion, you should be grateful for the many benefits your tax money has brought you. Isn't your beautiful temple in Jerusalem a good example of Roman generosity?"

Dismayed at being shuffled between officials, the disheartened men returned to Bethany. Apparently there was no other place to turn. "What options remain?" they asked each other. One of the men exclaimed angrily, "We need to stand together against this injustice. We are willing to pay a fair amount of taxes to Rome, but these Jewish tax collectors have lined their pockets with excess charges. I propose that we withhold any more tax payments until Jokim is replaced." In a show of solidarity, all the businessmen of Bethany declared a boycott against the unfair tax rate. They would pay no taxes until the issue was addressed by the authorities.

Several days after the alliance was rebuffed by the governor's representative, Jokim paid a visit to Bethany. His first stop was Benjamin's pottery shop. This time he was accompanied by two armed Roman soldiers. "I understand that you are unhappy with me," he said with a tone of sarcasm in his voice. "My supervisor, Zacchaeus, told me that you and a group of your friends paid him a visit and demanded that I be replaced. You accused me of fraud and extortion. Then you had the audacity to take your grievances to the governor.

Your actions were not appreciated by me or those who employ me. In fact, I am here to present you with your revised tax assessment. Unfortunately, I made a mistake on your earlier billing. This one is fifty percent higher. The soldiers are here to make sure I collect the difference."

Benjamin looked at the tax collector with astonishment and contempt. "You are a son of the devil himself. You won't get any additional payments from me today or any day in the future. The amount you charged earlier was already grossly unfair."

When the men of the village got word of the tax collector's visit to Bethany, they began to assemble outside Benjamin's pottery workshop. They could hear the voices inside become more heated. After several emphatic exchanges, Jokim, in a voice as authoritative as he could muster, demanded, "As a designated representative of Rome, I hereby order you to prison until your bill is paid. If your family or friends make the payment, you will be released. Take this man away." One of the soldiers reached over and grabbed Benjamin's arm roughly, pulling him forcibly toward the door.

Martha, who had been helping her mother prepare dinner, heard the commotion. She entered the shop through the back door just as the Roman soldier was accosting her father. Martha impulsively began pounding the soldier with her fists. "Leave him alone!" she screamed. "He hasn't done anything wrong!"

With his grip firmly on Benjamin's arm with one hand, the soldier slapped Martha across the face with the back of his other hand. She fell limply to the floor. Benjamin wheeled around and instinctively drove his clenched fist into the soldier's mid-section. Benjamin winced as his hand bounced off the protective leather armor. The second soldier drew a dagger from his belt and sunk it into Benjamin's back. Benjamin reeled forward and fell in a heap on the floor.

Martha, still groggy from the blow, opened her eyes to see her father lying next to her. He was bleeding profusely from his wound. She quickly collected herself, jumped to her feet, and began to wildly pummel the soldier who was holding the bloody dagger. The soldier stood stoically while Martha continued swinging at him until she was totally exhausted. Breathing heavily, Martha looked down at her wounded father. His skin appeared ashen, and a puddle of blood covered the floor around his torso. She kneeled down and checked his pulse for any sign of life. "They killed my father!" Martha cried out. "They murdered him!"

By now the crowd of villagers outside the workshop numbered more than twenty men. Hearing Martha's frantic shouts, they pressed forward against the front door and it swung open. The first men into the shop gasped collectively. They were shocked to see Benjamin lying on the floor in a pool of blood and Martha kneeling beside him crying. Their astonishment quickly turned to anger. The doorway into the workshop nearly collapsed as a wave of villagers rushed in and surrounded the intruders standing inside.

The soldiers tried to draw their swords, but the crush of so many bodies in the small space made their attempts impossible. The enraged men overpowered and disarmed the soldiers, but not without difficulty. The soldiers, trained to fight to the death, continued struggling fiercely until pinned to the floor. It took several men to tie their hands securely with ropes. The soldiers remained defiant, demanding to be released immediately. They warned that any actions against them would be punished severely by Rome.

Seeing that the soldiers would be of no help to him, the tax collector cowered in fear. "I swear I will pay you back all of the fees you were overcharged . . . with interest," Jokim promised. "Just don't hurt me. Let me go and you will never see my face again."

It was too late to plead for mercy. The mob of villagers shouted vulgarities and spit on their captives as they dragged them roughly out of the workshop. "Let's kill them!" the men shouted. "May Benjamin's blood be upon them!" After reaching an open field nearby, the angry crowd forced the three hostages to their knees and formed a circle around them. Each man picked up one or more large rocks that dotted the bone-dry landscape and prepared to stone them to death.

Several minutes earlier, Tobias had learned of a confrontation at Benjamin's home. He raced down the hill from the synagogue as the villagers were dragging three men toward the field. Tobias ignored them and kept on running until he arrived at the pottery shop. Out of breath but fueled by adrenaline, he rushed through the open door. His eyes were immediately drawn to Benjamin's body lying motionless on the floor, his head cradled in his wife Rebecca's lap. Martha sat on the floor next to them crying uncontrollably. "He's dead," Martha sobbed. "One of the soldiers murdered my father."

Anger and anguish filled every pore of Tobias' body and soul. But as quickly as these emotions overcame him, Tobias was jolted back to reality. If the villagers harmed or killed a Roman soldier, the entire garrison in Jerusalem would retaliate with a vengeance, outweighing any satisfaction gained by avenging Benjamin's death. Tobias knew that no act of defiance, no matter how justified, would go unpunished. Retribution for Benjamin's murder would not be the end of bloodshed in Bethany.

Tobias left the workshop and rushed to the field where the stoning was about to take place. "Stop! Stop at once! Men of Bethany hear me out!" shouted Tobias to the angry crowd. "You must let these men go unharmed. I am as outraged by Benjamin's murder as you are. But think about your lives and the lives of your families. Acting in haste right now would destroy everything that you have. We are no match for the Roman army. They will seek revenge for the death of their fellow soldiers, and all of us will be subject to their retribution. We have to swallow the bile in our throats and send these men away alive."

One by one the villagers dropped the stones they were holding. Tobias walked to the middle of the circle and spoke to the three hostages. "I wish to God you had not come to Bethany today. At this point I assume you regret your presence here as well. You need to understand that your actions nearly got you killed today. These men were ready to stone you to death for murdering Benjamin. As a matter of fact, they still could—unless you are willing to cooperate. After I untie your hands, I suggest you return to Jerusalem quickly before these men change their minds."

Tobias directed a warning to the soldiers. "I recommend that you say nothing about this matter to your commanding officer. It would be embarrassing if he found out that a group of unarmed villagers disarmed you. He wouldn't appreciate the near riot you incited here in Bethany. In return for your silence, we will not inform your supervisors that any of this happened. Is this agreeable with you?" The soldiers could do little else but nod their heads affirmatively. They had no weapons with which to defend themselves and no chance of overcoming the large crowd of enraged onlookers.

Tobias then turned to Jokim. "None of this would have happened without your avarice. You have treated the men of Bethany with contempt by stealing their profits for your own gain. They have every reason to take their rage out on you. Do you have anything to say that would change their minds?"

In a soft whimper, the tax collector reiterated a portion of the pledge he made earlier. "Just let me go and you will never see my face again. I will transfer to another district, and I promise to treat the people there fairly. My supervisor doesn't need to know that any of this happened." No one noticed that Jokim had neglected to repeat his earlier pledge to reimburse the overcharges he had collected.

After obtaining oaths from the three men to fully cooperate, Tobias untied them. As the trio rose slowly to their feet and brushed the dirt from their clothes, the villagers opened one side of the circle they had formed. It led toward the road to Jerusalem. Attempting to maintain a semblance of dignity, the soldiers stood erect with their shoulders back and chins up. In contrast, Jokim's shoulders were drooped and his gaze focused downward at the ground. In the midst of a chorus of obscenities from the crowd, the three of them walked away silently until they could be seen no more.

Lazarus was nearing Bethany when he passed two Roman soldiers and another man going in the opposite direction. He was returning from Jerusalem after filing legal documents on behalf of one of his Bethany clients. Lazarus recognized the tall skinny man as the tax collector, Jokim, whom his father and all the businessmen of Bethany detested. "Strange," Lazarus thought. "They look like they've been roughed up. Their clothes are torn and their faces and arms have bruises." Eager to get home to his wife, Lazarus dismissed the oddity and continued his journey.

The road led him past the synagogue. Tobias stood at the entrance with his back to the road. He didn't see Lazarus approaching. "Rabbi, how are you today? I hope you are well," Lazarus called out. Tobias turned to face him. As soon as their eyes met, Lazarus knew something was wrong. Tobias motioned for Lazarus to come to him.

"What is it?" Lazarus asked, fearing the worst. "You look troubled."

"Lazarus, I am so sorry. Your father is dead," Tobias answered in hushed tones. "He was murdered by Roman soldiers. They were arresting him for refusing to pay taxes."

Lazarus stifled an urge to scream. Despair filled his entire being. His heart felt as if it were going to explode. He couldn't fully comprehend the words he just heard. Without speaking, Lazarus turned and left Tobias standing there.

Lazarus' heart beat wildly as he ran down the road to his father's house. He threw open the door and saw a sight he could not have anticipated. His mother and several other women from the synagogue were washing the body of his father on a table covered with a tarp. The ritual cleansing was being done before anointing the corpse with oil and spices and wrapping it in burial cloths. Benjamin would be buried the same day he died in order to minimize decomposition in the hot climate.

Through eyes filled with tears, Lazarus stared at his father's face. It appeared peaceful even though his death had evidently been violent. Benjamin's blood-soaked cloak lay on the floor nearby. Lazarus held his mother close. He felt her tears fall on his neck as she sobbed quietly.

"How could this happen?" His calm voice intentionally disguised his inner turmoil. "I saw Tobias on my way into the village. He said that the soldiers were arresting Father when they killed him. He mentioned something about not paying taxes."

Martha, seeing that her mother was overcome with emotion, replied in a voice filled with anger, "You and the other businessmen demanded that the slimy tax collector, Jokim, be replaced. When you were turned down, everyone probably thought that was the end of the matter. It wasn't. Jokim got word of your complaint and decided to teach our village a lesson by demanding even more taxes. Today he brought Roman soldiers for support.

"Father was recognized as one of the village spokesmen, so Jokim visited his pottery shop first. When he refused to pay the outrageous amount demanded, the soldiers started to arrest him. I tried to intervene, but one of them threw me to the floor. Father tried to protect me, and the other soldier stabbed him to death."

"What happened then?" Lazarus asked.

"The men of the village rushed the three of them, tied them up, and dragged them to the field down the street. The villagers were going to stone them to death, but Tobias intervened. He convinced them that any satisfaction gained from killing them would be overshadowed by the bloodshed resulting from Roman revenge."

"I wish to God that I had been here to help," Lazarus exclaimed in remorse. "Maybe I could have prevented his death. Now all I can do is help bury him."

After final preparations were completed, the entire village formed a procession to accompany the body to the burial site. Weeping and wailing filled the air as the assembly of mourners trudged to the family tomb, a cave carved into a limestone outcrop jutting from a grassy hill just outside the village. Benjamin's embalmed body was taken through the narrow opening in the cave and laid on a stone bench. The walls inside were dotted with small man-made niches, many of which held ossuaries. The stone boxes contained bones of family members who had died in years past. As soon as Benjamin's body fully decomposed in the tomb, Lazarus and his family would place his father's skeletal remains in a new ossuary. The process would be repeated for future burials.

After a seven-day mourning period, Lazarus returned to his office. He and Levi had formed a partnership and co-owned a one-story building in the business district of Bethany. The location was convenient to their commercial clients as well as to individuals who needed the legal services of a scribe. Their business was doing well, and Lazarus felt the need to get back to work as soon as possible.

The silhouette of a man appeared in the doorway. Lazarus looked up from his documents. "Come in, please," invited Lazarus. "How can I help you?"

The man entered and stood in front of Lazarus' desk. He was tall and well built. His beard was long but well-groomed. Lazarus guessed they were about the same age. "Don't you remember me?" the man asked. "It's only been five years since we graduated from synagogue school."

"Simon, is that you? I wouldn't have recognized your face, but I recognize your voice."

"I've been growing this beard ever since we left school. I'm not surprised you didn't know it was me."

Lazarus felt a twinge of anxiety. He recalled the times when Simon and his friends had bullied him. He remembered asking God for help and how God had answered his prayer. But that was a long time ago. Lazarus wondered what type of man Simon had become and why he had suddenly reappeared in his life.

"It's good to see you again," offered Lazarus. "I've always meant to thank you for protecting me from your friends. After that day you stood up for me, I never had trouble with them again."

"I should be the one thanking you. The day you helped me answer Tobias' question was a turning point in my life. I suddenly realized that good things could result from applying myself rather than wasting my God-given abilities. From then on, I decided to put more effort into learning new skills, and it's paid off. I'm working with my father in his stone-cutting operation. I handle the business end of it, and he manages the employees."

"So how can I help you? Do you need some contracts drawn up?"

"Not exactly. It has to do with your father. First of all, I want to express my deepest sympathies for your loss."

"Thank you. I miss him so much. He was an inspiration to me. It was tragic how he could be murdered for something as trivial as taxes."

"That's really why I came to see you. I was in the crowd the day your father was killed. I heard that the tax collector was in Bethany accompanied by some soldiers so I followed a number of other men walking toward your father's workshop. When I got there, some of the men were already dragging the collector and soldiers out. I heard what had happened, and I joined them on the way to the field. We were all outraged and ready to stone them to death. Tobias stepped in and stopped the stoning before it started."

"That's consistent with what I've heard," Lazarus said. "I regret I wasn't there. Maybe I could have done something to intervene, and he wouldn't have been murdered. But it's over now. I appreciate your condolences."

"I want to offer you much more than sympathy. As a scribe and expert in the law of Moses, you will probably agree that justice was not done that day and hasn't been done since. I'm here to propose a way you can avenge the death of your father."

Lazarus did a double take. He had been, and still was, extremely angry about his father's callous and unnecessary murder. But until that moment, he had not considered the possibility of revenge. Lazarus considered himself to be at fault because of his absence almost as much as he blamed the soldier who did the stabbing.

Simon continued, "A few years ago I joined an underground society of Jews. You might have heard of our organization. We call ourselves Zealots because our group is fanatical about achieving independence from Roman rule. We despise both the Romans and their Jewish sympathizers, particularly tax collectors. All I need to do is tell them the story of your father's murder and identify Jokim and the guilty soldiers. My fellow Zealots will do the rest."

"What do you mean . . . they will do the rest?"

"You know what I mean. The men who killed your father will meet the same fate."

Lazarus remained silent for a considerable time. He remembered seeing the three men on the road as he returned to

Bethany. He might have killed them then and there if he had known what they had done. He saw flashbacks of his mother and sisters crying and his father's bloody clothes lying nearby. Recollections of the burial seemed like a bad dream.

"As much as I loved my father, I'm not sure that I want to see anyone else dead," Lazarus finally responded. "I want to see justice, but would killing three more people make the situation any better? Won't God be their ultimate judge?"

"You know the answer better than I do," Simon answered. "But didn't God tell Moses in the Torah that acts of violence should be paid back in a similar manner? A broken bone deserves payback with a broken bone. An eye is given for an eye, and a tooth for a tooth."

"Yes, the Torah does say that," Lazarus stated with authority. "But Jewish scholars later interpreted this to require monetary compensation, not a literal loss of body parts."

"There is no price that could be paid for the loss of your father," countered Simon. "In this case, a life for a life seems completely appropriate. In my opinion, killing the three of them would be justified. On the day of Benjamin's murder, it was probably best that the entire village didn't retaliate. But now that over a week has passed, you have the chance to get revenge without letting the Romans know who did it."

Lazarus paused to consider Simon's proposal. If he authorized the killings, he would be as guilty as the Zealots who carried them out. He had been so careful to live a life of obedience to the law. God had blessed him for it. Would a just God punish him for avenging his father's unjust murder?

"I can't condone the killing of anyone," Lazarus finally replied. "My conscience would not allow me to rest if I did. However, I can't stop you or anyone else from doing what they feel is right."

"I respect your decision," Simon responded. "Any blame for what happens next will be on my shoulders. Tomorrow I'm going to Jerusalem for a scheduled meeting of the Zealots. I'm going to tell them what happened, and I'm sure they will agree to avenge the death of your father. Nothing the Zealots do will be traceable back to you, your family, or the people of Bethany."

Word spread quickly through the village. A new tax collector had arrived from Jerusalem and was making the rounds to various businesses in Bethany. It was no surprise to anyone that Jokim had been replaced. After the death of Benjamin two months earlier, everyone was sure that he would be too frightened to show his face again.

The pottery shop that Martha now operated on her own was the third business that the new tax collector visited that morning. She heard a knock on the workshop door and looked up from the pottery wheel. Standing in the opening was a small, pudgy man carrying a parchment scroll and a money bag. "Good morning, sir. How can we help you?" asked Martha.

"My name is Matthew, and I've come to collect your quarterly tax payment on behalf of the government of Rome."

"What happened to our previous tax collector?"

"Unfortunately, Jokim was involved in a robbery recently. As he was returning to Jericho from Jerusalem, a band of thugs accosted him on the road. They not only stole the money he had collected, but they also beat him severely and slit his throat from ear to ear. I understand it was quite gruesome. The authorities believe that this awful deed might have been the work of the Zealots. They've been very active recently in undermining our efforts to collect taxes. To be honest, I'm in fear for my own life. I also heard that several Roman soldiers were killed in an ambush just outside Jerusalem. Those miscreant Zealots are going to bring the wrath of Rome down on us all."

"I can't say that I'm sorry to hear about Jokim," Martha admitted. "He was responsible for the death of my father. However, I agree that these are contentious times between the Jews and Romans. I don't see an easy way out of this. It will take a miracle. Perhaps it's time for God to send the Messiah he promised."

"I wouldn't hold my breath on that one," Matthew replied sarcastically. "I decided a long time ago that it's better to join than to fight. That's why I took this job working for the Romans even though everyone in the community hates me for it. But if the Messiah does come during my lifetime, I would have no problem switching loyalties. Until then, I'm making a good living doing what I do."

Chapter Five

DESPAIR

RACHEL GRIMACED AS she felt another contraction. The midwife placed a wet cloth on her forehead and spoke in comforting tones. "You're going to be fine. The baby is coming soon." In spite of her words of encouragement, the midwife knew something was wrong. She had seen these symptoms in only one other instance during her many years of delivering babies.

Earlier in her pregnancy, Rachel occasionally passed small amounts of blood. By the time she had reached full term, the flow was heavier and more frequent. Now, after an hour of contractions, bright red blood was oozing steadily onto the blanket on which Rachel was lying. Her lower abdomen began swelling. There was still no sign that the baby was ready to emerge.

The midwife called out to Lazarus, who was waiting expectantly in the adjoining room, "Please bring more blankets and water." The pool of blood caught his eye as he entered the room. His first reaction was disbelief. He had not expected something like this after almost nine months of a seemingly normal pregnancy.

"Are you in pain?" Lazarus asked.

"Not too much, but I feel very weak and dizzy," Rachel replied softly. "I don't know what's wrong. I'm so tired and want to sleep, but our baby is ready to be born."

Lazarus gently squeezed his wife's hand. Rachel's breath remained regular but shallow. She seemed at peace as she closed her eyes.

"There's nothing you can do but pray," whispered the midwife. "You might want to get some rest yourself. From what I can tell, this might take a while." She rolled Rachel's hips gently in one direction and then the other while replacing the blood-soaked blanket.

Lazarus stepped out of the room in silence. His eyes glistened with tears. Once out of earshot of his wife, he fell to his knees and bowed his head in prayer. "Lord, if I have ever found favor in your sight, spare my wife, Rachel. She's all that I value on this earth. And if it is your will, bring our child safely into this world. A year ago you took my father before his time. My heart can't take another loss like that so soon."

Throughout the day, Lazarus moved in and out of the birthing room. From what he could surmise, the situation was not improving. He had supplied the midwife with a number of blankets which quickly needed replacement. There was no indication that the bleeding was subsiding. Rachel drifted in and out of consciousness. The contractions had stopped.

"I'm certain your wife will die from loss of blood," the midwife admitted. "There's nothing I can do to save her. Our only option to possibly save the child is to cut into the womb and pull it out. I believe that the cord is attached at the opening of the womb and the lining has ruptured. However, if we do this, your wife will bleed to death even more quickly than if we did nothing. The longer we wait the less chance we have that your baby can be delivered alive."

Rachel's face was ashen from loss of blood. Her eyes were closed, and her lungs barely rose as she took slow, shallow breaths. There was little chance, apart from a miracle, that she would survive the night. But she was still alive. Lazarus' mind was racing. How could he bring their child into the world if it meant taking Rachel's life?

Thoughts of suicide kept creeping into his mind. Six months after both his wife and baby had died during childbirth, Lazarus was sinking further and further into depression. He wanted to die and be with his beloved Rachel and the son he never got to hold. The grief he felt was so powerful that Lazarus could not be consoled by his family or friends. He didn't eat properly and couldn't bring himself to go to work.

He was always tired but too agitated to sleep, irritable and prone to angry outbursts.

Realizing that their brother's condition was serious and perhaps life threatening, Mary and Martha struggled to convince Lazarus that his life still had meaning. Rebecca, still grieving over the loss of her husband, feared that she might lose her son. His family prayed fervently for Lazarus' recovery.

But Lazarus didn't recover. Instead, he fell deeper into the pit of despair that had engulfed him after Rachel and his unborn son died. One train of thought kept running through his mind. Why did God let this happen to his wife and child? Had he done something to incur God's wrath? Was he being punished for complicity in the death of the tax collector and soldiers? He had not ordered or performed the killing, but he had not tried to stop it from happening. Was he doomed to a life of misery, or could he do something to earn God's favor again?

Lazarus recalled the story of Job that he had studied in synagogue school. He and Job had much in common. God allowed everything that Job cherished to be snatched away. Job never knew why it happened. Now Lazarus faced a similar situation. Except in his case, Lazarus feared he was not as blameless as Job. Perhaps, unlike Job, he deserved what happened to him.

That night as he lay in bed alone, Lazarus prayed for guidance. "God of Abraham, Isaac, and Jacob, my heart is broken and my soul is crushed. My wife and child have been taken from me, and I have no one to turn to but you. From childhood I have done my best to obey you. But if you are punishing me because I failed you, I humbly ask for your forgiveness. Help me to find favor with you again. Show me what you want me to do, and lead me in the path you want me to follow. Bless me, Lord God, and give me peace."

Over the next few days Lazarus concluded that he needed a new start. He needed to put the bitter memories behind him and find some peace of mind. While determining what to do next, he recalled an encounter with two male customers at the pottery store many years earlier. His initial impression was that the men were odd. They were dressed plainly in matching white robes. Their demeanor was detached, and they spoke to each other in hushed tones. After selling them a few pieces of pottery, Lazarus asked where they lived. The men replied that they were from Qumran, a settlement located northwest of the Dead Sea.

After they left the pottery store, Lazarus asked his father about the strange visitors. Benjamin told him that an offshoot Jewish religious sect had settled in a compound at Qumran about one hundred years earlier. Most outsiders speculated that the founder had been a disgruntled Pharisee who left the established Jewish leadership to form his own sect. They came to be known as the Essenes.

According to his father, the Essenes were ascetics in the true sense of the word. They had no regard for material possessions and considered everything they had as communal property to be shared. The Essenes isolated themselves from the rest of society in order to remain pure. They strictly adhered to the law of Moses to a degree that exceeded even that of

Pharisees. Women were not allowed into membership and celibacy was mandated.

Lazarus wondered if the Essene community might be the answer to his prayers. Qumran was in an isolated area of the desert twenty miles from Bethany, and there was little contact between residents of the two communities. Living there would provide adequate separation from the site of his painful memories.

Lazarus also speculated that the Essenes' strict adherence to the law of Moses might be a way to redeem himself from God's wrath. By avoiding the temptations of everyday life, he would be able to more fully obey God's commands and get right with him again. A vow of celibacy would be no problem. No woman could ever replace his beloved Rachel.

Lazarus announced to his mother, sisters, and his business partner, Levi, that he was leaving for Qumran. He didn't know how long he would be there or if he would ever return to Bethany. He was going there to begin a new life. In his convoluted thought process, a fresh start meant abandoning all that remained dear to him.

The Essenes viewed Lazarus as an anomaly. Few outsiders sought their way of life. Those who applied for membership were screened closely to ensure they would fit into the uncommon culture. After arriving at Qumran, Lazarus went through a rigorous interview process. He had no problem qualifying. He was young, educated, healthy, and unmarried. More importantly, he was a scribe with extensive knowledge of the Mosaic law.

Lazarus began his first year of probation full of hope. During this period, a candidate for membership received extensive training in the Scriptures, interspersed with rigorous examinations on the subject material. The training was meant to assist in reaching a higher level of spiritual purity. A prospect lived in austere conditions outside the member housing area during this time. He was expected to adhere to all rules of the community and work for the common good.

If, after a year of acceptable conduct, Lazarus wished to continue the qualification process, he would have to successfully complete an additional two years of probation. During those two years, Lazarus could live in housing within the compound. However, he would not be allowed to participate in certain religious rituals, eat communal meals, or enter buildings that were reserved for members only.

If Lazarus finally achieved full membership, he would be required to donate everything he owned to the community coffers. Most men who had lived in regular society and were in a normal state of mind would never consider becoming an Essene. Lazarus, at this point in his life, was not in a normal state of mind.

Lazarus opened his eyes and squinted. The first rays of sunshine were seeping through cracks in the walls of the primitive mud hut that served as his living quarters. The cloth sheet covering the straw bed on which he slept was soaked with sweat. Dark of night didn't provide much relief from the desert heat. Before getting out of bed, he offered a silent prayer, thanking God for the new day and asking for his guidance and protection.

Lazarus retrieved his white tunic from a small wooden table. He had worn the same clothes every day since arriving in Qumran three months earlier. They would be replaced only if torn beyond repair. He put on the tunic and a pair of worn sandals and walked out the door of his hut, stooping to pass through the low opening. Hot air enveloped him as soon as he got outside. It reminded him of the heat from the kiln at his father's pottery shop.

Lazarus walked along a dirt path toward the member compound. He passed several Essenes walking toward the main building where communal meals were served. None of them said a word or acknowledged his presence. Lazarus continued down the path and entered a small stone building. On the table was his morning meal consisting of a small loaf of bread, a bowl of dates, and a cup of wine. Ezra, his instructor, stood nearby.

Lazarus entered the room silently and sat down at the table. Ezra said a prayer asking God to bless the food and their time together. While Lazarus ate, Ezra taught the lesson for the day, which addressed rules for observing the Sabbath.

Throughout the lesson, Lazarus was not allowed to speak. It was not until after the lecture that Ezra asked if there were any questions. As a graduate of synagogue school and a scribe by profession, Lazarus had already committed to memory all the Scripture references Ezra used in his lesson. However, his Jewish upbringing didn't prepare him for the Essene interpretation of the Sabbath rules.

"With all due respect," noted Lazarus, "I have been a devout Jew all my life and do my best to follow all the Mosaic laws. However, I have never been told by any religious leader or scholar that I can't defecate on the Sabbath. How can a natural bodily function like that be wrong?"

"We expect our members to obey the letter of the law," replied Ezra. "In the book of Exodus, God requires us to remain pure in mind and body. We must refrain from sinning and avoid anything that would make our bodies unclean. That is why we continually perform ritual washings. It is also why we require anyone who has a bowel movement to walk a half mile outside the community to a designated area where he can dig a pit, defecate, and cover the hole with dirt."

"What does that have to do with the Sabbath?"

"God has also prohibited us from doing any work on the Sabbath. Digging a pit and covering it is considered work. Therefore, we refrain from relieving ourselves during the entire twenty-four hours of the Sabbath."

"With all due respect, I suspect there must be quite a few violations of that particular Sabbath law."

"You would be surprised," replied Ezra, not realizing Lazarus' remark had been made tongue-in-cheek. "This temptation can be avoided by fasting the previous day and practicing bowel control. As you rightly point out, Essenes take a stricter approach to compliance with Sabbath laws than other

Jewish sects. During the Sabbath we are expected to avoid anything that might appear to be work. We eat meals but cannot prepare them on that day. We are not allowed to lift anything heavy or do anything else that requires more than minimal physical effort. The Sabbath is to be spent resting, contemplating God's word, and giving him thanks for the blessings he has given us. Anything that distracts us from doing these things is considered evil."

Lazarus didn't respond. In order to remain at Qumran and become an Essene, he would have to comply with every requirement whether it made sense or not. After Lazarus finished his meal and the lesson was over, Ezra said another prayer, asking God's help to keep their minds and hearts pure through the coming day.

Lazarus left in silence and began the long walk to the fields. He spent the rest of the day in the blazing sun, watering and weeding the crops. As darkness approached, Lazarus returned to the training building. Ezra had prepared the evening meal of bread, wine, and vegetable stew. His instructor said a prayer asking God's blessing on the food, and Lazarus ate in silence while Ezra taught the second lesson of the day.

On the way back to his hut, Lazarus bathed and washed his tunic in a cistern filled with water captured during seasonal rainfall. Before falling asleep, he thanked God for the day now over. It had been just like every other day of his stay in Qumran.

After completing his first six months of probation, Lazarus reflected on his experiences in Qumran. This seemed like a good time to evaluate whether or not his lifestyle change was accomplishing what he hoped it would. If it wasn't meeting his expectations, he was under no obligation to remain there.

Lazarus had considered joining the Essene sect for two reasons. The first was to escape the overwhelmingly painful memories of the loss of his wife and child. Although the pain could never be erased, hard work provided some measure of relief from the grief he felt. In Bethany, Lazarus was regularly awakened by nightmares of his wife's death. In Qumran, exhausted from a full day of manual labor, more often than not he slept through the night. Lazarus realized, however, that exhaustion was only a temporary panacea for his anguish.

The second reason he had considered becoming an Essene was to win back God's favor. If he had done something terrible to deserve God's wrath, he needed to become acceptable to God again. But after living what he considered to be a pious life for the prior six months, Lazarus wasn't sure if he was any closer to achieving his goal.

Even if his stay in Qumran had fully achieved both objectives, it was doubtful that Lazarus would ever become a full-fledged member of the Essene community. The more he learned, the more he realized, much like the clay in his father's workshop, he could not be formed into the shape they required.

Ezra did his best to indoctrinate his student, but he was fighting an uphill battle. The biggest obstacle was the past. Lazarus' belief system had been ingrained in him since his youth, so it would take a monumental paradigm shift to change it. Unlike Lazarus, Ezra had never experienced life outside of Qumran. He had been adopted as a young child by the Essene community, a practice that allowed the celibate sect to survive. Ezra had arrived in Qumran with a blank slate, but Lazarus entered with a lifetime of preconceptions.

In their initial training sessions, Ezra explained the origins of the Essene sect. Nearly two centuries earlier, the Jews had won independence from their Syrian Greek subjugators. When the leaders of the revolt, the Maccabee family, appointed one of their own family members as high priest, many devout Jews felt that this defiled both the priesthood and the temple. Jewish tradition required priests to be from the bloodline of Aaron, Moses' brother. The disgruntled dissidents formed new communities to distance themselves from the corrupted priesthood in Jerusalem and became known as Essenes, meaning "pious ones." Qumran was one of the first such communities established.

Throughout the training, Ezra stressed the moral superiority of the Essene culture. Essenes considered themselves to be the Sons of Light while the rest of the Jewish world was populated by Sons of Darkness. To remain untainted by those living in darkness, the Essenes isolated themselves from the rest of Jewish society in remote locations like Qumran.

In order to live in isolation, Essenes had to be self-sufficient. This was accomplished through a combination of hard work and adoption of a minimalistic lifestyle. Essenes placed no value in wealth, possessions, or status. Instead, they valued whatever allowed them to please God and shunned whatever might distract them from that objective. Even seemingly

God-pleasing actions such as marriage were considered distractions to be avoided.

Lazarus admired the efforts of Essenes to avoid evil and remain right with God. After all, that was one of the main reasons he had come to Qumran. However, he could not accept many of their other basic beliefs. Instead of offering sacrifices in the Jerusalem temple, the Essenes believed that sincere repentance, followed by ritual washing, provided forgiveness of sins. Lazarus considered bathing an unacceptable substitute for the shedding of blood on the temple altar.

Lazarus also had a problem with the Essene view of the Messiah. The Essenes envisioned the Messiah to be one of their own, descended from the priestly line of Aaron, who would restore the temple and the priesthood to their previous state of purity. Lazarus, like most other Jews, saw the Messiah as a strong leader who would restore the Jewish state into a strong independent nation similar to that established by King David and his son Solomon.

The most important bone of contention for Lazarus involved the concept of life after death. As a Pharisee, Lazarus believed that the physical body would die and decay but would be resurrected again on the last day. Those who obeyed God during their lives would spend eternity in heaven with God. The Essenes, similar to another Jewish sect called the Sadducees, denied the resurrection of the body. This was unacceptable to Lazarus, who believed that he and his wife and child and family would someday be reunited in bodily form in heaven.

In spite of his many misgivings, Lazarus decided to remain in Qumran for a while longer. He wasn't quite ready to return to Bethany, and he still harbored a flicker of hope that the Essene way of life might be the solution to his problems. However, that hope was diminishing quickly as time passed. Instead of relishing the solitary life he thought he needed, Lazarus increasingly missed the love and support of his sisters and mother. He even missed his occupation as a scribe. Perhaps God had directed him to Qumran to show him how blessed his former life had actually been.

The sun was straight overhead, and Lazarus was sweating profusely. The hoe he was using to dig weeds out of the wheat field seemed heavier than usual. Lazarus stood up to stretch his back. A man could be seen in the distance walking on the path leading to the field. It wasn't one of the Essenes because he wasn't dressed in white. As the man got closer, Lazarus thought that he recognized the gait. As he got even closer, Lazarus realized that the man approaching him was Caleb, his brother-in-law. Lazarus waved to him, making sure that Caleb could distinguish him from the rest of the workers. Caleb returned the wave and continued walking toward him.

"Hello, brother-in-law," greeted Lazarus with a smile. "What brings you to this desert paradise?"

Caleb returned the smile, but his expression quickly turned solemn. "Lazarus, I have some bad news. Your mother is very ill. We're not sure she will make it. I came here to let you know in case you wanted to see her before she died."

Lazarus felt a flood of emotions racing through his mind. He envisioned his mother's lovely face, her warm embrace, and her comforting voice. At the same time, he felt guilt for abandoning her and the rest of the family for so long. He wanted to scream and cry at the same time. After taking a moment to calm himself, Lazarus made the only decision he could. "Let's go," he responded. "We're wasting time here."

Lazarus dropped his hoe, and he and Caleb hurried down the path toward the compound. After reaching the front gate, they continued on the road to Bethany. Lazarus didn't stop to let anyone know he was leaving. His focus was fixed on getting to his mother.

In spite of the heat of the afternoon, Lazarus increased his pace. Caleb struggled to keep up with him. "Tell me about my mother's illness," Lazarus implored. "I left her nine months ago and haven't written to her during that time. If I had known she wasn't well, I would have returned home earlier."

"If it's any consolation, her illness came on suddenly," responded Caleb. "Yesterday morning Mary visited your mother to see how she was doing. She found Rebecca sitting in a chair staring at the wall. When Mary approached her, she looked up but didn't say anything. Your sister could see something was wrong. The right side of your mother's mouth was drooping and some drops of saliva were running down her chin. When Mary asked what had happened, she tried to talk but could only mutter unintelligible sounds. Mary was able to get her to her feet, but your mother seemed dizzy and had a difficult time walking. Mary finally got her to the bed and covered her up to keep her warm. She ran to get Martha. They have been with your mother since that time. As far as I know, your mother hasn't improved."

Four hours after they left Qumran, the two men arrived at his mother's house in Bethany. Lazarus entered the front door without knocking and hurried to the back bedroom where he found Mary and Martha standing near their mother's bed. "How is she doing?" Lazarus asked abruptly.

"Hello to you too," Martha answered with a touch of irritation in her voice.

"I'm sorry to be short. Greetings, sisters," Lazarus replied apologetically. "All I've been thinking about is Mother's condition. How is she?"

"She hasn't regained consciousness since I got her into bed," replied Mary. "That was over a day ago. She hasn't eaten anything during that time. Based on the difficulty I had getting her into bed, I think her right side is paralyzed."

"Is there anything we can do for her?"

"Only prayer will help. We have been keeping her as comfortable as possible," Martha responded. "We sent for a physician in Jerusalem who might be able to travel to Bethany. No one here can treat her. I wasn't sure if a doctor would come, but we needed to try."

"I am glad she's still alive. I was afraid she might die before I got home."

"We're glad you're back too," replied Martha. "But you really need to get cleaned up. I hope all of the Essenes don't smell as bad as you do."

"Actually, they are some of the cleanest people I've ever met," Lazarus told her. "Every time they do something they consider sinful, they wash in one of the ritual baths to become pure again. Sorry I smell so bad. I was working in the hot sun when Caleb found me."

"Given your recurring feelings of guilt, I imagine you were washing yourself all the time," Martha joked.

Lazarus smiled for the first time he left Qumran. "You always have a way to bring me back to reality. The truth is that I wasn't allowed to participate in ritual washings until my probation period was completed. But I was able to find water in which to bathe every day. At least I was able to clean the outside of my body."

Rebecca died the next day. She never woke up, so the family didn't have a chance to comfort her or say goodbye. Lazarus was devastated. Both of his parents, his wife, and his unborn child had passed away in a relatively short period of time. His fear that God was punishing him was reinforced by his mother's death. It appeared that his experiment with the Essenes had not helped him get closer to God. Lazarus decided he would not return to Qumran and made no effort to retrieve the few personal possessions he had left there.

Chapter Six

HOPE

IT WAS ALMOST noon, and Lazarus was still at home. Nearly two years had passed since Rachel's death, but the painful memory of her passing continued haunting him. For the first six months after she died, Lazarus struggled to get out of bed and wasn't able to leave the house. The next nine months were spent with the Essenes, during which his emotional health improved. However, his mother's death reversed most of the gains made in Qumran. Now, after experiencing setback after setback, Lazarus' life was about to change for the better.

His sister Mary knocked once and walked in the door. Her smile always cheered him up. "Good morning," Lazarus greeted. "Or is it afternoon? I was just getting ready to go to work."

"I was on my way to see Martha at the pottery shop and thought you might be home. I decided to stop by and see how you were doing."

"I'm doing a little better, thanks. I hope business is good at the inn."

"Passover week is about to start and all our rooms are booked. This happens during every major festival. The inns in Jerusalem are filled to capacity, and we get the overflow here in Bethany. Speaking of Passover, will you be joining Caleb, Martha, and me for the Passover meal?"

"Yes, I'd love to. Last year I wasn't in a position to celebrate anything."

"We all felt so sorry for you. It will be great to be with you again this year. By the way, something very odd happened yesterday. A rabbi from Galilee checked into a few of our last available rooms. He traveled here with twelve of his disciples and couldn't find any vacancies in Jerusalem. We talked a bit. I discovered that before he became a rabbi, he worked with his father as a carpenter in Nazareth. I told him I had a brother who made a similar career change."

"That is quite a coincidence," said Lazarus. "But it doesn't seem odd to me."

"That isn't what was strange," responded Mary. "He seemed to know you. Before I could tell him that you left the pottery trade to become a scribe, he commented that you made the correct choice in careers. He said he wanted to meet with you to discuss some legal matters. How could he know that you are a scribe if he never met you before?"

"I'm not sure," replied Lazarus. "Maybe he spoke to someone in Bethany about me. In any case, he sounds like a potential client. Bringing in new business would help make up for neglecting my half of the partnership with Levi for the past couple of years."

Lazarus greeted the man who had just entered his office. "Please have a seat. How can I help you?"

"Actually, I'm here to help you, Lazarus."

The comment caught Lazarus by surprise. He took a closer look at the man sitting across from him. His hair and beard were dark, thick, and worn relatively short. He had broad shoulders and thick forearms. Lazarus guessed that the man had a job that required physical labor. But the man's most memorable feature was his smile. It was wide and welcoming, framed by craggy lines that extended from his chin to his eyes.

"I don't believe we've met before. Unless you're trying to sell something, I don't know how you could presume to help me."

"I assure you I'm not here to sell anything. In fact, I want to give you something for free. The gift I have to give is the assurance that God loves you more than you know."

Lazarus paused for a moment to digest what the man had said. "You've piqued my curiosity. But with all due respect, unless you are God himself, how would you know what I think about him or what he thinks about me? Tell me, who are you and where are you from?"

"My name is Jesus. I was born in Bethlehem and brought up in Nazareth. I apprenticed with my stepfather as a carpenter, but I'm now a rabbi. My home base is Capernaum, but I teach in cities and towns all over Galilee."

"My sister told me you might stop by the office. She said that you wanted to discuss some legal matters. I expected you to ask for help in resolving a dispute or prepare a contract. Instead, you deliver a message from God. Tell me, rabbi, how do you plan on helping me?"

"I know you are hurting. People you love have been taken away from you. You feel you have done something to offend God and because of that he must be punishing you. You're looking for ways to get back into God's good graces, but you're looking in the wrong direction. I repeat, God loves you more than you know."

Lazarus was astonished. "How do you know so much about me? Where did you get this information? Was it from my sister? Or can you somehow read my mind?"

"I know more about you than you can imagine. My Father in heaven has revealed it to me. Someday you will understand completely who I am and why I have come. In the meantime, Lazarus, take comfort. Your sins will not condemn you because I will be condemned on your behalf. And when you die you will live again just as I will be raised from the dead."

Lazarus' mind was spinning. He couldn't grasp any of what he just heard. Was this man delusional, or even worse, dangerous?

"I appreciate your concern for my well-being," said Lazarus. "But I honestly don't understand what you're talking about, and what you're saying is making me feel uncomfortable. Unless there's something I can do for you, perhaps we should continue our discussion another time."

"I understand your uneasiness," replied Jesus as he stood up and prepared to leave. "It must be difficult discussing personal matters with a complete stranger. But you will see over time that I have your best interests at heart. Until we see each other again, remember that God loves you more than you know."

Thursday afternoon Lazarus arrived at his sister Mary's home to eat the Passover meal. The house was situated next to the Bethany inn owned by her husband Caleb. There was no response when he knocked on the front door. When Mary invited him earlier in the week, Lazarus had assumed he would be attending an intimate gathering in her home. Perhaps he was supposed to be at Martha's house instead.

Just then the scent of roast lamb wafted through the air. He followed the aroma to the inn's banquet hall annex. Once inside, he was surprised to see three long narrow tables configured in a "U" shaped pattern. A series of couches had been placed on the outer sides of the tables.

Mary and Martha were going in and out of the door to the kitchen. Lazarus began feeling anxious. "Mary, I went to your house thinking that the four of us would be eating the Passover meal there. I see quite a few tables and couches. Has there been a change of plans?"

"I'm sorry, but I forgot to tell you. Yesterday I invited Jesus and his disciples to celebrate the Passover meal with us. The arrangements they made in Jerusalem fell through. It was a last-minute thing, and I didn't think you would mind."

"Of course, I don't mind," Lazarus answered halfheartedly. "But you know how I am about socializing with people I don't know. I didn't tell you that your rabbi friend Jesus visited my office earlier this week. He wasn't asking for legal advice. In fact, he said he was there to help me. By the end of our conversation, I felt a bit uneasy."

"Well, Jesus will be here in any case. If you're too uncomfortable, you can always leave. I want you to stay, but it's your decision. If it makes any difference, I believe you might know one of his disciples. Do you remember the bully who used to harass other kids in the neighborhood? I think his name was Simon. Wasn't he in the same class with you in synagogue school?"

"It could be him, but I doubt it. The last time I saw Simon, he was working in his father's stone-cutting business. He also got involved with the Zealots. He isn't the type of person who would follow a rabbi."

"So, are you staying or not?" asked Mary with a trace of irritability in her voice. "If you are, why don't you go into the kitchen and see if you can help Caleb?"

Lazarus found his brother-in-law standing next to a brick oven. A lamb was roasting on a spit over the open flame.

"How is everything going?" Lazarus asked. "Can I help you with anything?"

"Everything is on schedule," answered Caleb. "Earlier today I killed the lamb, drained the blood, and skinned it. It was unblemished as far as I could tell. I removed the fat and kidneys and put them in the fire to burn as an offering to God. As you know, the Torah requires the Passover lamb to be slain at the temple in Jerusalem and its blood sprinkled by a priest on the altar before taking it home to cook and eat it. But these days the size of the crowds makes it impossible for the priests to sacrifice a lamb for every family. I think God will approve what we have done."

Since Caleb had everything under control in the kitchen, Lazarus returned to the banquet hall. Just then Jesus made his entry. He and his disciples removed their sandals, and Mary and Martha hurried over to wash their feet. Mary led Jesus to the seat of honor at the head table. The disciples began jockeying for a position near Jesus.

Lazarus recognized Simon immediately. Mary had been correct after all. "Hello, my friend," greeted Lazarus.

Simon wrapped his arms tightly around Lazarus. "It's great to see you again. I knew if I returned to Bethany, I would see someone I knew. It's been a few years since I last saw you. In fact, it was after your father was killed. I imagine you're still dealing with the heartache."

"I'll never forget how you consoled me after my father's death. So many things have happened in my life since then. It appears that your life has gone in a direction I wouldn't have expected. We need to sit down and trade stories."

"The Passover meal won't be an appropriate time. But we're all going to Jerusalem tomorrow morning so Jesus can do some teaching. Would you like to go with us? We can talk on the way there and back."

A sudden rush of adrenaline flowed through Lazarus like a wave crashing onto the shore. Whenever faced with doing something unfamiliar, Lazarus fought a bout with anxiety. It had plagued him all his life, at least as far back as he could remember. Most of the time the anxiety disappeared quickly and he forged ahead. At other times, anxiety caused him to avoid the unfamiliar situation entirely. In this instance, his curiosity proved stronger than his apprehension.

"Yes, I'd like to go with you. When are you leaving? I can meet you here at the inn."

"We're leaving just after daybreak. That will give Jesus most of the day to teach before we return to Bethany."

The Passover meal began promptly at six o'clock. Lazarus reclined with members of his family, and Simon joined Jesus and the other disciples. On each table were traditional ingredients of the meal including lamb, bitter herbs, nut-and-fruit paste, loaves of unleavened bread, and goblets of wine. The food was eaten communally without utensils. Each guest served himself or herself, and then passed the platter to the next person. Goblets of wine were also shared.

Passover was a festive occasion, a reminder to the Jews of their miraculous deliverance by God from the Egyptians centuries earlier. Jesus, who led the ceremony, began with the customary prayer. "Blessed are you, O Lord our God, king of the universe, who has created the fruit of the vine. And you, O Lord our God, have given us festival days for joy, this feast of the unleavened bread, the time of our deliverance in remembrance of the departure from Egypt. Blessed are you, O Lord our God, who has kept us alive, sustained us, and enabled us to enjoy this season."

After the prayer the first drink of wine was taken. As the meal progressed, eating and drinking were interspersed with traditional Scripture readings, prayers, hymns, and stories related to the first Passover. Jesus spoke with such conviction and realism that Lazarus wondered if he had been there in person with Moses.

Each portion of the meal recalled some aspect of God's mercy and saving power. The roasted lamb reminded them of the blood of the unblemished lamb sprinkled on each family's doorpost so the angel of death would pass over their homes. The bitter herbs represented the pain and suffering endured by the Israelites during four hundred years of slavery. Unleavened bread symbolized the haste with which the Israelites left Egypt.

After the meal was over, Jesus prayed the closing benediction. He concluded the evening with a personal message. "Tonight we celebrated God's deliverance of our people from slavery in Egypt many years ago. In a year from now, you will celebrate God's deliverance of all mankind from the slavery of sin. I am telling you this well in advance even though you will not fully understand until my work is completed. Go in peace."

Lazarus recalled Jesus' visit to his office earlier in the week. His final remarks at the Passover meal sounded much like what was said then. Once again, Lazarus had no idea what Jesus was talking about.

The next morning as Lazarus approached the inn, Jesus was standing outside with his disciples. Before leaving home to go to the inn, Lazarus had considered not going to Jerusalem, but the impulse passed as quickly as it came. Surprisingly, he actually looked forward to the trip. Perhaps the isolation he experienced in Qumran made him more willing to interact with unfamiliar people. Perhaps the repetitive daily routine he followed there made him more inclined to try new experiences.

The two-mile journey from Bethany to Jerusalem usually took less than an hour. The first mile and a half led north to the summit of the Mount of Olives. It was actually more of a hill than a mountain, rising only about three hundred feet above the elevation of Jerusalem. The uphill road to the summit had a gradual slope making it easy for Lazarus and Simon to talk.

"Simon, I hope you slept well. Since we talked last night, I've been wondering how you arrived at this point in your life. I never imagined you would become the disciple of a traveling rabbi."

"I'm as amazed as you are. Since we last saw each other, my life has taken several unexpected turns. Last night we talked a bit about the death of your father. About two years ago, my father passed away as well. Building projects involving stone-cutting had dried up around Jerusalem, so he and I looked for work in Galilee. We were working on a construction job in Capernaum when a large chunk of limestone became dislodged and fell on him. After the burial, I remained there."

"I'm sorry to hear about the death of your father. How did you deal with the loss?"

"I started going to synagogue worship as a means of managing my grief. Jesus was speaking during one of the services. His message made a huge impression on me, and I reached out to him afterward. He saw my pain and provided words of comfort that helped get me through it. Later, when Jesus invited me to follow him, I felt compelled to do so. I sold my house here in Bethany and moved to Capernaum. As you know, my mother died when I was young so there were no longer any ties to this community. Now here I am, learning as much as I can from a teacher I greatly respect."

"That's quite a series of events," said Lazarus. "I just wish your father was still alive."

"Thank you. You and I were both very close to our fathers," remarked Simon. "Now, what about you? I'd be interested in what you've been up to lately."

"I wish I could say that everything has gone well. Unfortunately, I've had some struggles over the past few years," replied Lazarus. "You never got to meet my wife, Rachel. She was the love of my life. We were expecting our first child when she and our baby boy died during childbirth. I can't describe the pain and anguish I experienced. The level of depression I felt was overwhelming. There were times when I thought about ending my own life."

"I'm very sorry to hear that. I never married, so I can't imagine losing a wife and child. How did you get through it?"

"I'm not sure that I'm through it yet. Several months after Rachel died, I left Bethany to live with the Essenes in Qumran. You've probably heard about them. They are a separatist sect of Jews who feel the priesthood is corrupt. I went there to start a new life. After nine months in Qumran, my mother became ill so I returned to Bethany. She died shortly after I got back. Her death added to my emotional upheaval."

"I'm so sorry to hear about your mother. It seems like you're getting hit with one blow after another. I hope things settle down for you soon."

The two men walked for several minutes before Lazarus broke the silence. "Now that the depressing topics are out of the way, maybe we can talk about more pleasant matters. I find it fascinating that you quit your stone-cutting job to become Jesus' disciple. Something similar happened to me. While you and I were in synagogue school, I was apprenticing with my father to become a potter. I told him I wanted to become a scribe. You visited my office after my father died. Now I get to teach Mosaic law, settle legal disputes, and create legal contracts."

"I remember you were quite the scholar. I'll never forget the time you gave me the answer in class that got me out of a day of school. Tobias probably still wonders how his worst student was able to answer that question correctly."

Lazarus grinned and changed the subject. "I'm curious about Jesus. You said he helped you cope with your grief after your father died. Earlier this week he came to see me at my office. Somehow he knows the problems I'm dealing with and apparently wants to help. Why would Jesus care about someone he doesn't know? What's in it for him?"

"I understand your skepticism. After being with him for two years now, I can honestly say that Jesus is the most self-less person I have ever known. He is sincere in his desire to help people, particularly those who are less fortunate. I suspect that Jesus has an inherently loving spirit. He is constantly teaching us to love each other, even to the point of loving our enemies."

"I shouldn't be so cynical," remarked Lazarus. "I have a habit of looking for the worst in people. By the way, my fellow scribes have been talking about the miracles Jesus is performing in Galilee. They're looking forward to seeing him do the same here in Jerusalem."

"I'm not surprised that he's becoming well known outside of Galilee. Since I started following Jesus, I've witnessed more miracles than I can recall. To be honest, I've become almost numb to the extraordinary things he does. The other disciples feel that way too. We expect Jesus to work miracles every day."

"Tell me about some of them."

"Well, most of his miracles involve healing. Last night you met Peter. His mother-in-law was very sick with a high fever. Jesus just touched her hand and the fever was immediately gone. She got out of bed and made us dinner. He's healed people who were paralyzed or had blood diseases or leprosy.

He's even cured people who were blind and deaf from birth. All it takes is a word or touch from Jesus."

"That's unbelievable. If I hadn't heard it from you, I would discount it completely."

"It gets even more incredible. Jesus actually brought two dead people back to life. One incident happened in the village of Nain, just south of Nazareth. We entered the village as a funeral procession was passing by. Jesus saw how devastated the widowed mother was by the loss of her son. He walked to the litter on which the body was being carried and ordered the boy to get up. To the shock of everyone there, including me, the boy sat up and walked to his mother as if nothing had happened."

"That's amazing. Tell me about the other incident."

"We had just returned to Capernaum when we were met by a man named Jairus. He was the ruler of a synagogue there. His daughter was very ill, and he wanted Jesus to come to his house and heal her. Jesus agreed to go, but before we could get there, some of Jairus' servants met us on the road and said his daughter had already died. Jesus told him to have faith that his daughter would get well. When we got to Jairus's house, a crowd had already gathered to mourn. Jesus told them that the girl was just sleeping, and they laughed at him. Jesus took Peter, James, and John into the house along with the parents. Several minutes later they came out of the house, and the girl was alive and walking with them. Later we asked Peter what had happened. He told us that Jesus simply held her hand, told the girl to get up, and she did."

"I'm speechless. What kind of man can bring people back to life? Definitely not an ordinary one. I imagine Jesus attracts a lot of attention wherever he goes."

"His miracles have changed everything. At the beginning of his ministry, we could walk through the streets of any town without being recognized. Now it's impossible to get away from the crowds. They seek him out no matter where he goes."

"I wish that Jesus had been around when Rachel was giving birth and when my mother fell ill. They might not have died. He probably could have brought my father back to life too. But I'm curious. Has Jesus done any miracles that don't involve healing people?"

"The answer is yes. The first miracle I witnessed had nothing to do with healing. Shortly after I became a disciple, Jesus and the rest of us were invited to a wedding for one of his relatives. It was held in Cana, a town halfway between Capernaum and Nazareth. The wedding feast was supposed to last five days, but near the end of the fourth day Jesus' mother told him that the supply of wine had run out. I'm not sure how she knew that. Maybe she was helping with the food preparation.

"Anyway, after he found out, Jesus asked a couple of servants to fill up a half dozen jars with water. They must have been about thirty gallons each. After they filled the jars, Jesus told the servants to take them to the wine steward. We watched as the wine steward tasted the liquid in the jars. To our amazement, the steward began gushing over the quality of the wine he had just sampled. He even called the bridegroom over and questioned why he had saved the best wine for the final days of the feast. The bridegroom had no idea what the steward was talking about, but he was overjoyed that the wedding guests would have wine to drink."

"I'm very impressed," remarked Lazarus. "How did you and the rest of the disciples react?"

"We were stunned. None of us had seen anything like that before. No one could have done what Jesus did unless God was with him. It reconfirmed our decision to follow him."

"Have any of his miracles affected you personally?"

"Absolutely. The one I remember most vividly is when all of us nearly lost our lives. Have you ever been to the Sea of Galilee?"

"No, I haven't. In fact, I've never been farther north than Jericho."

"Many of the cities and towns where Jesus has taught are on the shores of the Sea of Galilee. Before meeting Jesus, several of the disciples lived in Capernaum and worked as fishermen. We used their boats to take us wherever Jesus wanted to teach. Sailing is much faster and less strenuous than walking. But the Sea of Galilee is known for its variable weather. Violent storms can pop up without warning.

"One night Jesus decided to sail from Capernaum to Gerasa. Evenings were usually a good time to travel. Jesus could relax after a day of teaching and healing and avoid any crowds who tried to follow. All of a sudden, one of the worst windstorms I have ever experienced hit the sea. Waves several feet high buffeted the boat. We tried to steer into the wind to avoid capsizing, but the waves were so powerful they lifted the bow completely out of the water. We were afraid the boat might flip over backward."

"Where was Jesus when this happened? Was he as frightened as you were?"

"I was just getting to that. Believe it or not, he was sleeping soundly at the back of the boat. He must have been completely exhausted from the day's activities. We probably should have handled the crisis ourselves, but we panicked and woke him up. To our astonishment, Jesus commanded the wind and the waves to calm down. As soon as he spoke, the wind stopped and the surface of the water became smooth as glass. The whole event was surreal."

"What did Jesus do afterward? Was he angry that you woke him?"

"He made it seem like nothing out of the ordinary had occurred. Jesus asked us why we had been afraid. He said that if we had enough faith, we wouldn't have been frightened. Later, when we were alone, we marveled at how even the sky and sea did his bidding."

"As I said before, if I hadn't heard these stories from someone I know, I wouldn't have believed them. I hope I'll get to witness one of his miracles myself."

"I wouldn't doubt it," said Simon. "He might perform several while we are in Jerusalem."

Time was passing quickly, and Lazarus wanted to ask a few more questions about Jesus before they arrived. "I heard from some of my fellow scribes that Jesus was involved in several confrontations with the Jewish leadership in Galilee. Is that the case? If so, I wonder how that might impact how he feels about me."

"You heard correctly, my friend, but I'm not sure you want to know the details."

"Why is that?"

"Several religious leaders in Galilee have tried to either test Jesus or embarrass him. Some appeared to be motivated by curiosity and others by jealousy. In every instance, Jesus got the best of them and they went away frustrated and angry. I'm sorry to say that many were Pharisees, the Jewish sect to which you belong. Some were also scribes, the profession in which you are employed."

"I assure you that I am an independent thinker. If my fellow Pharisees and scribes had issues with Jesus, it doesn't mean that I will. However, I'd be interested to know what caused the bad blood."

"In my opinion, the hostility of Jewish leaders toward Jesus started when he began to gain popularity. They couldn't figure out how this man, with no formal training as a rabbi, could attract such a large following. Some of them started shadowing Jesus from town to town and soon discovered that he didn't fit their image of a conventional rabbi. He taught with authority and could perform miracles. They began seeing him as a threat to their leadership status in the community. As a result, they attempted to discredit him. The scribes in Galilee, experts in the law as you are, tried to accuse him of disobeying the law of Moses."

"What did they claim Jesus did to violate the Mosaic law?"

"At first it wasn't so much what he did, but rather what he didn't do. For example, he didn't always wash his hands before eating. When the scribes questioned him on this, Jesus accused them of being clean on the outside but dirty on the inside. In essence, he was calling them hypocrites."

"I've got to admit, as a teacher of the Law I would be inclined to support my fellow scribes on this issue. The Torah is clear that washing one's hands before eating is required. The same is true of washing the pots and pans used to prepare the food. I haven't seen or heard anything that would eliminate those requirements."

"In any case, after being unsuccessful in their initial attempts to discredit Jesus, the Jewish leaders ramped up their efforts. Instead of focusing on what he didn't do, they tried to find fault with what he was doing. As you know, God commanded the Jews to rest on the Sabbath and not do any work. The leaders criticized Jesus for walking through grain fields and eating the kernels on the Sabbath. Actually, they were afraid to accuse him directly, so they blamed us, his disciples, instead.

"They also criticized Jesus for healing on the Sabbath. He pointed out that God created the Sabbath for people's benefit, not to their detriment. To illustrate what he meant, he asked them whether or not they would untie their donkey on the Sabbath in order to lead it to a water trough. The answer, of course, was yes."

"I can see Jesus' thought process," remarked Lazarus. "He's advocating a practical standard for the law. But God doesn't ask us to be practical. Instead, he asks us to obey his commands literally and without fail. Once again, the Torah is clear. We are prohibited from working on the Sabbath. I have to agree with my fellow scribes on this issue as well. Tell me, were there any other concerns that the scribes had with Jesus?"

"Yes. They questioned his authority. One day a paralyzed man was brought to Jesus to be healed. The room was so crowded that his friends had to lower him from a hole they made in the roof of the building. Before Jesus healed him, he told the man that his sins were forgiven. The scribes picked up on this immediately and accused Jesus of blasphemy because only God could forgive sins. Jesus asked them if it was easier to heal the man or forgive his sins. When they didn't answer, Jesus proceeded to heal the man."

"What you just said reminded me of something," noted Lazarus. "I told you that Jesus came to visit me at my office this week. Even though I had never met him before, he told me that my sins would not condemn me. At the time I wondered, just like the scribes in Galilee, how he could speak for God, especially when it comes to forgiveness. How would you describe Jesus' relationship to God?"

Simon thought for a moment before answering. "Jesus has given us clues, but he hasn't made that relationship clear yet. Ironically, Satan might have provided the best explanation. One morning while Jesus was teaching in a Capernaum synagogue, an evil spirit accused Jesus of trying to destroy him and his fellow spirits. The demon called Jesus 'God's Holy One' just before Jesus cast him out of the man."

"That's interesting. The writings of Isaiah the prophet described a redeemer who will deliver Israel from its enemies.

He called that redeemer 'God's Holy One'. If the demon called Jesus by that name, might Isaiah's prophecy refer to Jesus?"

"I think it's possible if not probable. I have another incident to tell you about. The morning after Jesus miraculously calmed the Sea of Galilee, we landed the boat on the shore near Gerasa. A man possessed by a number of demons approached us. They controlled him so completely that he ran around naked and lived in a graveyard. Just before Jesus cast them out of the man into a herd of pigs, the evil spirits called Jesus 'Son of the Most High God'."

"You jogged my memory again. During Jesus' visit I asked him how he knew so much about me. He said that his Father in heaven provided the knowledge. I thought he was deranged. After hearing everything you told me about him, his relationship with God appears extremely close."

Once they reached the summit, the spellbinding view made the uphill walk worthwhile. To the west lay the city of Jerusalem surrounded by massive walls interspersed with spectacular gates. Just beyond the east wall of the city they could see the temple complex known as the Temple Mount. The layer of gold overlaying the façade of the temple sanctuary gleamed in the sunlight. The magnificent panorama never failed to impress Lazarus.

The journey became less strenuous as they descended the final half mile to their destination. Just before reaching the low point of the Kidron Valley, they passed the Garden of

Gethsemane, a virtual forest of olive trees. In contrast to the Mount of Olives where the ground consisted of chalky limestone interspersed with rocks, the soil in Gethsemane supported a thick growth of grass and wildflowers. Once the men reached the valley floor, they crossed a shallow stream called Brook Kidron. From there it was a brief uphill climb to a flight of stone steps leading to the Eastern Gate, one of the main entrances to Jerusalem.

After entering the city, the men went directly to Solomon's Portico, a covered porch that lined the east side of the Temple Mount. Word spread quickly that Jesus was there. A crowd formed around him and he began to teach. Lazarus recognized some of the men in the crowd as fellow scribes who worked in Jerusalem. Lazarus wondered if they were there to learn or to find fault.

The rest of the morning and the afternoon passed quickly. The crowd listened eagerly to Jesus' every word. Lazarus had not heard him teach before, and he now understood why Jesus attracted large numbers of people whenever he spoke. He taught with unusual clarity, speaking in parables that made spiritual concepts understandable to his listeners. He spoke with authority and conviction, unlike most other rabbis. It was as if God himself were delivering the message.

What impressed Lazarus the most that day was Jesus' viewpoint on keeping the law. While Jewish scholars like himself emphasized literal interpretation, Jesus stressed a broader approach. According to Jesus, the commandment to not kill went beyond murder to include hating someone. Adultery extended beyond cheating on a spouse to lusting after a woman. Lazarus realized that if this were the case, then no Pharisee or scribe, including himself, could ever claim to be sinless, and Lazarus' efforts to win God's favor by keeping the law would be futile.

As sundown approached, Jesus blessed the crowd and announced he would be back to teach the next day. After the crowd dispersed, Jesus said he had one more thing to do before the journey back to Bethany. He led Lazarus and the disciples to the northeast corner of the city where they stopped at the Pool of Bethesda. The water in the man-made pool was believed to have healing powers whenever the water was stirred up. Blind, crippled, or otherwise disabled invalids sat around the pool hoping to be the first ones in the water when it moved.

At one end of the pool a man sat sobbing. Jesus asked if he could help. The man told Jesus that his legs had been paralyzed for nearly forty years, and there was no cure for his condition. He explained that he'd attempted to be healed for a long time but couldn't get into the pool quickly enough.

Jesus, his eyes filled with compassion, asked the man if he wanted to be cured without waiting for movement of the water. Startled, the man replied yes. Jesus told him to pick up the mat on which he was sitting and get up and walk. The man looked up at Jesus and slowly propped himself up on his hands and knees. From that position, he cautiously moved his feet under him and stood up. The man shuffled a short distance, taking small steps at first. Soon he lengthened his stride, and a huge smile spread across his face. After walking a few times around the perimeter of the pool, the man returned to the spot where Jesus had healed him, but Jesus had already gone.

As they walked home to Bethany, Lazarus remembered Simon's prediction that he would witness a miracle. What Jesus did was far more amazing than he could have imagined. After witnessing what Jesus had done, Lazarus couldn't understand how Simon and the other disciples would ever become desensitized to seeing Jesus perform miracles.

The next morning Lazarus accompanied Jesus and his disciples back to the temple. The twinge of anxiety he felt the previous morning didn't recur. Instead, he was excited for the opportunity to hear Jesus teach and perhaps see another miracle. Jesus attracted another large crowd in Solomon's Portico. As he was teaching, the man he had cured the previous night approached, bowed respectfully, and said, "Thank you for enabling me to walk again. I couldn't thank you last night because you left too soon."

"It was late and we wanted to return to Bethany," Jesus replied. "How are you doing now?"

"Words can't express how great I feel. I never expected something this incredible to happen. But not everyone is as excited as I am. This morning some of the Jewish leaders scolded me for carrying my mat in violation of Sabbath rules. I told them about the miraculous healing. They asked me who healed me, and I said I didn't know. I hadn't gotten a chance to ask your name. They asked me when I was healed, and I told them it was around sundown."

"You have my permission to tell them that Jesus from Nazareth healed you. Now that you can walk, you should be going throughout the city telling everyone how I helped you."

Soon after the man left, a group of scribes appeared. Lazarus recognized most of them. "We just found out that you healed a paralyzed man last night after the Sabbath had begun," one of them said with contempt in his voice. "As experts in the law, we need to remind you that such activities on the day of rest are forbidden by God. What do you have to say for yourself?"

Jesus replied, "All I have to say to you is that God is my Father, and my Father never rests from doing good, even on the Sabbath."

The scribes looked at Jesus contemptuously. One of them said, "Not only have you broken the law of Moses, but you are now claiming to be the Son of God. When the high priest and the Sanhedrin hear about your blasphemy, you won't be safe in Jerusalem any longer. If you are as intelligent as people say you are, you will return to Galilee and stay there."

Jesus smiled at the scribes and said nothing. After they went away, Jesus continued teaching the crowd. He expanded on what he had told the scribes, revealing that he had been sent by his Father to give forgiveness and eternal life to those who believe in him. Simon turned to Lazarus and said, "Jesus just answered the question you asked me yesterday. He just confirmed what the demons said about him. God is Jesus' Father, and Jesus is God's Son."

After Passover week was over, Jesus returned to Capernaum with his disciples. Back in Bethany Lazarus monitored reports about Jesus' activities during the months that followed. According to what he heard, throngs of people continued to follow Jesus from town to town in Galilee to hear him teach and perform miracles. He was healing the blind, the deaf, lepers, and the demon-possessed. One account even told of Jesus feeding thousands of people with only a small amount of bread and a few fish.

As Jesus' popularity with the general public grew, hostility toward Jesus from Jewish religious leaders was growing as well. News from Galilee indicated that Pharisees were plotting to kill Jesus after he healed a man's shriveled hand on the Sabbath. Lazarus wondered what was going on behind the scenes in Jerusalem.

Whenever Lazarus wanted to find out what was happening locally, he went to visit Nicodemus, a fellow scribe and Pharisee. The two men had formed a bond of friendship over the years ever since Lazarus trained with Nicodemus shortly before he met Rachel. Both men were comfortable sharing information about business and personal matters.

Nicodemus was well connected in the city by virtue of his membership in the Sanhedrin. The Sanhedrin, also known as the Council, was composed of seventy-one of the most educated and wealthy men in Jerusalem. As a governing group, they served as the highest authority in Jewish religious, legal, legislative, and political issues. The high priest presided over the Sanhedrin.

Six months after the Passover, Lazarus traveled to Jerusalem to meet with Nicodemus. "Hello, my friend," greeted Lazarus. "It's been a while since we last talked. I haven't had any legal cases or contract work that required me to come here from Bethany."

"It's good to see you again," replied Nicodemus. "I hope you and your sisters are well. Business has been booming here. There are disputes about almost everything. It seems like people are only concerned about themselves lately. I remember the old days when everyone got along well enough to settle things without going to court. The upside is that both my business schedule and my pocketbook are full. So, what brings you here to Jerusalem?"

"Actually, I came to see you," answered Lazarus. "I wanted to get your opinion about a rabbi in Galilee named Jesus. I'm sure you've heard of him. I met him during Passover several months ago. He stayed at the inn in Bethany that my sister Mary and her husband operate. For some reason, Jesus seemed to take an interest in my welfare. Initially he struck me as a bit peculiar. But a friend of mine named Simon who is now one of his disciples tried to convince me otherwise. I came here to ask what you know about Jesus and what the Sanhedrin thinks about him."

"I wouldn't tell this to anyone other than a trusted friend like you. I met with Jesus during Passover week as well," admitted Nicodemus.

"You know you can count on me to be discreet," said Lazarus. "But weren't you risking your position on the Sanhedrin by meeting with him? Jesus has become a very controversial figure."

"That's why I arranged to meet him at night in private. The two of us met in the garden outside my home. My curiosity was piqued after several people I know and respect in Galilee witnessed some of Jesus' miracles. They also heard him teach. All of them heaped praise on him. They said he must be doing these things with the help of God. I wanted to discover for myself whether what they were telling me was true. Most of my colleagues in the Sanhedrin expressed the opposite viewpoint."

"What did you find out during your meeting?" quizzed Lazarus.

"Jesus told me that he was sent by God for a particular purpose," replied Nicodemus. "That purpose was to save mankind from death. He referred to an incident described in the book of Numbers when the Israelites were traveling to the promised land. The people complained to Moses it was taking too long to get there. God punished their lack of trust and patience by sending poisonous snakes that bit and killed many of them. After the people cried out for mercy, God told Moses to make a snake out of bronze and attach it to the top of a pole stuck in the ground. Any Israelite who looked at the bronze snake didn't die even if they were bitten. Jesus said he would be lifted up in a way similar to the snake. He said that those who look to him in faith will never really die but would live eternally."

"That story brings back memories. I earned a day off from synagogue school because I knew what happened to the bronze snake. But I'm curious. Did Jesus give more details on how he was going to save everyone?"

"He just said he would be lifted up. Taken literally, it would mean Jesus is going to be suspended on a pole where everyone can see him. But that doesn't make sense, so he must have been speaking figuratively. In any case, it appears that in order to live forever, people will need to believe that he will save them from death."

"That sounds a bit vague. After speaking to Jesus, who do you think he really is?"

"I'm still not sure. Jesus called himself Son of Man during most of our conversation. But he also called himself the Son of God and claimed he came from heaven. I didn't notice the distinction while we were talking. Later, after I had time to think about what he said, my first thought was that if he came from heaven, he might be an angel. But that wouldn't make him either God or a man. Then I imagined he might be both God and man at the same time. That wasn't logical either. At this point, all I can say is that Jesus is no ordinary man."

"You seem very impressed by him," remarked Lazarus.

"I am," replied Nicodemus. "Before meeting him, I would have probably agreed with those who called him a fraud. After listening to what Jesus had to say, I felt much differently. At the beginning of our conversation, Jesus said that in order for people to understand and believe what he was teaching, God's Spirit had to be poured out on them like water. As Jesus spoke, I felt moved by his words. Maybe that was the spirit he was talking about."

"I'm still not sure what to think about him," Lazarus observed. "But the more I hear from people I know and trust like you and Simon, the closer I'm coming to believe that Jesus was sent to us by God."

"I almost forgot," added Nicodemus. "You asked me what the Sanhedrin thinks of Jesus. Recently the Council launched a concerted effort throughout Galilee and Judea to discredit him in the eyes of the general public. They are afraid that Jesus will become so popular that he and his followers will try to overthrow the Sanhedrin as the religious and political governing body in our country. They are also afraid that if a radical change in the nation's leadership were to occur, the Roman government might feel threatened. That could jeopardize the already tenuous relationship between Jews and Romans."

"Simon told me about efforts to sabotage Jesus' ministry in Galilee. You just confirmed who is behind those efforts. Simon said their plans weren't working out so well."

"He's right. So far, the Sanhedrin's efforts to discredit Jesus have failed miserably. He has embarrassed them at every turn and become even more popular as a result. At this point the high priest and most of the Sanhedrin are so paranoid that they're considering killing Jesus in order to silence him. I'm afraid that if he comes back to Jerusalem, he'll be in real danger."

"I didn't get the impression that Jesus would try to replace the Sanhedrin or overthrow the Romans," observed Lazarus. "Based on what he told me at Passover, his goals are spiritual and not worldly."

"I can't agree with you more about Jesus' character and motives. But try telling that to the Sanhedrin. Their minds are made up. Personally, I don't see this ending well for Jesus."

A few days after returning to Bethany from his meeting with Nicodemus, Lazarus was preparing the evening meal after a long day of work. He answered a knock at his front door and found Jesus standing there. "I can't believe it's you!" Lazarus exclaimed. "Of all the people I might imagine paying me a visit today, you would probably be last on the list. I didn't think you would be returning to Bethany until next Passover."

Jesus smiled. "I hope you aren't too disappointed. Perhaps you will be kind enough to invite me in."

"I'm sorry," Lazarus apologized. "I didn't mean to be rude. Actually, I'm very happy that you're here. Please come in and join me for dinner."

During the meal, Jesus explained why he was in Bethany. "You and I met during the Passover this spring. The Festival of Weeks was held this summer. Now that the fall season has arrived, I'm here to attend the Festival of Booths. As you know, these are the three occasions in the year when God requires all Jewish men to visit the Jerusalem temple."

"Do you know that you are in danger here in Jerusalem?" asked Lazarus. "Rumor has it that the high priest and the Sanhedrin are plotting to kill you."

"Yes, I'm well aware of their plans," replied Jesus. "But threats against my life are nothing new. Earlier in my ministry I was teaching in the synagogue in my home town of Nazareth. After I scolded the congregation for not believing my message, they dragged me to a nearby cliff and were about to throw me off the edge. As you can see, they didn't succeed. My death will happen when my Father wills."

"If you know you are in danger, then why did you come back here? Did Simon and the rest of your disciples come along to help protect you?"

"No, I came alone. My four brothers, actually my step-brothers, are already in Jerusalem for the festival. They think I'm still back in Galilee. When I go to Jerusalem tomorrow, word of my arrival will spread quickly."

"Where are you staying? The festival lasts a full seven days. Did my sister have room at her inn?"

"If you don't mind, I would prefer to stay at your house. I wanted to discuss some matters with you concerning your future and mine."

"Of course I don't mind. You are welcome to stay as long as you like. What do you plan to do in Jerusalem? I'd like to go there with you."

"I was just about to invite you. I plan to teach at the temple. I want people to know who I am and why I have come. By the next Passover in another six months, it will be time for me to give up my life and then take it back again. Then every-one will know that what I told them about me is true. And you, Lazarus, will be the one to foreshadow my resurrection."

Lazarus remained silent. As often happened during his con-versations with Jesus, he didn't understand what Jesus meant. He decided to wait until later to ask questions.

The next morning, Jesus and Lazarus left Bethany for Jeru-salem. The Festival of Booths was already in its third day. Jewish pilgrims from all over Israel and surrounding countries filled the city. The festival was originally established at the time of Moses to celebrate the fall harvest. Later, it also commemorated the temporary tent housing in which the Israelites lived while traveling to the promised land.

When they arrived in Jerusalem, Jesus went to the Temple Mount and stood under Solomon's Portico. As he predicted, it didn't take long for word to spread that the rabbi from Galilee had arrived. A large crowd gathered around Jesus. Many were attracted by his reputation as a healer and a teacher. Others were there to find fault with him. Those who heard Jesus for the first time were amazed that a former carpenter from Galilee with no formal training as a rabbi could be so knowledgeable. No one who stopped to listen to Jesus was disappointed.

By the seventh and final day of the festival, Jesus had attracted an even larger following. After listening to him teach, the crowd was divided on who Jesus really was. Some called him a prophet. Others claimed he was the Messiah. Several Pharisees, fearing Jesus' growing popularity, summoned the temple guards to arrest him. Intimidated by the crowd surrounding him, the guards refused to comply with their request.

After another exhausting day, Jesus and Lazarus returned to Bethany to spend the night. As they walked the two-mile journey home, Lazarus breathed a sigh of relief. The near confrontation with temple guards made him extremely anxious. He had been certain that Jesus would be arrested and possibly killed.

"I'm glad the Festival of Booths is over," remarked Lazarus, relieved that he wouldn't have to spend another stressful day with Jesus in Jerusalem. "I assume you'll be going back to Galilee tomorrow."

"Actually, I intend to visit the temple again tomorrow. I have some unfinished business I need to take care of. The Sanhedrin isn't committed enough to following through with their death threats. I am going to give them some additional incentive while I'm here in Jerusalem. When the time comes to take my life, the Jewish leaders will be ready and eager to do so."

Lazarus looked at Jesus in disbelief. "Did I hear you correctly? Are you saying that you want to be killed by the Sanhedrin?"

"What I am saying is that I am committed to doing my Father's will. You might recall the first time we met in your office I told you that your sins will not condemn you because I will be condemned on your behalf. You had no idea what I was talking about. Since then, you have heard me teach and seen my miracles. It is time to add some clarity to what you have seen and heard.

"You heard me say to the festival crowd that that I was sent from heaven by God my Father. He sent me to be the perfect sacrifice for the sins of all people. Unlike the sacrifices offered in the temple, my death and the shedding of my blood will be the last and only sacrifice necessary for sinful mankind to be forgiven. You will not be condemned for your sins because of what I will do on your behalf."

"I'm struggling with what you just told me," Lazarus responded. "Everything I have learned from a lifetime of studying the Torah has told me that I can win God's favor by obeying his laws. Now you seem to be telling me that becoming acceptable to God is solely dependent on what you will do for me."

"Lazarus, you are starting to understand. Someday God's Spirit will make everything clear. Until then, everything about me and my mission will be confusing, especially when events seem to be out of control. Even my disciples who are with me every day will lose confidence in me. But God's plan to save sinners will be completed, and you will see it happen before your eyes."

"Confused is a good word to describe how I feel right now," admitted Lazarus. "But it might help if you can clear up something that I've been wondering about all week. Several people in the crowd at the temple argued that you must be the Messiah. Others claimed you couldn't be. If I may be so bold, which opinion is accurate? Are you the Messiah or not?"

"Before I answer your question, my friend, I need to ask you a question. What is your definition of the term Messiah?"

"Along with most other Jews, I believe that the Messiah will be a descendant of King David. The prophet Isaiah has written that someday one of David's descendants will become a king. That king, the Messiah, will unite the Jews from all over the world and return them here to the land of their ancestors. Under the Messiah's leadership, the glory of David's kingdom will be restored and even surpassed. Our oppressors will be defeated, and peace and justice will reign once again. Isaiah compares the coming of the Messiah to a new branch that sprouts out of a tree stump that has been cut down."

"Well said. I can tell that you are a student of the Scriptures. Based on your definition, why would people in the crowd call me the Messiah?"

"I don't think they're basing their opinion on your relationship to King David, even if there is one. I think it's because of your miracles. If you can heal people with only a word or a touch and can feed thousands with hardly any bread or fish, you should be able to defeat an enemy army."

"That could be. But as you pointed out, there are a number of Jews, including prominent religious leaders, who think I couldn't be the Messiah. Why do you think they still feel that way even after they have seen me perform miracles?"

"There could be many reasons, including your lack of formal education and the fact that you come from Galilee. But, in my opinion, the main reason you will never be considered to be the Messiah by the Jewish leadership is that you have claimed to be the Son of God. That would mean there are multiple gods. Jews believe that there is only one God, and they are commanded to worship him alone. They believe the coming Messiah will be a special man, but not God. God will be with him and make him a strong and capable leader, able to free the Jews from foreign control."

"Once again, well said. I can see why some Jews might reject the notion that I might be the Messiah. But now I'd like to know your opinion. You have seen my miracles and listened to me teach. Simon has testified to you about me. Tell me, Lazarus, who do you think I am?"

Lazarus paused for a moment to collect his thoughts. "Honestly, I don't know what to think. If I saw you standing among a group of people, I would think you were an ordinary man. Yet you have done things that no ordinary man could do and you teach in a way that no ordinary man could teach. You are an enigma to me."

"I have a feeling that you aren't being completely candid. Are you holding back your real opinion in order to spare my feelings?"

"Sometimes I think you can read my mind. To be completely honest, I expect the Messiah to be more dynamic and driven than you seem to be. I can't picture you gathering Jews together from all corners of the earth or leading an army into battle against the Romans as Isaiah indicated. I'm also not convinced that you are the Son of God as you claim to be. It's clear to me that you are a unique individual, but at this point I would have a difficult time believing you are the Messiah whom I and most other Jews are expecting."

Jesus looked lovingly at Lazarus and smiled. "It is finally time for me to answer your original question. You are correct. I am not the Messiah that you and most other Jews are expecting. Your definition describes a king who will restore the nation of Israel to world prominence by defeating its enemies in battle. You quoted Isaiah to support your viewpoint. However, if you read the writings of Isaiah more carefully, you will see that the Messiah he was talking about is a much different type of king who will bring fairness, honesty, justice, and peace to the Jews as well as the Gentiles."

"Are you saying that I'm looking for the wrong Messiah?" asked Lazarus.

"I suggest you reread the later sections of Isaiah. There he describes the Messiah as a sinless servant of God who gives up his life as a sacrifice to pay for the sins of all people."

"Was Isaiah talking about you when he wrote about a suffering servant? Are you *that* Messiah?"

"Yes, I am *that* Messiah. My Father sent me, his Son, from heaven to restore the perfect relationship between him and mankind that existed before sin entered the world. Because he is a God of justice, that broken relationship cannot be repaired without righteous retribution for sins committed. As a result, I, the sinless Son of God, came into the world as a man to endure the punishment that sinners deserve. My death will be the perfect sacrifice that Isaiah prophesied would happen. Once I have paid for the sins of all people by my suffering and death, my Father will raise me from the dead. Those who believe in me and trust what I have done for them will become acceptable to God in spite of their sinfulness. Their faith will provide assurance that they will live with me in heaven forever."

"What you have just told me sounds very complicated. Yet it has an element of simplicity that appeals to my sense of logic. What I heard you saying is that sinful people, including me, can't stop sinning or make up for the sins they have already committed. Therefore, a just God who is also loving and merciful had to intervene in order to save sinners from eternal punishment."

"You spoke the truth, my friend. Your heart and mind have been opened to that truth by God's Spirit. No one can know me or the Father without the Spirit's guidance."

"Did I just hear you mention your Father, yourself, and God's Spirit in the same sentence? I was having a difficult time accepting your claim that there are two Gods. Now you are introducing another one. How can that be if God has made it perfectly clear that he is the only one that we should worship?"

"Unfortunately, I can't explain it in terms that your human mind can comprehend. The Father, the Son, and the Spirit are three separate persons in one God. The Father created the world. He sent me, his Son, to save the world from sin and death. The Spirit proceeds from the Father to convince the world to believe in me. This concept of God has to be accepted by faith and not by reason. This the one and only God that you are commanded to worship."

"My head is spinning. This is too much for me to take in. I almost wish you and I hadn't met. My notion of God was much simpler before you entered my life, even though I had no idea how to please him."

"You will understand in time. You will learn that there is nothing you can do to please God on your own. I am the only one who can make you and other sinners acceptable to him."

"I must admit, my opinion of you has changed during our walk back to Bethany. You are definitely not the Messiah I had been expecting, but you might be the Messiah that I and other sinners need. I want to believe you, but I will reserve final judgement until what you have told me today is proven true. In the meantime, I'd like to know why you are revealing all of this to me. From the first time we met, you seemed to single me out for special attention. Why pay any atten-tion to me at all?"

"As I told you then and will say now, God loves you more than you know. He has selected you for a special purpose. Future generations will hear the name Lazarus and be reminded that I have achieved victory over sin and death."

The next morning Lazarus accompanied Jesus back to Jerusa-lem. Soon after he arrived, Jesus resumed teaching. It didn't take long for a large crowd to gather even though the Festival of Booths had concluded the day before. The morning and most of the afternoon passed without incident until a loud commotion was heard coming from the nearby Court of Gentiles.

A number of men were forcefully dragging a woman toward Jesus as she struggled to escape from their grip. Lazarus recognized them as local Pharisees and scribes. The men threw her down roughly at Jesus' feet. "Rabbi, we caught this harlot cheating on her husband with another man. We brought her here to get your opinion. The law of Moses says that we should stone her to death for this crime. What do you think we should do?"

Jesus looked at the woman and then back at the Jewish leaders. "I see you have brought only a woman. Where is the man that you found her with? Doesn't the law require both the man and the woman to be stoned?"

The Pharisees and scribes looked at each other in surprise. One of the scribes finally answered, "It was the woman who seduced him. The man is well-respected in the community. He swore that she enticed him into sleeping with her against his will. She pestered him until he finally gave in to her. We found him to be innocent in this matter. It's the woman who should be punished."

While the scribe was speaking, Jesus squatted down and started writing with his finger in a layer of dust on the floor. Lazarus couldn't make out what he was writing, but he knew that the Jewish leaders weren't there to ask Jesus' advice. They were there to embarrass him. Whatever answer he gave, Jesus would offend someone in the crowd. If Jesus said the woman should be released, he would be accused of opposing the law of Moses. If Jesus agreed that she should be stoned, he would be criticized for being too harsh.

The Jewish leaders continued to pester Jesus for an answer, but he continued to write. Finally, Jesus stood and looked into the eyes of each Pharisee and scribe. "You asked for my opinion, so here it is. I suggest that whoever among you has never sinned should throw the first stone." Jesus then squatted down and resumed writing in the dust.

The scribes and Pharisees looked at each other with blank expressions. The crowd watched them intently, waiting to see what they would do. Jesus had turned the tables on the Jewish leaders. Once again, Jesus had humiliated those who tried to discredit him.

After a few minutes of silence, the oldest accuser walked away, his eyes fixed on the ground. The rest of the men left, one by one, until the indicted woman was the only person remaining. Jesus helped her to her feet and asked, "Where are those who wanted to stone you?"

"They've all walked away," she answered.

"Don't worry. I'm not going to denounce you as those men did," said Jesus. "Go home and don't sin anymore."

Jesus turned back to the crowd and resumed teaching. They were amazed at how he had so effortlessly put the religious leaders to shame. The people listened to his message even more intently than they had earlier.

A short time later another group of Pharisees and scribes appeared at the back of the crowd. At that point Jesus ramped up his rhetoric, stating that God was his Father and that he had existed before Abraham was born. One of the Pharisees called Jesus a liar. He and his companions tried to shove their way through the crowd, threatening to take Jesus away and stone him. As the Jewish leaders attempted to reach Jesus, they were surrounded by his supporters. During the commotion, Jesus and Lazarus escaped into the temple, where they would be safe until it was time to return to Bethany.

That evening after returning home, Lazarus realized why Jesus wanted to stay another day. He intended to provoke the Pharisees and scribes to the point they wanted to kill him. He was preparing the stage for his death at a later date. The next day, Jesus began his journey back to Capernaum in Galilee.

Jesus returned to Bethany three months after the Feast of Booths. Another festival, the Feast of Dedication, was being observed in Jerusalem. The eight-day celebration commemorated the Jewish victory over their Greek overlords and rededication of the temple nearly two hundred years earlier. The successful revolution gave the Jews independence for the next one hundred years until the Roman occupation began. The immediate aftermath of that revolution had resulted in the establishment of the Essene sect.

"I can't believe Mary isn't helping me," complained Martha. "She's in the other room with all of you while I am getting everything ready by myself." Lazarus had just come into the kitchen. It was the final evening of the Feast of Dedication. On that night Jews lit the eighth candle of the menorah in remembrance of the one-day supply of oil that had miraculously lasted eight days during the temple rededication. Martha had invited Jesus and his disciples to join her and her family for dinner.

"I'm sure Mary will be here soon to help out. She's just being hospitable to our guests," offered Lazarus. "By the way, when is dinner going to be served?"

"You're asking the wrong person the wrong question at the wrong time," said Martha bluntly. "It might be ready sooner if you helped out. You men are spoiled. If it weren't for us women, you would probably starve to death."

Lazarus had heard Martha's tirade against men many times before and knew better than to contradict her. "I'll let Mary know that you need her," he assured. Lazarus hurried back to the adjoining room, where Jesus and the others were gathered.

"We had an exciting day today, didn't we?" Peter said. "I've lost count of the number of times people have threatened to stone Jesus." Lazarus and the other disciples nodded in agreement.

"What happened while you were in Jerusalem?" Mary asked.

"It was business as usual most of the day," replied Peter. "Jesus was teaching in Solomon's Portico. A large crowd had gathered and several of them asked Jesus if he was the Messiah. Some Pharisees and scribes became offended when Jesus said he was God's Son and picked up stones to throw at him. When they tried to grab him, Jesus' supporters stepped in to allow us all to escape."

"Don't take what happened today lightly," warned Jesus. "This was a preview of things to come. Soon you will see my enemies succeed in putting me to death. At that time, you will be filled with fear and great sadness."

Just then Martha emerged from the kitchen. "Mary, I thought you would listen when Lazarus asked you to help me," Martha said impatiently. "But here you are, still sitting with the men while I slave in the kitchen."

Mary looked at Lazarus, who was gazing sheepishly at the floor. Neither of them said anything. Martha then turned toward Jesus. "Rabbi, doesn't it bother you that I'm preparing the meal all by myself? Please tell Mary she should help me out."

Jesus looked lovingly at Martha and smiled. "Martha, you have always been meticulous in whatever you do, and I commend you for the hard work you've done today. It hasn't gone unnoticed. But perhaps you could have prepared a less-than-perfect meal. That would have given you some time to do what Mary is doing, sitting here listening to me."

Mary apologized to her sister and accompanied Martha into the kitchen. Later, Lazarus thanked Mary for not exposing his communication failure. That evening at dinner, traditional psalms were read and the story of the temple rededication was retold. At the end of the meal, Jesus announced that he and the disciples were leaving the following morning to teach at a few towns along the Jordan River.

Chapter Seven

NEW LIFE

LAZARUS WINCED AS he bent over and clutched his right side. The pain in his lower abdomen had been getting worse over the past twenty-four hours. He could barely eat or sleep or even get out of bed. Waves of nausea caused him to vomit regularly, increasing his pain.

Mary and Martha were alerted by Levi, Lazarus' business partner, that their brother hadn't come to work as scheduled. They immediately went to his house and found him moaning in agony. He was disoriented and his speech was incoherent. A local physician was summoned, but his medical skills were limited. His only advice was to apply warm, wet cloths to the distressed area and chew on ginger root to lessen nausea. Unfortunately, none of these remedies eliminated his distress.

By evening of the second day the pain was unbearable and unrelenting. It was then that Lazarus felt a quick, sharp sting in his lower belly. The sting was followed by a lessening of the pain. "Maybe I'm going to feel better now," thought Lazarus. He lifted himself from the bed and took a few small steps but could go no farther. His strength had been sapped. He shuffled slowly back to the bed and lay back down.

The next morning Lazarus was sweating profusely. He was shivering in spite of a number of blankets covering him. Mary, who had stayed to take care of her brother, felt his forehead and immediately realized his fever was out of control. In a weak, halting voice Lazarus informed his sister that the pain had moved from his right side and was slowly spreading through his entire abdomen. The nausea became even worse.

Seeing that the situation was becoming hopeless, Mary left the house to summon rabbi Tobias. When she reached the synagogue, Mary explained what had happened to their brother and asked Tobias to visit Lazarus and pray over him. "I will be glad to go with you, and I will certainly pray for him," Tobias said. "But from what you are telling me about his condition, my prayers may need some assistance. Hasn't your friend Jesus healed many people throughout Galilee and Judea? I heard he was staying here in Bethany."

"Jesus was here for the Feast of Dedication, but he left four days ago," answered Mary. "He and Lazarus have formed a special bond, and I'm sure he would want to help. It appears we need a miracle to save our brother's life."

"If Jesus is still a reasonable distance from here, you could send a messenger to let him know Lazarus needs him back in Bethany right away," Tobias advised.

"Jesus said he was going to a small town on the eastern shore of the Jordan River called Bethabara. I'll send a messenger there at once," replied Mary. "You are very wise man, Tobias. Thank you."

It took the messenger just four hours to travel the twenty miles to Bethabara. Once he arrived, it took the messenger only a few minutes to locate Jesus. A large crowd was gathered near the Jordan River just a mile from town to hear him and possibly witness a miracle or two.

The messenger skirted the crowd and walked directly toward Jesus. The disciples saw him coming and tried to stop him, but he was determined to reach his destination. "Greetings, rabbi," the messenger said respectfully. "I just arrived from Bethany and have some important news from your friends Mary and Martha. I am sorry to inform you that their brother Lazarus is seriously ill. They don't know how long he has to live, and they are asking you to come there right away to save his life."

Jesus replied, "His illness will not end in his death. It will give glory to my Father and to me. Go back to Bethany and tell Mary and Martha that Lazarus is in God's hands and that I will be there soon." The messenger thanked Jesus and hurried back to Bethany. To the surprise of his disciples, Jesus returned to the crowd and resumed teaching.

Suddenly Lazarus realized his pain was completely gone. A moment before, his body had been wracked with pain. In the blink of an eye, he went from pure agony to feeling no discomfort at all. What Lazarus didn't know was that he was in the final stages of death. His nervous system no longer functioned, his heart had stopped, his internal organs had failed, and his brain was shutting down. His soul was preparing to leave his body.

In the last vestiges of life, Lazarus visualized his surroundings from a detached vantage point above the bed. He saw his sister Mary bending over his motionless body. She cradled his hands in hers, praying through her tears that his life could be spared. His sister Martha, usually the stoic one, sobbed uncontrollably nearby. Lazarus' focus moved to his own face. His eyes were closed and his lips were slightly parted. Gradually the picture before him faded until it was completely black. Lazarus had died.

Immediately everything changed. Darkness was replaced by indescribable brightness. A feeling of joyful ecstasy came over him. Lazarus felt the presence of God. His soul was now in heaven. In spite of being separated from his body, Lazarus could visually identify his surroundings. A countless number of angels were singing and praising God, giving him honor and thanks for creating them and allowing them to live with him forever. The sights and sounds were overwhelming.

As he looked around to take in the wondrous surroundings, Lazarus recognized the souls of his mother and father approaching. He felt their joy as they greeted him and knew that they could feel his joy as well. His parents motioned for him to turn around. Lazarus immediately recognized the souls of his wife, Rachel, and his unborn son. The indescribable grief he had experienced from losing them on earth was instantly forgotten, replaced by overwhelming joy he now felt from being reunited with them in heaven.

But as great as his elation was from being with his loved ones again, Lazarus' greatest pleasure resulted from his proximity to God. Unconditional love permeated the entirety of heaven. It radiated from God himself and filled the entire space. At that moment there was nothing Lazarus wanted to do more than sing songs of praise and thanks.

Two days after receiving the news from Mary and Martha, Jesus had not mentioned Lazarus to his disciples or indicated that he wanted to travel to Bethany. He continued drawing crowds near the river with his message of the coming of the God's kingdom. Finally the disciples questioned him about Lazarus, wondering if he had forgotten about the sisters' urgent request. He replied that they would leave for Bethany the next morning.

Before they left Bethabara, some of the disciples expressed their concerns. "Jesus, we fully support traveling to Bethany in order to help Lazarus. But you need to consider the danger you're putting yourself in. You have many enemies in Jerusalem. The Jewish leaders are always looking for a reason to put you in jail or, even worse, put you to death. They have spies everywhere, even in Bethany. You will need to be very cautious during your visit there."

Jesus answered, "I'm not worried. I have always taught openly in public without regard for my own welfare, and I'm not going to stop now. I trust my Father will keep me safe until it is time for me to complete my mission. No matter what happens to me, I will go to Bethany tomorrow to wake up my friend Lazarus, who has gone to sleep."

"That's good news about Lazarus," they said. "When he wakes up, he will certainly feel better."

"That's not exactly what I meant," responded Jesus. "I mean that Lazarus has actually died. Because we have stayed here this long, you will have the opportunity to witness another miracle, one that you will never forget."

Thomas added, "I'm ready to go to Bethany and on to Jerusalem. Brothers, let's all commit to remain with Jesus even if it results in our deaths."

Jesus and his disciples had remained in Bethabara for two days after the messenger brought news of Lazarus' illness, and it took another two days to reach the outskirts of Bethany. The disciples were astonished that Jesus continued teaching along the way.

Mary and Martha received word that Jesus was nearing the village. The sisters were at the inn being comforted by friends of the family, some of whom had come from Jerusalem after hearing that Lazarus had died. Martha left to meet Jesus while Mary stayed behind.

When Martha found Jesus, she expressed her annoyance with him. "Lazarus has been buried in the family tomb for four days. He died the day we sent the messenger to Bethabara. We expected you to come back with him, but for some reason you didn't. I know you could have healed him if you were here. Nevertheless, I know God will do whatever you ask him to do."

Jesus assured Martha, "Your brother will live again. I am the one who brings people to life after death. Those who have faith in me will live forever. Do you believe me, Martha?"

"I do believe you. You are the Promised One, the Son of God sent into the world."

Martha returned to the inn and informed her sister that Jesus wanted to see her. Mary left immediately to meet him as he made his way toward town. When Mary found him, she voiced her frustration just as Martha had done, "Jesus, if you had been here earlier, my brother wouldn't have died."

Jesus' eyes began to moisten. Mary stood next to him openly sobbing. He had just been accused by Mary and Martha of failing to prevent the death of their brother. Filled with sorrow and compassion, Jesus broke down and cried.

Those who accompanied Mary remarked how much he must have loved Lazarus.

After recovering his composure, Jesus asked Mary where Lazarus was laid to rest. She offered to show him and sent word to Martha to join them. When Martha arrived, they all left for the place where Lazarus was entombed. It was the same limestone sepulcher in which their father and mother had been buried.

On the day Lazarus died his body had been covered with spices, wrapped in burial cloths, and placed on a flat bench in the tomb. The tomb was then sealed with a large boulder to keep out intruders. In a few weeks after the body decomposed, the rock would be rolled away. At that time his sisters would gather Lazarus' bones and place them into an ossuary, just as they and their brother had done for their parents.

When they arrived at the tomb, Jesus asked his disciples to roll the stone away from the entrance. Martha, ever the pragmatist, warned that the body was already partially decomposed and would certainly stink. Undeterred by her comment, Jesus walked to the front of the opened tomb and prayed, "Heavenly Father, please bring life back to Lazarus. I thank you for hearing me. I know that you always answer my prayers. If it is your will, show everyone here that I am the one you have sent."

When he finished praying, Jesus shouted into the tomb, "Lazarus, come out!" The sound echoed off the rock walls inside. All eyes were glued to the entrance. For a moment nothing happened. The silence was deafening as everyone listened for any activity in the tomb.

Then the seemingly impossible occurred. A sound like leaves rustling was heard coming from inside the tomb followed by the sound of footsteps shuffling toward the entrance. Then, as Jesus had commanded, a man partially wrapped in burial cloths emerged at the opening. The onlookers gasped in disbelief. It had to be Lazarus. Incredibly, Jesus had raised him from the dead.

Lazarus squinted as sunshine washed over him. After awakening, he had removed the burial cloth that covered his face. His eyes were adjusting from the darkness of the tomb. He felt relaxed and rested, but he was confused by what was happening around him. He tried to determine exactly where he was and how he had gotten there, but his mind drew a blank.

Lazarus soon began to recognize his surroundings. Apparently he was in the Bethany cemetery surrounded by a crowd of deliriously happy people. His sisters were embracing him, sobbing with happiness and praising God for his return to them. Other relatives and friends were cautiously touching him and wishing him well. But try as he might, Lazarus couldn't remember how or why he was standing there.

Then his eyes fell on Jesus standing nearby. Jesus returned his gaze with a smile that gave Lazarus comfort in spite of his confusion. Simon, Lazarus' friend and a disciple of Jesus, helped him remove the remaining strips of burial cloth. He could now move around freely. Simon removed his own cloak and wrapped it around Lazarus.

"Jesus, I'm not sure what has happened or why I'm here," Lazarus confessed. "But I know that somehow you are involved. Please tell me what is going on."

Before Jesus could reply, Mary blurted out, "Brother, until a few minutes ago you were dead and buried. You died four days ago. Jesus prayed and God brought you to life again."

Lazarus looked at his sisters and then at Jesus. He thought for a moment, trying to recall anything that might have happened to him. "I do remember being sick in bed for a few days and both of you were taking care of me. But after that I don't remember anything until I was standing at the entrance of the family tomb. It's as if I went to sleep only to wake up in a different location and wearing different clothes."

Jesus smiled again and said, "God has raised you from the dead, just as I will die and be resurrected. It is to your benefit that you don't remember what happened after you died. If you did, you would never again be satisfied living in this world. You have been made alive again to show that I am sent by God. I will make it possible for everyone who believes in me to live forever in heaven. Soon you will be a witness to my victory over sin and death."

"I am your servant," said Lazarus. "Use me as you wish."

Chapter Eight

BETRAYAL

"Y OU BOTH NEED to leave Bethany and get as far
from here as you can," warned Nicodemus. He
had traveled from Jerusalem that morning to speak to Jesus
and Lazarus. Two weeks had passed since Lazarus had been
brought back to life. Word of the miracle spread quickly, and
by now nearly everyone in Judea had heard about it. People
from all over the surrounding area were coming to Bethany
to see Jesus and the man named Lazarus he had raised from
the dead.

Nicodemus continued, addressing Jesus directly. "The day
Lazarus was resurrected, a few men who had witnessed the
miracle traveled to Jerusalem and told several members of

the Sanhedrin what had happened. No action was taken at that time, but yesterday the high priest called an emergency meeting. He was worried that you had become so popular that the Jews would try to make you a king. If that happened, he believed the Romans would crush any such attempt at forming a new government. Then the temple and the entire nation would be in jeopardy. Jews would lose the limited independence we are currently enjoying."

"Caiaphas and the rest of the Sanhedrin are more worried about retaining power and personal wealth than they are about the welfare of the Jews," replied Jesus. "People have wanted to make me king several times. One incident happened after I fed five thousand men with only a couple of fish and five loaves of bread. The Jewish leaders knew that was only talk, and nothing ever came of it."

"This is different," countered Nicodemus. "This time the Sanhedrin is plotting to kill you. It's the first time since I've been a member of the Council that we have targeted anyone for death. I and several other Pharisees voted against having you killed. But Caiaphas has convinced the rest of the members that it would be better for you to die than for the entire nation to be destroyed. A warrant is out for your arrest, so it is only a matter of time before they find you, especially if you remain in Bethany."

"I can understand why Jesus needs to hide," said Lazarus. "But why are you warning me to leave Bethany as well?"

"I was just getting to that," said Nicodemus. "Caiaphas holds you accountable for Jesus' current popularity. He believes that if you are eliminated, people will forget about the resurrection miracle more quickly. The Sanhedrin is planning to kill you along with Jesus."

"That would be ironic," noted Lazarus with a smirk on his face. "I died and was raised from the dead two weeks ago. If this death threat is carried out within the next week or so, I would undoubtedly be the only person in history to die twice in the same month."

"Lazarus, I'm glad you've kept your sense of humor in spite of being in danger," Jesus said with a smile. "It wasn't long ago that you would have been paralyzed with fear in this situation. I have a feeling that you are beginning to trust what I have told you about myself. In order to remain calm during the coming days, you will need to put your trust in me."

Turning toward Nicodemus, Jesus continued, "Lazarus and I owe you a debt of gratitude. You risked your leadership role in the Sanhedrin by coming here to warn us. As I revealed to both of you, I will be condemned to death, but not right now. The Passover is two months away. At that time, I will be delivered to the Sanhedrin by one of my disciples. Lazarus and I need to leave Bethany and go to a safe and solitary place until then."

After Nicodemus returned to Jerusalem, Jesus called his disciples together. "I've decided we should leave here for a while. The Sanhedrin is plotting to kill both me and Lazarus. As I have told you before, the mission that my Father has given me to do will result in my death. It will happen soon, and I want to spend some time with you before I leave this world."

"What about Lazarus?" asked Simon. "I'm concerned for my friend. Will he be coming with us?"

"Yes, he will. Lazarus has much to accomplish before he loses his life again."

The next day Jesus and his twelve disciples, accompanied by Lazarus, began their journey to Ephraim. It was a small town located in a remote area fifteen miles northwest of Bethany, surrounded by a series of low, barren hills. No main roads passed through Ephraim, making it an ideal hideaway.

During their time in Ephraim, Jesus spoke directly and plainly about what was going to happen. He told them he would be arrested and that they would all desert him. He would be put on trial and sentenced to death. Three days after dying, he would rise again, just as they had seen Lazarus resurrected.

The disciples tried their best to understand, but they couldn't fathom that Jesus might leave them so soon. In spite of Jesus' clear and persistent explanation of his mission, the disciples clung to the hope that he was the promised one sent to restore the kingdom of David. Lazarus knew better. He had accepted Jesus' declaration that he was not the Messiah everyone else expected.

As the Feast of Passover approached, Jesus announced it was time to leave Ephraim and return to Bethany. They arrived there on the Friday morning prior to Passover week. Jesus and the disciples spent that afternoon visiting with Tobias at the synagogue. During their visit Tobias asked Jesus if he would read from the sacred scrolls at Sabbath worship the next day. Jesus agreed.

The next morning Bethany's residents walked up the hill to the synagogue for worship. After entering the building, the men sat on the right side and the women on the left. In the center of the room was the raised platform on which the synagogue leaders and guest dignitaries were seated. At the far side of the synagogue was the ark containing the sacred scrolls including the Torah and books of the Prophets.

The service began with the *Shema* recited by the entire congregation: "Listen, O Israel. Jehovah our God is the only true God. You must love Jehovah your God with all your heart, and with all your soul, and with all your might." A common prayer was recited followed by a moment of silence for any personal prayers that members might have. This was followed by a reading of the Scriptures.

Tobias left his seat on the platform to retrieve one of the sacred scrolls. Jesus had selected the writings of the prophet Isaiah. Jesus took the scroll from Tobias, walked to the lectern located at the center of the platform, and began to read:

> *"He had no beauty or majesty to attract us to him, nothing in his appearance that we should desire him. He was despised and rejected by mankind, a man of suffering, and familiar with pain. Like one from whom people hide their faces he was despised, and we held him in low esteem.*
>
> *"Surely he took up our pain and bore our suffering, yet we considered him punished by God, stricken by him, and afflicted. But he was pierced for our trans-*

gressions, he was crushed for our iniquities; the punishment that brought us peace was on him, and by his wounds we are healed. We all, like sheep, have gone astray, each of us has turned to our own way; and the Lord has laid on him the iniquity of us all.

"He was oppressed and afflicted, yet he did not open his mouth; he was led like a lamb to the slaughter, and as a sheep before its shearers is silent, so he did not open his mouth. By oppression and judgment he was taken away. Yet who of his generation protested? For he was cut off from the land of the living; for the transgression of my people he was punished. He was assigned a grave with the wicked, and with the rich in his death, though he had done no violence, nor was any deceit in his mouth.

"Yet it was the Lord's will to crush him and cause him to suffer, and though the Lord makes his life an offering for sin, he will see his offspring and prolong his days, and the will of the Lord will prosper in his hand. After he has suffered, he will see the light of life and be satisfied; by his knowledge my righteous servant will justify many, and he will bear their iniquities. Therefore I will give him a portion among the great, and he will divide the spoils with the strong, because he poured out his life unto death, and was numbered with the transgressors. For he bore the sin of many, and made intercession for the transgressors." [7]

---

7   Isaiah 53:2b-12 (NIV)

Jesus rolled up the scroll and handed it back to Tobias. All eyes were on Jesus. He began to teach them, saying, "You, like your fathers before you, have been waiting anxiously for the Messiah promised long ago. But you have been looking in the wrong direction. You expect a mighty warrior who will restore the glory days of King David and King Solomon. You look for a liberator who will free you from Roman rule.

"Who is this man Isaiah is talking about? Could he be the Messiah? By your definition, certainly not. Isaiah describes someone who is unattractive, despised, and trampled on. Isaiah describes a servant sent by God to be a sin offering. Although innocent of any wrongdoing, he willingly suffers and dies so that many can be forgiven. Isaiah's description is not the Messiah you are expecting to see, but he is the Messiah whom God has already sent. I tell you the truth, the one about whom Isaiah prophesied is standing here in front of you."

Jesus sat down, and Tobias offered a closing prayer. The men and women in attendance exited the synagogue with quizzical looks on their faces. Lazarus could tell that they had heard Jesus' words but didn't understand what he had said. Regardless of Jesus' message, their hopes still rested on a Messiah who was a conqueror and not a servant.

That evening Mary and Martha hosted a dinner celebrating the return of Jesus and Lazarus from Ephraim. After the sun set and the Sabbath officially ended, all the guests for Martha's celebration were gathered in the banquet hall at the inn. While Martha finished the cooking, Mary placed bowls of olive oil and cups of wine on the tables and set out trays with bread, raw vegetables, and fruit. Martha brought out a pot filled with lamb stew. After everyone had reclined, Jesus said a prayer of thanks. The food and wine were passed around the tables and each person ate his or her fill. The evening proved to be a festive occasion filled with laughter and storytelling. Lazarus enjoyed himself in spite of his general aversion to social gatherings. Being brought back to life had given him a different perspective on interpersonal relationships.

As the evening came to a close, Mary walked into the banquet hall from the kitchen and moved to a position directly behind Jesus. In one hand she held a bottle carved out of alabaster stone. The white polished surface of the bottle indicated that it was not just an ordinary piece of pottery. A towel was draped over her opposite arm. As she removed the wax cap from the bottle, a sweet, earthy scent of spikenard filled the room. The guests' attention was immediately captured by the strong but pleasant odor, and all eyes turned to Mary.

Jesus sat up and hung his legs over the side of the couch on which he had been reclining. Mary placed the towel on the floor under his bare feet and poured the contents of the bottle over them. Mary then untied the braid in her hair allowing its entire length to cascade over her shoulders. She kneeled and began wiping the excess liquid from Jesus' feet with her hair. When she had finished, Mary gathered up the bottle and towel and walked silently back into the kitchen. No one uttered a sound. They were waiting to hear what Jesus might have to say.

However, it wasn't Jesus who broke the silence. Judas, the disciple who kept track of the group's finances. reprimanded

Jesus In a voice tinged with disrespect, "Why did you let that woman waste good perfume? That bottle and its contents probably cost more than a year's wages. Didn't you realize all the good we could have done with the money received from selling it? We could have used the proceeds to support your ministry and maybe even given some of it to the poor."

"Judas," Jesus replied gently, "Mary did what she did because she loved me. I've told you several times in recent days that I am about to lose my life. She has anointed my body with perfume even before I am dead. The poor will always be around for you to help, but I won't. Mary has done the proper thing in God's eyes."

Lazarus, who was seated near Judas, could see that he was embarrassed and angry. Jesus' words, although spoken in a conciliatory tone, appeared to greatly offend Judas. His frown turned into a scowl as he glared at Jesus. Lazarus thought he heard Judas mutter under his breath, "He won't get away with this."

Late the next morning, Jesus gathered his disciples together in front of the inn before leaving for Jerusalem. It was Sunday, the first day of the Jewish week. The Passover meal was scheduled to take place on Thursday evening, the first night of the seven-day festival. Jesus had invited Lazarus to accompany them, and he accepted without hesitation

"Do any of your friends here in Bethany own a donkey?" Jesus asked Lazarus. "I would like to ride from here to Jerusalem and back each day. I want to conserve my energy for later in the week." The disciples looked at each other quizzically. They didn't understand why Jesus would need to be rested, but none of them chose to ask.

"There's a stable about half a mile northeast of here just outside Bethpage on the road to Jerusalem," Lazarus replied. "It's near the summit of the Mount of Olives. Horses and donkeys are boarded there. We can rent one on the way to the city."

Jesus turned to the brothers Peter and Andrew and asked, "Will you go ahead of us to Bethpage? Select a young donkey that has not yet been ridden and wait for the rest of us to get there. Perhaps Lazarus is willing to show you the way to the stable." Lazarus nodded his consent.

Peter addressed Judas. "Andrew and I will need enough money from the common purse to pay the rental fee. What do you think they will charge for a week's rent?"

Jesus interrupted before Judas had a chance to reply, "You won't need any money. Just tell the owner that Jesus of Nazareth needs the donkey."

The three men left for Bethpage. Upon arriving at the stable, they saw a number of horses and donkeys tied up in individual stalls. The unmistakable odor of fresh manure wafted through the building. Andrew and Lazarus wandered through the stable while Peter went to find the owner.

A few minutes later, Andrew spotted a stall containing a jenny and her foal. Each was tethered with a rope to a metal ring mounted on the back side of the stall. Andrew walked cautiously toward the foal, taking care to keep his distance from the jenny. He untied the young donkey and led it out of the stable. Its mother craned her head to see where her foal was being taken and then turned back to her food trough.

As Andrew and Lazarus emerged from the dimly lit stable into the sunshine, they saw a tall, crusty man walk out of a nearby building and approach Peter. "What are you doing with my donkey?" he asked. "Who gave you permission to untie him?"

"My brother and I are disciples of Jesus, the rabbi from Nazareth in Galilee," Peter replied. "He needs it to ride between Bethany and Jerusalem during the Passover."

"Did you say Jesus? Isn't he the one who raised a local man named Lazarus from the dead a month or so ago?"

"Yes, he is the one. And the man you see with my brother over there is Lazarus."

The stable owner walked over to Lazarus and looked him over from head to toe. He reached out and touched Lazarus' arm. "I can't believe you were really dead."

"It's true. I am living proof that Jesus is sent from God, who has power over death."

The stable owner waved his hand toward the road. "Go. Take the foal as long as you need it. There will be no charge."

A short time after the young donkey was procured, Jesus and his followers arrived at Bethpage. The small contingent accompanying Jesus included the remaining ten disciples and a few

Bethany residents. Jesus mounted the foal, and the procession left Bethpage for the final mile and a half trip to Jerusalem.

After reaching the summit of the Mount of Olives, the beauty of Jerusalem was visible across the Kidron Valley. The glorious Temple Mount was the centerpiece. Herod the Great had begun reconstruction of the temple nearly fifty years earlier, transforming it into an awe-inspiring monument to the God of Israel. The building project was so extensive that even after half a century the work was not yet completed.

During their descent to the city, a party of Jewish pilgrims traveling to Jerusalem from Galilee for the Passover overtook them. When the pilgrims found out that Jesus was in the group they were passing, a few of them ran ahead to announce he was coming. Word quickly spread throughout Jerusalem that the miracle-worker, the one who had just raised a dead man to life, was about to enter their city. By the time Jesus reached the valley floor, hundreds of people had lined the road outside the East Gate waiting for a glimpse of him.

Enthusiasm mounted as Jesus got closer. Some in the crowd began chanting, "Blessed is the king who comes in the name of the Lord! God bless the coming kingdom of our ancestor David. Praise to the Son of David!" The entire crowd was caught up in the excitement. Many laid their cloaks on the ground in front of Jesus and cut down palm branches to wave at him.

As they neared the East Gate, Judas slipped away from the procession into the crowd with his head down and shoulders slumped. Lazarus noticed him leave and assumed he was going to take care of some money matters. Minutes later,

Jesus and his entourage entered the city amidst the cheers of his admirers.

Once Jesus reached the Temple Mount, he went directly to Solomon's Portico, where he normally taught when in Jerusalem. This day, however, the entire area was filled with visitors. Because Passover was one of three major festivals requiring travel to Jerusalem, it attracted Jews from all over the world in a mass pilgrimage. During the Passover celebration, the population of Jerusalem swelled from around ninety thousand full-time residents to an estimated two hundred fifty thousand residents and visitors.

Seeing that his favorite teaching spot was unavailable, Jesus relocated to the Court of Gentiles. In spite of the noise and other distractions caused by vendors exchanging currency and selling sacrificial animals, a large crowd gathered to listen to Jesus' message. Later Jesus went into the temple, where he spent the rest of the afternoon in prayer, asking God for help during the coming days. At the end of the day, Jesus and his followers returned to Bethany to spend the night.

The following morning, in stark contrast to the day before, Jesus and his entourage entered Jerusalem unnoticed. He selected a location in the shade under Solomon's Portico and began teaching worshippers who stopped to listen on their way into the temple. The crowd grew larger as word spread that the rabbi who had raised a dead man from the grave was there.

As the day progressed, Jesus repeatedly glanced toward the Court of Gentiles, where he had been compelled to teach the day before. The Court of Gentiles, which occupied most of the Temple Mount, was loud and congested. Vendors called out to prospective customers, hawking the animals and birds that would be sacrificed in the temple. The bulls, sheep, goats, and birds being sold created raucous sounds and unsavory odors. Money changers shouted their exchange rates to Jewish pilgrims obligated to pay the mandatory half-shekel temple tax.

Lazarus could sense that Jesus was increasingly bothered by what was taking place nearby. He didn't expect what happened next. Jesus left Solomon's Portico and walked purposefully toward the vendors' booths. Grabbing a rope lying near a goat pen and doubling it to increase the impact, he began whipping the vendors and money changers who were unfortunate enough to be within reach. He then proceeded to topple every chair and table in sight.

Jesus' eyes bulged and the veins on his neck stood out as he continued his rampage against the group of startled businessmen. They scattered in every direction to escape this seeming madman. Once he had driven the objectionable men and animals out of the Court of Gentiles, Jesus called out in an impassioned voice, "This can't happen in my Father's house. The temple is intended for worship and prayer. These men have made it into a sanctuary for crooks and swindlers."

Lazarus had never seen Jesus this agitated, but he wasn't surprised at how Jesus reacted to the desecration of the temple. Word of what Jesus had done quickly spread throughout the city. He continued to teach in parables, perform miraculous healings, and speak about the coming kingdom of God. People from all over Jerusalem, visitors and residents alike, came to hear Jesus speak.

All of this notoriety did not go unnoticed by the Jewish leaders, particularly the Sanhedrin. Their fear that Jesus could win the hearts of the majority of Jews was becoming a reality. If so, their authority over Jewish politics and religion would be at risk. The spotless image that the Pharisees and scribes tried to portray was also threatened by Jesus. He never shied away from exposing their hypocrisy.

In an attempt to undermine Jesus' credibility, on Tuesday afternoon a Sanhedrin member who happened to be a chief priest pushed his way through the crowd. In a voice filled with venom, the chief priest questioned him, "Who do you think you are? Who gave you the authority to teach falsehoods that contradict the law? Who gave you the authority to do miracles and forgive sins?"

Jesus answered, "I will reveal my authority if you first answer my question for you. By what authority did John baptize? Did his authority come from God or from himself?"

The chief priest and the crowd were all familiar with John. He was a distant relative of Jesus who preached repentance and announced the coming of the Messiah. Before he died, John baptized many people, including Jesus, in the Jordan River. John had recently been imprisoned and beheaded by Herod Antipas after criticizing Herod for divorcing his wife in order to marry his brother's ex-wife.

The chief priest was speechless. Jesus had put him in a difficult predicament. On one hand, if he said that John's authority came from God, he would be contradicting the high priest and other members of the Sanhedrin who opposed John's teaching. On the other hand, many in the crowd believed that John was a prophet sent by God. If the chief priest said John's authority did not come from God and implied that John was a fraud, the crowd might stone him. Since he was in a no-win situation, the chief priest could only reply sheepishly, "I don't know."

The chief priest turned and walked away in shame. "This humiliation can't continue," he muttered to himself. "Jesus is going to have to die soon."

Wednesday morning an emergency meeting of the Sanhedrin was held at the home of Caiaphas the high priest. He had invited only members of his own Sadducee sect and intentionally excluded any Pharisees. The topic of the meeting was what to do about Jesus. Three months earlier, the Sanhedrin had voted to have Jesus and Lazarus killed and issued warrants for their arrest. Now that both of their targets were in Jerusalem, the Sanhedrin needed to decide how and when to accomplish their plan.

Caiaphas did not trust the Pharisees enough to allow them to participate in the discussion. At the previous emergency meeting he noticed that Nicodemus and a few other Pharisees had voted against killing Jesus and Lazarus. He couldn't be sure where their loyalties lay.

The chief priest who had been outsmarted by Jesus the previous day began the discussion. "This Galilean has been a thorn in our side ever since he started to teach and do miracles three years ago. Jesus has consistently made us look foolish in the eyes of the people. Although we have tried to catch him in some sort of error or lie, he has always been able to evade our questions or change the subject. Yesterday he refused to answer a simple question I asked him. Instead of answering, he made a mockery of me in front of a crowd of people outside the temple. This lack of respect for Jewish leadership can't be tolerated anymore. We need to do something now."

A second chief priest chimed in. "I have news that might provide a solution to our problem. You recall that on Sunday Jesus entered Jerusalem to wide acclaim. While that love fest was going on, one of his disciples, he said his name was Judas Iscariot, slipped away and entered the temple. He went to the hall where we hold our daily Sanhedrin meetings. The meeting was already over, but I happened to be there at the time. I asked if I could help him, not knowing that he was one of Jesus' disciples. Judas said he heard the Sanhedrin was offering a reward to anyone who could deliver Jesus to the high priest. He wanted to know if what he heard was accurate."

The chief priest continued. "I replied that the offer was legitimate and asked him why he was inquiring about it. That's when he told me that he was a disciple of Jesus. From what I gathered, he recently had a squabble with Jesus and wanted to see him arrested and jailed. I don't believe he knows that we are actually planning to have Jesus killed. But that would be his problem, not ours."

Caiaphas asked, "How do we contact this Judas character? Can we speak to him this afternoon? We need to act quickly.

In a few days, it will be the Sabbath, when nothing can be done. Tomorrow is the Passover meal. That will be our best chance to make our move because the entire population of Jerusalem will be inside their homes commemorating that special day. No one will notice that Jesus has been arrested."

"Jesus is at the Temple Mount every day with his disciples," replied the second chief priest. "I'll send one of my servants right now to bring Judas here. While we're waiting for him to arrive, we can discuss how to get rid of Jesus. Lazarus' fate can be decided later."

The servant was dispatched and found Judas in Solomon's Portico alongside Jesus, who was teaching a large crowd. He managed to catch Judas' eye with a beckoning nod. No one else noticed the gesture. Seeing the servant motion to him, Judas slid unobtrusively around the edge of the crowd. The servant explained that the high priest wanted to talk to him immediately. He reminded Judas of his visit to the Sanhedrin meeting hall earlier in the week.

Judas looked back toward Jesus for a moment and then spun around, motioning for the servant to show him the way. Once he arrived at the high priest's residence, Judas was directed to stand at one end of a large wooden table. At the far end was Caiaphas. "We understand that you inquired if there was a reward for information leading to the arrest of Jesus. Is that true?"

Judas replied, "Yes, I did. But I'm having second thoughts about providing any information. After all, he is my rabbi. However, if I were to cooperate, how much money are we talking about?"

"I see that your cooperation is tied more closely to profit than loyalty. What type of information can you give us? That will determine how much you would get."

Judas paused for a moment and then replied, "Jesus plans to eat the Passover meal tomorrow night here in Jerusalem. I'm not sure where that will be. After the meal, if he follows his normal routine, Jesus will return to Bethany. I can find out exactly where and when he will be going and leave before the meal is over. Assuming you can assemble enough temple guards to arrest Jesus, I will lead them to him before he leaves for Bethany. I will identify Jesus to the guards if they don't know who he is. That's as far as I'm willing to go. So how much is this worth to you?"

"Arresting him tomorrow night doesn't leave us much time to complete our plans before the Sabbath. However, we may have no choice. Jesus will certainly leave the area and return to Galilee soon after Passover week is over. We might never have an opportunity like this again. We're willing to give you twenty pieces of silver for your assistance."

"That's less than a week's wages," an emboldened Judas replied. "I wouldn't give him up to you for less than thirty pieces of silver. Also, I need your pledge that you will not hurt Jesus. He thinks you're plotting to kill him, but I don't believe that you would be that vindictive. He may have been overly critical of you in the past, but he is innocent of any crime. I want you to promise to arrest him and put him in jail and nothing more. I just want to teach him a lesson for the way he treated me."

Caiaphas looked around the room as if he were looking for consensus. No one objected to the increased cost or the conditions Judas imposed. The decision to kill Jesus had already been made and wouldn't change. "You have a deal," Caiaphas responded. The high priest opened a metal box on the table in front of him and counted out thirty pieces of silver. "Here is your fee. Spend it wisely. We will have the temple guards assembled here at my house tomorrow night. We expect you to be here as soon as you find out where we can arrest Jesus."

Judas picked up the coins and counted them. Without saying a word, he dropped them into his money pouch and walked out of the room. When he returned to the temple grounds, Jesus was still teaching in the same spot. As Judas merged back into the crowd, Jesus glanced at him and smiled. Judas looked away, a tear forming in his eye.

The day of Passover preparation had finally arrived. Just as he did every other day that week, Jesus made the journey by donkey from Bethany to Jerusalem. When Jesus and his disciples arrived at the temple, Jesus asked Peter and John to arrange the Passover dinner that evening.

"That will be difficult," noted John. "Most of the dining places have already been reserved by the mass of people here to celebrate. Is there a specific location you had in mind that we don't know about?"

Jesus answered, "As you walk out of the south gates of the Temple Mount into the city, you will see a man carrying a jar of water. Follow him to his house. When you get there, ask if he has a spare room for a Passover meal. Tell him it is for Jesus and his disciples. He will show you a room upstairs that we can use. It's fully furnished. We can observe the Passover there."

Peter replied, "I am confident that what you have told us will happen, but we would like to take Lazarus along with us in case we need to look elsewhere. He's the only one of us who lives in the area and is much more familiar with the city than we are."

"Apparently, your trust in me is not as strong as you think," replied Jesus. "But feel free to take Lazarus with you if he is willing."

The three men exited the temple and walked down a narrow street lined with commercial buildings. A man carrying a water jar was coming toward them. They looked at each other in amazement, waited for him to pass, and reversed direction. The man finally stopped in front of a two-story building in the Lower City section of Jerusalem.

As the man opened the front door and started to enter, Peter called out, "Are you the owner of this building? If so, we need to talk to you."

"Yes, I am. How can I help you?"

John asked, "May we come inside to talk?"

The man entered the building and gestured for the three strangers to follow him inside. The first floor was a large open space that was dimly lit. It appeared to be a storage area of some sort.

"My name is Peter and my companions are John and Lazarus. We are followers of Jesus of Nazareth. He asked us to find a room in which to eat the Passover meal tonight. Do you have any space we might be able to use?"

"My name is Demetrius. I'm a businessman of Greek origin. I use the first floor of this building as a warehouse for the rugs I import and sell locally. I live on the second floor. Fortunately for you, I have a room upstairs that might serve your purpose very well. It's large enough for a sizeable group to dine comfortably. The tables and couches are already set up. My wife and I used to entertain quite often when she was alive. I'm sorry to say that she died two years ago. I left the room just as it was before her death."

"I am sorry to hear about your wife. So, are you agreeing to let us use that the room tonight?" asked John.

"Yes, I am," the man replied. "Even though I am Greek, I've heard quite a bit about Jesus from my Jewish friends. He has built a reputation throughout Judea for his teaching and miracles. I would be honored to have him dine here."

"We will also need to prepare the meal. May we use your kitchen to roast the lamb and prepare the rest of the food?" asked Lazarus.

"This should work out well," Demetrius responded. "Because I'm not a Jew, I don't celebrate Passover. I was planning to have dinner at a friend's house tonight. You can have the run of the upstairs all afternoon and evening. By the way, how many people are you expecting?"

Peter replied, "There will be fourteen men including Jesus."

"I usually don't keep much food or wine around the house," said Demetrius. "But feel free to help yourself to anything you can use."

"Thank you so much for your help," declared John. "The three of us will spend the afternoon buying supplies and preparing the food. Jesus and the rest of the disciples will arrive later. I have a feeling this will be a very memorable Passover meal."

Later that afternoon Jesus and the other disciples arrived at Demetrius' building. The aroma of roast lamb filled the air. "Were there any problems with the meal preparation?" Jesus asked. "It certainly smells good."

"Everything went well," said Peter. "We're ready to celebrate the Passover."

Lazarus led the men upstairs into the room that served as the dining area. Three long tables were configured in a U-shaped pattern with couches placed on the outer sides. "The three of you have done an excellent job," Jesus observed. "Thank you for your efforts in making my last meal so memorable." No one in the room, including Lazarus, caught the significance of what he had just said.

Jesus took his place at the head table. Peter, James and John attempted to position themselves at Jesus' right side, the place of honor. As they vied for position, Jesus called out, "Judas, why don't you come and recline next to me at my right hand?

We don't get to talk much anymore. Perhaps we can catch up during the meal."

Judas looked at Jesus with a shocked expression on his face. Jesus rarely singled him out for the kind of special attention he gave to his three favorite disciples. Realizing that all eyes were on him, Judas dutifully walked to the head of the table and took his place next to Jesus. The other disciples jockeyed for the remaining positions closest to their teacher. John was able to secure the seat at Jesus' left side. Peter reclined next to John, and James reclined next to Peter. Simon motioned to Lazarus to fill an empty spot next to him. By the time they had all settled in to their places it was nearly sundown, the traditional starting time of the Passover meal.

Instead of beginning the celebration with the opening prayer, Jesus stood up from his couch. The disciples watched quizzically as he took off his outer cloak and walked toward the door. The bowl of water and towel they had used to wash their feet as they entered the room was lying near the entrance. Jesus tossed the towel over his shoulder and carried the bowl to the couches where Lazarus and Simon reclined. As the others looked on in amazement, Jesus began to wash Lazarus' feet. After drying Lazarus' feet with the towel, he moved on to Simon and repeated the process. Jesus advanced from disciple to disciple in silence until he reached Peter.

"If you plan on washing my feet," Peter said, "I'm asking you not to do it."

Jesus replied, "If I don't wash your feet, then you aren't my disciple."

"In that case," said Peter, "don't just wash my feet. Wash my hands and head as well."

After he was finished, Jesus returned to his place at the table. Every eye was on him, waiting for an explanation of his actions. Jesus didn't disappoint. "Even though I am your leader, I have stooped to wash your feet. In the same way, you need to become a servant to each other and all those who love me."

Ordinarily the Passover meal was a festive occasion held to celebrate the Jews' miraculous deliverance by God from the Egyptians. However, this night was different. Jesus seemed preoccupied with his own thoughts. He was more quiet than usual. When he spoke, his voice was tinged with sadness.

After the traditional Passover rituals were completed and the meal was eaten, Jesus broke apart one of the loaves of unleavened bread. He passed one half to Judas and the other half to John. He told them to break off a piece and hand the remaining loaf to the man next to him. When everyone had received a piece of bread, Jesus instructed them to eat it. "This bread is my body given up for you," he said. "Every time you partake of it, remember me."

Jesus then lifted one of the wine goblets and drank from it. He passed the goblet to John, telling him to take a drink and pass it along. When they all had some of the wine, Jesus said to them, "This is my blood that is shed for the forgiveness of your sins. Every time you drink it, remember me."

Lazarus listened intently to Jesus' words. What Jesus had told him in their private conversations was becoming clearer. The death of the unblemished lamb at the first Passover allowed the Israelites to escape from bondage in Egypt. Similarly, Jesus would be sacrificed to save his followers from the slavery of sin. Lazarus recalled Jesus' words spoken the first day they met: "Your sins will not condemn you because I will be condemned on your behalf." Jesus' predictions were beginning to be realized.

Jesus then made a startling statement. "One of you will betray me into the hands of the Jewish leaders tonight." After a moment of stunned silence, the disciples began questioning each other, trying to determine who would do such a thing. Each of them, including Judas, denied the charge. John, reclining next to Jesus, asked who he was talking about. "I will dip this piece of bread into the sauce of the lamb and give it to my betrayer," Jesus said. He dipped the bread and handed it to Judas. In a voice not much louder than a whisper, Jesus told Judas, "Go and do what you have planned. I will see you in the Garden of Gethsemane."

Judas got up from his couch and left the room. It all happened so quickly that the other disciples did not connect Jesus' betrayal announcement with Judas' hasty exit. John had an inkling of who the betrayer might be, but even so, he couldn't believe that any of the disciples would ever be disloyal to their beloved teacher.

It was nearly ten o'clock when Jesus provided additional instructions to his disciples. He reemphasized the need to show love to others and be a servant to all. In a voice tinged with sadness, Jesus revealed once again that he would be leaving them soon to be with his Father in heaven. He promised to return someday and take them to be with him. He vowed to send God's Spirit to guide them until he returned.

Peter exclaimed, "Why can't I go with you? I want to be where you are even if it means my own death."

Jesus answered Peter's request with a question. "Are you really willing to die for me? Even though you think you are, I know better. In fact, before the night is over and the roosters begin to crow, you will deny that you know me a total of three times."

After the meal, Jesus led the disciples and Lazarus into the darkened streets of Jerusalem. They followed him out the East Gate and onto the road leading to the Mount of Olives, thinking they were on their way back to Bethany. Instead, Jesus turned off the road and onto a path leading into the Garden of Gethsemane.

The night air was cool, and the disciples pulled their cloaks tightly around them. Everyone was silent, and everyone was tired. Jesus appeared to be deep in thought. He asked them to stay awake and pray for him. Then he took Peter, James, and John several yards beyond the others and asked them to stay awake and pray as well. He walked farther into the garden alone and began praying.

Kneeling with his face toward the ground in an almost prone position, Jesus prayed so fervently that beads of sweat formed on his forehead. "Father, you sent me from heaven to earth to restore mankind to righteousness. But I am greatly distressed over what will soon happen to me. If it is possible, spare me from the suffering I am about to endure. But in any case, let your will be done."

After praying a while longer, Jesus returned to the three disciples and found them asleep. Lazarus and the rest of the disciples were also sleeping. "Couldn't you stay awake for a brief time?" Jesus asked them. "You need to pray so that you will survive what is going to happen soon." Jesus then returned to where he had been and repeated the same prayer. Finding the disciples asleep again, Jesus prayed a third time.

It was about eleven in the evening when Jesus saw dots of light approaching from the direction of the city. As the lights got closer, he recognized the glow of torches carried by a large contingent of men walking quickly toward him.

Jesus called out to the sleeping disciples, "Get up! It's time for me to be handed over to those who want to harm me!" The disciples awoke to the sound of footsteps approaching. Their glazed eyes began to focus. A unit of temple guards and a few members of the Sanhedrin were coming up the path. At the head of the procession was Judas.

The guards were armed with clubs and swords. Their swords were drawn as if they were ready to attack. The startled disciples rallied around Jesus, forming a barrier between him and the intruders. Judas and his retinue stopped several yards in front of the disciples.

Judas stepped toward Jesus. At the same time, Jesus parted the line of disciples and walked forward until he stood directly in front of Judas. Judas greeted Jesus, embraced him, and kissed him on the cheek. Immediately four of the temple guards encircled Jesus and started to lead him away.

Peter, who had brought a sword with him, pulled it from its sheath and swung it wildly at one of the guards. The sword made a swooshing sound as it moved through the night air. The guard ducked his head, but Peter managed to slice off a piece of his ear. Blood flowed from the wound as the guard screamed in pain.

Jesus took control of the situation. "Stop, all of you! Put your weapons down and listen to me. I will go with these men willingly. Even though I am innocent of any crime, it is God's will for me to be condemned for the sake of those who believe in me."

Jesus bent down and picked up the severed piece of ear and held it up to the wound. To everyone's amazement, the lopped-off portion became reattached, and the bleeding stopped. The stricken guard exclaimed that his pain had disappeared. One of the other temple guards remarked, "What kind of man has the power to heal like that?"

Desiring to avoid additional bloodshed, the captain of the guard ordered his men to bind Jesus' hands behind him and take him to the home of the high priest, where the Sanhedrin had assembled. Before being led away, Jesus implored, "Let my followers go peaceably. They are not the ones you came to arrest." The captain nodded in agreement. Turning to the disciples and Lazarus, the captain warned them to leave immediately or they would be arrested. Seized by fear and forgetting their promises to be loyal to the death, all of them scattered into the night, leaving Jesus standing alone with his captors.

Chapter Nine

THE PASSION

LAZARUS STOOD BENT over from the waist with his hands on his knees. His heart was pulsing wildly as he gasped for breath. He didn't know how far he had run or in what direction he had gone, but he clearly remembered the rush of adrenalin that caused him to flee in panic minutes earlier.

Lazarus was at a figurative crossroad. His first inclination was to find the road to the Mount of Olives and return to Bethany alone. Jesus had clearly said he needed to die in order to do his Father's will. He wouldn't want any help even if he could get it. Additionally, Lazarus was in danger himself. The Sanhedrin would be trying to kill him next.

After trying to rationalize why he should return home, Lazarus realized there was no excuse for his cowardice. He had run away in fear when Jesus needed him. How could he have deserted his friend after Jesus had given him a second chance at life? How could he even think about running off to Bethany? Instead, he needed to find out what was happening to Jesus. The captain of the guard had said they were taking Jesus to the house of the high priest. That is where he had to go.

Lazarus surveyed his surroundings. In the darkness the silhouettes of olive trees surrounded him. "I must still be in the garden," he thought. "It feels like I ran for miles." Peering through the trees toward the horizon, he located the outline of the city wall backlit by the light from candles and lamps burning in the homes of Jerusalem residents.

Lazarus began walking slowly toward the city, stepping carefully through the dark and unfamiliar terrain. Once he found the road leading to the East Gate, he lengthened his stride. He was afraid, confused, and had no idea what he was going to do once he got to Caiaphas' house. But the concern he felt for Jesus overcame his fears.

The high priest's house was an impressive stone structure on the west side of Jerusalem. The grounds were surrounded by a high wall. The entrance was gated and led to a large court-yard located at the front of the residence. Two guards were posted at the gate to provide a level of security appropriate for a man of the high priest's standing.

Lazarus approached the gate and was met by one of the guards. "I'm here at the request of Nicodemus, a member of the Sanhedrin," Lazarus said in half-truth. "The Council is meeting here tonight. I'm a scribe assisting him in the trial of the man named Jesus."

Earlier in the evening the guard received orders to allow meeting attendees through the gate. He waved Lazarus into the courtyard. In the middle of the courtyard was a fire pit filled with burning logs. Around the fire several men and women were warming themselves against the chill of the evening. Lazarus assumed that they were members of Caiaphas' household staff.

As he approached the fire, he was surprised and elated to find Peter sitting there. Lazarus caught Peter's attention and motioned for him to step away so they could talk privately. "I can hardly believe what happened tonight," Lazarus said in a subdued voice. "I panicked and left Jesus there in the garden. After I stopped running, I felt guilty and decided to come here and find out what was happening to Jesus. Do you know where he is and how he's doing?"

"I haven't been here very long myself," responded Peter. "You weren't the only one to run away. The rest of us took off in every direction. John and I hid behind some bushes nearby and watched as the guards took Jesus away. We followed them at a distance. They stopped for a short time at the home of Annas, the high priest's father-in-law. When they came out of Annas' house, Jesus was still bound with ropes but appeared to be unharmed. John and I then followed them here to Caiaphas' house. John apparently knew one of the people inside and got us both through the gate. We learned that Caiaphas had called a meeting of the full Sanhedrin into session. John left a few minutes ago to see if he could locate the other disciples, and I stayed to watch for any developments here."

"I think I can help," said Lazarus. "My friend Nicodemus should be in the meeting. If so, he can tell us what's happening. We need to keep track of Jesus in case they plan to move him elsewhere."

The two men walked back to the fire and sat down. Unexpectedly, one of the servant girls pointed to Peter and said in a loud voice, "I think this man is one of Jesus' followers. His Galilean accent gives him away." The people sitting around the fire looked up at Peter.

Peter's immediate reaction was denial. "I don't know what you're talking about."

Another person near the fire confirmed the servant girl's claim. "I was there earlier this week when Jesus rode into the city to a hero's welcome. I remember seeing this man walking along with him."

Once again Peter responded defensively, "You must be mistaking me for someone else."

Finally, another man chimed in, saying, "My uncle Malchus and I are servants of the high priest. We were both there tonight when Jesus was arrested. One of Jesus' followers cut off part of my uncle's ear and Jesus healed him. I swear that you're the one who swung the sword."

In a voice mixed with fear and anger, Peter replied, "By the name of the Almighty God, I don't know this Jesus you're talking about!"

Lazarus looked at Peter in amazement. The man who earlier in the evening claimed he would fight to the death for Jesus had just denied knowing him, not just once but three times. At that moment a rooster crowed. Peter's face turned ashen, and his chin fell to his chest. He pulled his cloak over his face and sobbed heavily. Before Lazarus could say anything, Peter ran from the courtyard and into the darkness of the street.

After Peter's abrupt departure, Lazarus looked across the courtyard toward Caiaphas' house. Light was coming from one of the windows partially hidden from view by some shrubbery. He moved toward the window, making sure that no one would notice. Peering inside, Lazarus observed a large room with a high ceiling, illuminated by a number of candles and oil lamps.

Lazarus recognized the high priest sitting on a high-backed chair at the far side of the room. The chair sat on a pedestal that raised him to a position much like a king on a throne. The other members of the Sanhedrin sat around several rows of tables facing the high priest.

Jesus, his back toward Lazarus and his hands bound behind him, stood facing Caiaphas. His head was bowed toward the floor, and his shoulders were slumped. He appeared to be completely exhausted. Lazarus could clearly hear what was being said through the open window.

"Gentlemen, we've listened to several witnesses so far. Unfortunately, they have not given a consistent argument for finding this man guilty of any crime," observed Caiaphas. "How should we proceed?"

One of the Sadducees stood and offered a suggestion. "We all know that his teachings and his actions are heretical. Why don't we let Jesus convict himself? The more he talks, the deeper the hole he will dig for himself."

One by one, the Jewish leaders proceeded to question Jesus. "Why do you associate with known sinners such as tax collectors? Why do you think you have the power to forgive sins? By whose power do you heal people? Why don't you and your disciples follow the ceremonial laws? What did you mean that you would destroy the temple and build it up again in three days?"

The interrogation lasted for nearly an hour. Jesus' response to each question was silence. The questioners' impatience grew as they demanded answers but didn't get them. They spoke in louder and increasingly accusatory voices as time passed. Finally the high priest shouted in frustration, "Enough! We aren't accomplishing anything with these questions. We need to get to the bottom of this right now. I ask you, Jesus, in the name of the God of Abraham, Isaac, and Jacob, do you claim to be the Messiah?"

Lazarus could feel the tension building. Jesus raised his head slowly, looked directly at Caiaphas, and replied, "If I told you that I was, you wouldn't believe me anyway. But I can tell you I will soon be sitting in heaven at the right hand of my Father, and when I return you will see me in all of my glory."

"Did I hear you correctly? Are you saying that you are the Son of God?" asked Caiaphas incredulously.

"What you say is true," Jesus replied.

The high priest, his mouth wide open, glared at Jesus. He jumped to his feet, grabbed the edge of his robe, and ripped it apart. "We have heard all that we need to hear. This man has finally condemned himself. He has committed blasphemy by claiming he is God. What is the punishment for blasphemy?"

The majority of the Sanhedrin stood, chanting in unison, "He deserves to die!"

"How should he die?" shouted Caiaphas.

The chief priest whom Jesus had made a fool of earlier in the week answered, "Stoning is too humane for what he has done. He should be crucified." The room was filled with roars of approval.

After blindfolding Jesus, several of the Sadducees began pummeling him with their fists. He winced in pain. In voices filled with contempt, they mockingly ordered Jesus to name the person who struck him. They spit on Jesus and shouted curses at him. After they finished abusing him, the high priest gave the temple guards orders to take Jesus outside and beat him even more severely.

Caiaphas called the meeting back to order. "We have agreed that Jesus must be punished by death, but we have a problem. The Romans have ruled that no Jews can be put to death for a capital crime without permission from the Roman government. In our case that ruling must come from Pontius Pilate, the governor. We will need to convince him that Jesus is a criminal deserving of death. It's still the middle of the night, and Pilate is probably asleep. At daybreak we will take Jesus to him and make our case."

When the majority of the Sanhedrin stood to condemn Jesus, Nicodemus and some of his fellow Pharisees did not join in the emotional outburst. Instead, they remained seated to show their opposition to the verdict. As soon as the uproar died down, Lazarus located Nicodemus, who happened to be sitting not far from the window. After hearing someone behind him whisper his name, Nicodemus turned his head and recognized his friend. He stood up slowly and walked to the window. "When you can get away, meet me outside near the back of the courtyard," said Lazarus. "There's a small grove of trees that will provide some privacy so we can talk."

When they met, Lazarus spoke with emotion. "I can't believe what's going on. Even though Jesus told us time after time that he would have to die at the hands of the Jewish leaders, I hoped it wouldn't happen so soon. Did you know Jesus was going to be arrested tonight?"

"I'm as surprised as you are," Nicodemus replied. "If I had heard about this earlier, I would have tried to warn Jesus. I found out tonight that Caiaphas and the other Sadducees on the Council held a secret meeting yesterday. During that meeting, one of Jesus' disciples, Judas Iscariot, agreed to betray

Jesus for thirty pieces of silver. He was supposed to lead the temple guards to Jesus so they could arrest him."

"I was in the Garden of Gethsemane with Jesus when Judas led them there," said Lazarus. "Several days ago, Jesus scolded him for criticizing my sister, Mary, after she had washed his feet with expensive perfume. I wonder if that is what triggered his disloyalty."

Nicodemus continued, "I have no idea what Judas' motives were. But sometime after the high priest and Sadducees met with Judas, Caiaphas sent a message to the entire Council to meet here tonight. We were told to be here at ten o'clock but weren't told why. Shortly after midnight, the temple guards dragged Jesus into the meeting room. I soon found out that we were going to try him as a criminal. As you might expect, this was a sham trial in every sense of the word. The witnesses lied and contradicted themselves. Jesus had no chance to call witnesses. No one spoke on his behalf. It would have been no use even if anyone had. The verdict was decided before the trial started."

"As Jesus was taken out of the room to be beaten, I thought I heard Caiaphas mention something about the Roman governor. What was said?" asked Lazarus.

"Caiaphas plans to take Jesus to Pilate in the morning. The Sanhedrin can convict Jesus for blasphemy and sentence him to death. However, before the sentence is carried out, the governor has to approve the death penalty."

"What are you going to do now?"

"I'm going home to try to get a few hours of sleep. I want to be there when Jesus is tried before Pilate. You're welcome to come to my house and sleep in one of the bedrooms. You look a bit tired yourself."

"Thank you for the invitation, but I can't accept. I want to locate Jesus' disciples and tell them what's happening to him. You need to go back into the meeting. The Sanhedrin wants me dead too. You shouldn't be seen talking to me."

Lazarus left the courtyard and headed in the direction of John Mark's house. John Mark had become a follower of Jesus as a result of his friendship with Peter. John Mark's home was in the northwest section of Jerusalem not far from Pontius Pilate's palace. When it was impractical to travel the two miles back to Bethany due to weather or darkness, Jesus and his disciples usually stayed at John Mark's house overnight.

The windows of the house were dark. Lazarus knocked once, aware that it was late in the evening. A minute later, Lazarus knocked again. This time he could hear footsteps on the other side of the door. "Who is there?" Mary, John Mark's mother, asked.

"It's me, Lazarus. I'm trying to locate Peter and the rest of Jesus' disciples. Jesus was arrested by the Sanhedrin tonight."

Mary swung the door open and greeted Lazarus warmly. "Come in," she said, closing the door behind him. "I'm glad you're here. My son is gone for the night so I'm here alone. Peter was here earlier. He was in terrible shape, sobbing and babbling incoherently. I finally got him calmed down enough to make some sense. He kept repeating that he had let Jesus down. He appeared to be exhausted, but I couldn't convince him to stay and get some rest. He left shortly after arriving and didn't say where he was going. I haven't seen any of the other disciples so far."

At that moment another knock sounded at the door. Mary opened it a crack and recognized the visitor. It was John. He greeted Mary and then turned toward Lazarus. "I'm glad to see you. Peter and I found each other in the Garden of Gethsemane, but we couldn't locate you or any of the other disciples. We followed Jesus to the high priest's house. I left Peter there and went to the homes of several of Jesus' followers, but no one had seen any of you. In any case, I was successful in getting word of Jesus' arrest to quite a few of his followers."

"I found Peter in Caiaphas' courtyard soon after you left him," said Lazarus. "I watched the Sanhedrin condemn Jesus to death on trumped-up charges. This morning they're going to take him to Pilate in order to get permission to kill him. I came here hoping to find you and Peter and the other disciples."

"Where is Peter?" asked John. "Why didn't he come here with you after you found out what was happening to Jesus?"

"I have some bad news. Do you remember when Jesus told Peter he would deny him three times? That's exactly what happened. Peter left the courtyard sobbing. Mary told me that he came here for a short time but left again. He must have been devastated by what he had done. I hope he doesn't do anything drastic and harm himself."

The high priest stood on the terrace outside the entrance to Governor Pilate's palace, a magnificent structure originally built for Herod the Great. At almost any other time of the year, Pilate would not have been in Jerusalem. His primary residence was in Caesarea Maritima, a port city on the shore of the Mediterranean Sea. To appease the Jews, Pilate visited Jerusalem for major religious celebrations such as the Passover.

Earlier that Friday morning, Caiaphas had sent word to Pilate that he needed to discuss a matter of great importance. He and the other members of the Sanhedrin could not go into the palace because Jewish law would declare them unclean. This would disqualify them from taking part in the remainder of Passover week. As a result, they waited outside for Pilate to come to them.

Caiaphas was accompanied by most of the other Council members. Nicodemus did not join the high priest's entourage, preferring instead to watch from the bottom of the palace steps along with a crowd of people who had stopped to see what was happening. Lazarus and John stood nearby but not close enough for anyone to associate them with Nicodemus.

Governor Pilate finally appeared at the entrance. "What do you want to talk about that's so urgent?" he asked the high priest gruffly.

"The man you see shackled in front of you has committed crimes against Rome," replied Caiaphas. "Among other misdeeds, he has encouraged our people not to pay taxes to Caesar. Even more treasonous, he has claimed to be King of the Jews. We are bringing this to your attention in order to see that his unlawful actions are stopped."

Pilate was clearly annoyed at being bothered so early in the morning. He replied sarcastically, "Those accusations don't seem worthy of punishment. It sounds to me like this man is simply delusional. Based on what you just told me, I don't see him as a threat to the Roman government."

"I respect your viewpoint, Governor. But what I have told you is far from the worst of it," Caiaphas responded. "This man has made a mockery of the Jewish religion as well. He has claimed to be God. We consider this to be blasphemy, and according to Jewish law he deserves to die. But Roman law prohibits us from putting him to death without your permission."

"The last accusation sounds like something that you, as high priest, should handle yourself. However, I see your dilemma regarding the death sentence, and I appreciate you coming to me for permission before taking action. Let me talk to this man briefly before I make my decision."

Pilate took Jesus aside. "Tell me the truth. Do you claim to be the King of the Jews? Even more bizarre, do you believe that you are a god? Be careful what you say. Understand that your answers are critical to your future well-being."

"You have been told that I am a king," Jesus replied. "I can't disagree with those who told you that. But my kingdom is not here on earth. If it were, my subjects would have prevented my arrest. My kingdom is in heaven."

Pilate looked at Jesus in astonishment and asked, "If your kingdom is elsewhere, why are you here?"

Jesus answered, "I have come to proclaim the truth. Those who want to hear the truth will listen to me."

"Is there really such a thing as truth?" responded Pilate. He sighed and brought Jesus back to Caiaphas.

"I don't see anything about this man that warrants his death," Pilate stated flatly. "In fact, I feel sorry for him. He appears harmless. In my opinion you should release him and try to find better things to do with your time."

"With all due respect, Governor," Caiaphas responded, "I think that these matters are important enough for us to appeal your decision. I had hoped the Sanhedrin wouldn't have to challenge your authority, but I believe that Emperor Tiberius Caesar would not be pleased to hear that his representative in Judea has not acted in the best interests of the people he was appointed to rule."

"That sounds like extortion. I don't appreciate anyone, including you, going behind my back to Caesar."

"Call it what you will, Governor," Caiaphas said in a smug tone, "but I and the rest of the Sanhedrin are committed to see this man punished for blasphemy. If we have to take other measures to obtain approval to put him to death, we will certainly do so."

Pilate frowned. His relationship with Rome was tenuous, and Caiaphas knew it.

"I might have a solution that could satisfy both your people and Rome as well," Pilate countered. "As you recall, each year I have allowed the release of one prisoner from prison at Passover. I have always let the Jewish people decide who that person is. I get a boost in popularity for giving the people a choice, and someone who is worthy of freedom is set free. I propose that we give the people of Jerusalem a choice between

Jesus and some other prisoner they name. That will tell us what the general population really thinks of Jesus. It will also remove me and the Roman government from the decision-making process."

Caiaphas replied with an air of confidence, "I am willing to take that chance. A crowd is already starting to form here at the bottom of the palace steps. If we wait a little longer, we will have a large enough sample to determine how the Jews feel about Jesus." Unbeknownst to Pilate, Caiaphas and the Sanhedrin had recruited many of their supporters to gather in front of Pilate's palace.

It didn't take long before a throng of people filled the area. A number of Jesus' followers had joined the crowd, but they were greatly outnumbered by backers of the Sanhedrin. The entire assemblage could clearly view Jesus standing next to Pilate and Caiaphas at the top of the palace steps. The two factions became more and more vocal, arguing with each other about how Jesus should be treated.

Seeing that the crowd might start a riot, Pilate called for silence. Once they calmed down, Pilate was able to speak. "People of Jerusalem, I have been told by your high priest that this man named Jesus from Nazareth has committed serious crimes against Rome and the Jewish nation that are worthy of his death. In particular, this man has allegedly called himself your king. He also allegedly claims to be the Son of God. In spite of these and other accusations, I have questioned him and found him innocent. But in the interests of justice and fair play, I have decided to allow you, the Jewish people, to decide his fate.

"As you know, each year during the Passover celebration, I have released a prisoner of your choosing from jail. This year I am going to vary that process a bit. I am proposing that Jesus be released. But in keeping with past practice, I am still giving you a chance to select someone else to set free. Do any of you have an alternative selection?"

The crowd remained silent. Sanhedrin supporters had not been told they would be called on to name a prisoner for release. Their instructions were simply to voice their disapproval of Jesus. To make matters more complicated, Pilate had endorsed Jesus as his choice. If anyone dared to propose an alternative, that person might be considered disloyal to Pilate.

Seeing that no one stepped forward to name someone other than Jesus, Pilate gave the crowd another chance. "I repeat, what prisoner other than this man Jesus should I release?"

Jesus' supporters held their breath. If no one spoke up to counter Pilate's recommendation, Jesus might be set free. A release granted by Pilate might not prevent the Sanhedrin from punishing him, but at least they wouldn't be allowed to put Jesus to death.

Pilate looked at Caiaphas and grinned. "It appears your supporters don't have a problem with me releasing Jesus."

Realizing his plan to execute Jesus was slipping away, Caiaphas swallowed hard and blurted, "We want you to release Barabbas." He regretted the choice as soon as it came out of his mouth. Under extreme pressure, the high priest couldn't recall any other criminals currently in the Roman prison. A few years earlier, Barabbas had started a failed rebellion against Roman rule. But instead of considering Barabbas a hero, the Jews despised him for provoking the wrath of the Roman army against the entire nation. Caiaphas realized too late that the general population's hatred of Barabbas made it more likely that they would choose to release Jesus instead.

Pilate responded in disbelief. "Caiaphas, are you joking? Barabbas is a terrorist who has shown no remorse for his crimes against Rome. I assure you that he will attempt another insurrection, which will fail as badly as the first. Next time Rome will not be as lenient with the Jews. In contrast, based on what I have observed this morning, Jesus has done nothing more than make you and your Sanhedrin cronies jealous of him. Nevertheless, I have given my word to provide the crowd with a choice. If there is any justice at all, they will choose to release Jesus."

Pilate turned to address the crowd. "Your high priest has just asked me to release Barabbas rather than Jesus. Whom of the two shall I set free?"

For a moment the crowd remained silent. Then one of the men in the crowd shouted, "Free Barabbas!" Upon hearing this, the crowd became energized. "We want Barabbas! We want Barabbas!" they bellowed. The protests of Jesus' followers were drowned out by Sanhedrin supporters.

Pilate still had not given up hope for releasing Jesus. He raised his arms to request silence and once again addressed the crowd. "I'm not sure you understand the possible consequences of the choice you just made. You are choosing to release a convicted terrorist, Barabbas, who has inflicted terrible harm on this community and will probably do so again. You could have chosen to free Jesus. He has never been formally charged with a crime until now. So, I am going to ask you again. Which man should I release, Jesus or Barabbas?"

Ignoring the guidance of the Roman governor, the majority of the crowd once again chanted, "We want Barabbas! We want Barabbas!"

Pilate motioned for his servant to bring him a bowl of water. He washed his hands and said to Caiaphas, "Take him away and do what you will do. I tried my best to see that justice was done. But you and your cohorts have perverted justice. My hands are now clean of this matter."

"I greatly respect your viewpoint, Governor, and sincerely thank you for your approval in this matter. But there is one other thing I need to ask of you," stated Caiaphas. "The crime of blasphemy that Jesus committed deserves a death that is slow and painful. You Romans have perfected the art of inflicting pain. At the trial of Jesus last night, the Sanhedrin decided that he should be crucified. Unfortunately, our Scriptures do not make allowances for crucifixion. Your soldiers are the only ones equipped to carry out such executions. We respectfully ask that you help us make this happen."

"How dare you make such a request of me?" Pilate asked incredulously. "I just told you I am no longer involved in this travesty. Now you are asking me to use Roman resources to assist you in killing this harmless man. You will have to change your plans."

"With all due respect, you might want to reconsider that decision," replied Caiaphas. "By allowing the Sanhedrin's sentence of crucifixion to be carried out, I guarantee you will endear yourself to me, the Sanhedrin, and the entire Jewish nation. I will personally commend you to the government in Rome for cooperating on our behalf."

Pilate paused for a moment. The frown on his face showed he was not pleased with the high priest's threats. He turned to his administrative assistant and confided, "I'm exhausted. The morning is only a few hours old, and it seems like an entire day has just passed. I'm not sure this man Jesus is worth the effort I've put into saving him. What difference does it make that I complied with the wishes of the Jewish leaders? I authorize the crucifixion of dozens of men every month. I'm sure that some of them are innocent of the crimes for which they are accused. Why should I risk my position as governor for someone who means nothing to me?"

Pilate then addressed the legion commander. "Take this man to the Antonia Fortress and have him whipped and beaten. Put a robe on him and a crown of thorns on his head. Then bring him back to me." The Antonia Fortress was a military complex located just outside the northwest corner of the Temple Mount. It served as the headquarters of the Roman army in Jerusalem.

A short time later, the Roman soldiers brought Jesus back to Pilate. Blood dripped down his forehead, the result of the crown made of thorns jammed into his head. Blood soaked through the back of the purple robe that the soldiers had put on him after he was whipped. Jesus was barely able to stand upright. Pilate raised his arms to quiet the crowd, which had grown even larger. "Here is your king," Pilate shouted. "What do you want me to do with him?"

The outcome was predetermined. Caiaphas had planted men in the crowd to provide the desired answer. "Crucify him!" someone yelled. "Crucify him!" shouted another. Cries of "Crucify him!" echoed through the crowd.

"The people have spoken," said Pilate in a contrived show of solidarity with the Jews. "Take this man away to be crucified."

As the crowd dispersed, Lazarus, John, and Nicodemus remained at the bottom of the palace steps. "There was nothing I could do," Nicodemus said apologetically. "Caiaphas and the others were determined that Jesus should be executed. However, there is something I can do in Jesus' memory. A friend of mine named Joseph who is also a member of the Sanhedrin has a family gravesite just outside the city. He and I are both supporters of Jesus. Last night we agreed that if Pilate approved the Sanhedrin's request to put Jesus to death, we would ask Pilate's permission to bury Jesus' body in Joseph's tomb. Otherwise, it would be dumped in a common grave with real criminals."

"That's a great expression of your love and respect for him," Lazarus observed. "But looking ahead, what do you think that the Sanhedrin will do after Jesus is dead? My bet is that they will try to erase any trace of Jesus and his teachings. That will mean eliminating his followers, including all of us."

Nicodemus replied, "Much of what occurs later depends on how you react. If you go back to your previous jobs in your hometowns and stay quiet, there's a good chance you won't be bothered. But if you remain in Jerusalem and attempt to keep Jesus' legacy alive, you will probably be persecuted and maybe even killed."

"Let's deal with what's happening now," said John. "God might have some last-minute miracle planned to keep Jesus alive."

Lazarus couldn't believe his ears. John was one of Jesus' closest disciples. Had he not been listening to Jesus for the past three years? "Do you really think there's a chance that Jesus won't be put to death?" asked Lazarus incredulously. "He told us plainly when we were in Ephraim that he would have to suffer and die."

"Until now all of Jesus' disciples, including me, thought that Jesus would be the one to free the Jews from Roman rule," replied John. "We saw so much potential in him given his ability to do powerful miracles. We hoped his death wouldn't happen until after he reigned for years as our king. I still have hope that his life will be spared somehow."

"Didn't Jesus also said he would be raised from the dead in three days?" asked Lazarus. "What did you think about that statement?"

"We all assumed that he was talking about the Day of Judgement when everyone will be resurrected. He was always speaking in parables. We were never sure whether he was talking literally or figuratively. You must have an opinion. What do you think will happen?"

"When I first met him a year ago, I had no idea who Jesus was. But since then, I've come to trust him. It isn't just because he brought me back from the dead. It's also because whatever he promised has come true. Jesus told me that God loves me more than I know, and he was right. He said his followers would be confused when things got out of control, and that's taking place now. You are entitled to your own viewpoint, but I believe that what Jesus told us about his death and resurrection is happening before our eyes."

John and Lazarus left Nicodemus in search of Jesus. It didn't take long to locate him. High-pitched wails of female mourners were coming from a nearby street. They were calling out Jesus' name and pleading with God to save him. After rounding a corner near the source of the sound, they caught up with the distraught women who were trailing a squad of Roman soldiers. Many of the women were long-time supporters of Jesus' ministry.

The soldiers were marching alongside two men, one of whom was Jesus. The purple robe that Pilate's soldiers had put on Jesus was gone and replaced with his original clothing. The crown of thorns was still on his head, and dried blood had crusted on his forehead and hair. The man walking next to Jesus was struggling to carry two large pieces of wood fastened together into a cross.

John and Lazarus followed at a distance. Jesus looked exhausted. He could barely manage to shuffle one foot in front of the other. His body, obviously wracked with pain, was bent forward at the waist. The procession moved slowly. Every so often, one of the soldiers would shout at Jesus to move faster and then strike him with a leather whip.

Finally the procession reached the northwest gate of the city. Outside the gate a narrow dirt road led to a low hill called Golgotha, named for its resemblance to the top of a skull. Two men sentenced to death for stealing were already hanging on crosses situated about twenty feet apart.

The man who had carried Jesus' cross dropped it between the two thieves. Roman soldiers laid Jesus on his back on top of the wood, his hands extended outward on the arms of the cross. His feet were placed on a small wooden platform secured to the cross.

Going from limb to limb, the soldiers pounded nails through Jesus' hands and feet into the wood of the cross. Ropes were tied around his arms and legs to help support his body weight. Jesus winced and then cried out in pain as the cross was raised to an upright position and dropped into a hole dug in the ground. His hands and feet bore the brunt of the abrupt landing. The soldiers shoveled dirt back into the hole and packed it firmly.

It was now nine o'clock in the morning, and the sun was shining brightly. The three crosses cast shadows down the western side of the hill. A large crowd, consisting primarily of Jesus' followers, had gathered at Golgotha. The mourning women stood as near to the cross as the soldiers would allow. No one was there to show support for the two criminals.

One of the women in the crowd was Mary, the mother of Jesus. John and Lazarus stood next to her. In an effort to comfort her, John put his arm around her shoulder. Mary looked up at him appreciatively. "Before Jesus was born, the angel Gabriel appeared to me and told me that my son would be great and be called the Son of God. He was supposed to become a king just like his ancestor David, and his kingdom would never end. If the angel's words were true, how could Jesus be hanging from a cross, his life coming to a horrible end?"

Mary continued recounting her memories. "When my husband, Joseph, and I brought Jesus to the temple for presentation to God, we met an old man named Simeon. He told us that our son would cause dismay as well as joy to many people in Israel and that he would be rejected by many of those who heard him. Simeon's final comment was addressed to me. He said someday I would feel as though I had been stabbed by a knife. At the time, I wasn't unduly concerned. Now I realize that Simeon's warning was prophetic. My heart feels like it is being cut out of my chest."

As the day wore on, several members of the Sanhedrin gathered some distance from the cross, congratulating each other for ridding themselves of the annoying rabbi who had always put them to shame. They taunted Jesus. "If you are the Messiah and Son of God, then come down from the cross. If you do, then we will believe."

In spite of their elation over his crucifixion, Jesus still managed to annoy the Jewish leaders. On orders from Pontius Pilate, the soldiers had nailed a sign at the top of Jesus' cross that was visible to anyone passing by. The sign read, "This is Jesus of Nazareth, King of the Jews." The sign was written in Hebrew, Greek, and Latin. Caiaphas indignantly appealed to Pilate to change the wording or remove the sign altogether, but he refused.

Following the lead of Jesus' detractors, both thieves ridiculed Jesus. But as the day wore on, one of them appeared to have a change of heart. The thief had seen the anguish expressed by Jesus' friends, who obviously loved him deeply. He saw the kindhearted manner in which Jesus handled the situation, even asking God to forgive the soldiers who had nailed him to the cross.

Finally, after listening to the incessant taunts of his fellow criminal, the thief had enough. "Stop your insults. Unlike us, this man hasn't done anything wrong." He turned toward Jesus and looked at the sign posted over his head. "I'm not sure exactly what kind of king you are, but please remember me when you establish your kingdom."

"Today you will be with me in heaven," Jesus promised.

As noon approached, the inexplicable occurred. Without warning, a bank of dark clouds suddenly appeared overhead. The clear, bright day became as black as night. The thick overcast completely obliterated the sun. It was as if the only candle in a windowless room had been snuffed out.

For the next three hours the darkness continued. In the gloom Jesus' followers could barely make out the silhouette of their teacher. The darkness was accompanied by an eerie silence. The only sounds heard were intermittent sobs of the women and groans of the three men being crucified. As time passed, the groans were replaced by heavy, labored breathing. The lungs of the dying men were slowly collapsing due to pressure caused by suspending the full weight of their bodies with only their outstretched arms.

Just before three o'clock in the afternoon, Jesus focused his gaze on his mother standing below him. She was crying, and John continued to console her. Jesus, in a voice filled with love and concern, addressed them both. "Don't be worried,

Mother. John will now become your son—John, care for my mother as if she were your own."

Jesus had not had anything to drink since the Passover meal the night before. "I am thirsty," he said through parched lips, caked with dried saliva. One of the soldiers heard Jesus' request and retrieved a jar of cheap wine that he and the other soldiers were sharing. He poured some of the wine on a sponge, broke off a branch from a hyssop plant growing nearby, and skewered the sponge with the end of the branch. He raised the saturated sponge up to Jesus' chin. With great difficulty, Jesus lowered his head and drew some wine into his mouth.

Before the soldier could lower the sponge to the ground, Jesus looked up into the sky and cried out in a loud voice, "My work is finished!" His chin fell to his chest and his body slumped forward. At that moment the ground began to shake violently. The tremor lasted for nearly a minute but seemed much longer. At the same time, the clouds that had blanketed the sky for three hours dispersed as fast as they had appeared. The sun, which had been completely hidden, now shone brightly in the western sky. It was as if a new day had dawned in the middle of the afternoon. After observing these extraordinary events, the centurion in charge of the work detail was moved to exclaim, "This man must have been a god come to earth."

Tears flowed freely beneath the cross. Their leader, friend, and teacher had died an untimely death. Those who had placed their hopes on Jesus now felt abandoned and alone. The future looked bleak and uncertain. With heavy hearts, Jesus' followers began to leave for home. Nothing more could be done that afternoon other than pray for guidance.

John escorted Mary to his house, where she would now live. Lazarus stayed behind and watched as the Roman soldiers prepared to dispose of the bodies. Pilate had given his word to the high priest that Jesus' corpse would be removed before sundown in accordance with Sabbath laws, so the soldiers worked quickly.

They first had to make sure that the three men, still hanging on their crosses, were dead. Most victims of crucifixion died of asphyxiation within six hours of being suspended on the cross. Exceptions occurred when the crucified man was able to prop himself up on the small platform to which his feet were nailed. If his legs remained strong enough, less pressure on the lung cavity could delay asphyxiation.

When the soldiers examined the two thieves, they found them barely alive and broke their lower legs with a large mallet. When they got to Jesus, they saw he was already dead. Instead of breaking his legs, one of the soldiers took a spear and stuck it into his side just below the rib cage. Fluid from the sac around his heart mixed with blood flowed from the wound, assuring the soldiers that Jesus had died.

After removing the bodies from the crosses, the soldiers prepared to load them onto a cart and take them to a common grave outside the city. Before they could stack Jesus' body on top of the other two corpses, two well-dressed men approached. One of them handed a parchment document to the centurion and said, "My name is Joseph. I have come to claim the body of Jesus. This is an order from Pilate authorizing me to bury him. My friend Nicodemus is here to help me."

The centurion examined the document and found it to be official. "You may take his body away," he authorized. "It will save us some extra work. This has been quite a day for all concerned. Based on what I witnessed, we might not have seen the last of this Jesus."

Lazarus called out to Nicodemus, "Hello, my friend! I'm glad you made it on time. They were just about to take Jesus away along with the two criminals."

"Lazarus, I'm thankful you're still here. If you are willing, we could use your help getting Jesus' body to the tomb. By the way, this is Joseph, the man from Arimathea whom I told you about this morning."

Joseph and Nicodemus lifted Jesus' lifeless corpse onto the back of a donkey while Lazarus held its halter. They situated the body between two sacks of spices that were tied together and draped over the back of the animal. The spices, a mixture of myrrh and aloe, would keep Jesus' body from decaying quickly. The three men walked for a quarter mile to an abandoned limestone quarry that now served as a cemetery for wealthy families of Jerusalem.

Joseph had been born and raised in the town of Arimathea, located several miles north of Jerusalem. After moving to

Jerusalem as a young man, he became wealthy by buying and selling choice properties within the city. Joseph had recently purchased a newly excavated sepulcher that he intended to use as a family burial site. It would now be shared with a rabbi by the name of Jesus.

When they got to the tomb, the three men carried Jesus' body through the opening. The tomb itself was fairly wide but had a low ceiling. A rock bench had been carved into the far end on which to lay the dead body until it decomposed. After laying Jesus' body on the bench, the men went back outside to get the spices and some strips of linen cloth. They rubbed the myrrh and aloes mixture on the body and then wrapped it with the linen strips. After exiting, the men rolled a large round stone over the entrance in order to keep out grave-robbing vandals.

To their surprise, they saw two women approaching. Lazarus recognized them as Mary Magdalene and her cousin Mary, the wife of one of Jesus' followers named Clopas. The women had supported Jesus throughout his ministry in Galilee and both had been present at the crucifixion.

Lazarus asked, "What brings you here? I thought everyone went home but me."

"We stayed behind because we wanted to find out where Jesus was buried," Mary Magdalene answered. "We were going to anoint his body after the Sabbath."

"We already anointed his corpse and wrapped it in burial cloths," said Joseph. "But we didn't have time to apply an additional layer of spices over the linen strips because the Sabbath was about to begin. We left the extra spices in the tomb. You might want to come back and finish the job we started."

While Joseph was speaking, a small military detachment marched toward them. Lazarus' heart beat faster. Now that the Sanhedrin had eliminated Jesus, had Caiaphas given orders to arrest him? Lazarus considered running in the opposite direction but decided that would only attract unwanted attention.

When the soldiers reached the tomb, Lazarus recognized the captain of the temple guard who had arrested Jesus in the Garden of Gethsemane. Lazarus stood behind Nicodemus, trying to remain as inconspicuous as possible.

"Greetings," said the captain. "We're looking for the tomb where a man named Jesus has recently been buried. We were told that it would be in this cemetery."

Joseph replied, "I can help you with that. This is the tomb you're looking for. We just completed his burial and were getting ready to leave. We haven't done anything wrong, have we?"

"No, you're fine," replied the captain. "We're here because the high priest sent us. He found out that someone had claimed Jesus' body and was planning to have it buried here. Caiaphas is worried that Jesus' followers will come and steal his body. We weren't told why that would be a concern, but we've been ordered to seal the tomb shut and stand guard for the next three days. If anyone attempts to remove the body, we have orders to arrest them and deliver them to the high priest."

Mary Magdalene addressed the captain, "Sir, if I may be so bold, my cousin Mary and I were planning to come back sometime after the Sabbath to apply more spices to the body. If you and your men are still here, would you allow us to enter the tomb? Perhaps you could even help us move the stone from the entrance."

Suspecting that her request might be a ruse to allow Jesus' followers to get into the grave, the captain replied, "I'm sorry, but we don't plan to let anyone into the tomb during our appointed watch. What you do after that is your business."

Anxious to leave before he was recognized, Lazarus interjected, "Captain, we appreciate your dedication to duty and hope you don't have to ward off any grave robbers, but it's getting late and the Sabbath is nearly here. We need to get back to Jerusalem."

When they got to the city gate, Joseph and the two Marys went on ahead. Nicodemus asked Lazarus if he planned to return to Bethany that evening. If not, Lazarus was welcome to spend the night at his house. The emotional rush from the last two day's events had worn off, and Lazarus was feeling tired. He accepted the offer.

It was nearly noon on Saturday when Lazarus woke from a deep sleep. He had slept for over twelve hours. Lazarus got dressed and went looking for Nicodemus. He found his friend outside sitting in a walled garden at the rear of the house.

Nicodemus looked up when he saw Lazarus. "Come and join me," he offered. "I just got home from Sabbath worship at the synagogue. I saw that you were still sleeping soundly so I didn't wake you. By the way, this is the same garden where I met with Jesus last year during the Passover. It's hard to believe that he's no longer with us."

"I remember you telling me about your meeting," Lazarus recalled. "Jesus told you he would be lifted up like the bronze snake that Moses made to protect the Israelites from snake bites. All they had to do was look at the bronze snake in order to live."

"At that time I had no idea what Jesus was talking about," said Nicodemus. "Now that you mention it, Jesus was lifted up. But he wasn't placed on a pole—he was nailed to a cross. That couldn't be a coincidence."

"I agree," Lazarus responded. "What he said to you was prophetic. But that isn't the only thing that Jesus said about the future. You might recall our discussion with John at Pilate's palace after Jesus was sentenced to death. I reminded John that Jesus had also predicted that God would raise him from the dead three days later."

"That would be tomorrow," noted Nicodemus. "He was crucified on Friday, today is Saturday, and tomorrow is Sunday."

Lazarus added, "Now that he has died, everything Jesus said about himself has been proven true. Now only one prediction remains unfulfilled—rising from the dead."

"Are you awake?" whispered Mary Magdalene. "I saw you stirring." It was Sunday morning, the day after the Sabbath, and the sun had not yet peeked over the Mount of Olives. John Mark had invited her and her cousin Mary to stay at his house during Passover week along with several other women from Galilee. They had all supported Jesus' ministry and sometimes traveled with him and the disciples to religious festivals.

Her cousin Mary was lying on a cot nearby. "Yes, I'm awake, but I didn't sleep much at all last night. I still can't believe what happened Friday. I thought Jesus would live forever. No one else could perform the miracles he did. He even brought our friend Lazarus back to life. Now that he is dead it seems there's no hope."

"I agree, it does seem hopeless," said Mary Magdalene. "Even so, we can show our respect for Jesus by finishing the job of anointing his body. I hope the soldiers have completed their guard duty. If so, we can get into the tomb. Are you ready to go?"

"Absolutely," Mary answered. "It looks like everyone else is asleep. If we're quiet enough, we should be able to leave the house without disturbing anyone."

Just before daybreak, the women walked through the North Gate of Jerusalem. Suddenly the earth began to pitch and roll beneath their feet. "Did you feel that?" exclaimed Mary Magdalene.

"It's probably just an aftershock from the earthquake that struck after Jesus died," replied Mary. "I wouldn't be too worried about it."

Several minutes later they caught a distant glimpse of the tomb. Their hopes rose when they didn't see any guards near the opening. As they got closer, Mary Magdalene saw that the large stone that had blocked the entrance to the tomb was already rolled out of the way. "God is good," she said excitedly. "It appears we can get into the tomb with no problem at all."

After they reached the entrance, the women filled the oil lamp they had brought and lit it. They would need it to illuminate the dark tomb. Mary Magdalene went in first, followed by her cousin. The women glanced toward the far wall and the stone bench, where the body should have been. To their surprise, they saw nothing but carefully folded strips of linen on the rock surface of the bench. The bag of spices that Joseph and Nicodemus had left there two days ago was lying on the floor, filling the air with the sweet scent of myrrh. But Jesus' body was nowhere to be seen.

The women looked at each other in disbelief. "Who would have removed him from the grave? Where would they have taken him?" cried Mary Magdalene, tears welling up in her eyes. Suddenly, they were blinded by a brilliant light coming from the far wall of the tomb. Shaking with fear, they saw the forms of two men in shimmering white robes sitting on opposite ends of the stone bench.

One of the men said in a calm and reassuring voice, "Don't be afraid. We know you are here looking for the body of Jesus. As you have already seen, he is not here. He has been raised from the dead by his Father in heaven just as he promised. Now, go back to Jerusalem and tell the others what I have told you."

Just as quickly as they appeared, the two men were gone. After extinguishing the lamp, Mary Magdalene and her cousin bolted out of the tomb, running toward the road leading back to the city.

When Lazarus awoke Sunday morning at Nicodemus's house, his friend wasn't there. Around noon, Nicodemus walked through the door. "I was hoping you would be up and around by now," Nicodemus said. "I have something very interesting to tell you. I was attending the daily meeting of the Sanhedrin at the temple when we were interrupted by one of the chief priests on duty. He apologized for disturbing us and said that the captain of the temple guard had news for the high priest. Caiaphas signaled to let him in the room.

"The captain reported that a violent earthquake struck at sunrise in the area where his men were guarding the tomb of Jesus. While the earth was shaking, what appeared to be an angel dressed in a shining white robe came down from the sky and rolled the stone away from the entrance. The guards were so frightened that they ran for their lives. They returned to the temple and reported what had happened."

"That's interesting. I didn't feel an earthquake at all, probably because I was sleeping so soundly," commented Lazarus. "Do you remember the two women we saw at the tomb on Friday, Mary Magdalene and her cousin Mary? They planned to finish anointing Jesus' body this morning. I wonder if they saw anything."

"That isn't all I was going to tell you," continued Nicodemus. "When Caiaphas heard the captain's story, I assumed he would be furious. I thought he would call the guards liars and accuse them of dereliction of duty for deserting their station. But he didn't get angry at all. I got the impression he believed the report, even the part about the angel."

"I'm surprised at his lack of reaction as well," remarked Lazarus. "What happened next?"

"After the captain left the meeting, Caiaphas told one of the chief priests to go to the cemetery and find out if Jesus' body was still in the tomb. If the body wasn't there, he was to pay each of the guards on duty that morning a large sum of money to tell everyone that Jesus' disciples stole the body while they were sleeping. The high priest even offered to provide the guards with an alibi if anyone, including the Governor, inquired why they had failed to do their jobs. I imagine this will be their story even if the evidence shows that Jesus' body wasn't stolen."

"What do you mean 'if the evidence shows'?" Lazarus asked. "Don't you remember what we discussed in the garden the day after Jesus died? I noted that all of Jesus' predictions took place except one. After what the soldiers reported this morning, there should be no doubt in your mind that Jesus' final prediction did come true. He must have risen from the dead."

Lazarus arrived at the home of John Mark early that evening. Since Jesus' death, the house had become the de facto gathering place for his supporters. It was centrally located and spacious enough to accommodate a large number of Jesus' followers.

The entire household was buzzing with excitement. Lazarus was quickly brought up to speed on the news. Mary Magdalene and her cousin had seen the empty grave that morning and passed along the angel's message that Jesus had risen. After hearing their account, Peter and John had raced to the tomb and found it empty, just as the women had said. Mary Magdalene had returned to the tomb and actually saw Jesus alive. Jesus had also appeared to Peter later in the day. Lazarus couldn't wait to tell Nicodemus that Jesus' resurrection had been verified several times.

A loud knock on the door interrupted their conversations. Fearing a visit from the Jewish authorities, everyone remained silent. Another loud knock was followed by a familiar voice. "Open the door. It's me, Cleopas, and my brother. We need to tell you what happened on our way back to Emmaus."

Peter unbolted the door and the two men strode into the room. "We have seen the Lord!" Cleopas exclaimed. "As we were making our way back home this afternoon, a man we didn't recognize caught up to us. He asked if he could join us and we agreed. As we were walking, the subject of Jesus' crucifixion came up. We explained how we were followers of his and were devastated by what had happened, particularly since we were counting on him to free the Jews from Roman domination. We told him about the morning's events which made it appear that Jesus might be alive.

"We were taken by surprise when the man reprimanded us and called us foolish. My brother and I listened intently as he quoted the Scriptures to show that God had promised a Messiah who would save Israel, not from the Romans but from sin and death. He went on to explain that the Messiah would have to die in order to accomplish his mission but would then be raised up and glorified by his Father in heaven.

"We were totally captivated by his understanding of the Scriptures. When we got to Emmaus, he accepted our invitation to stay for dinner. When he prayed over the food, we both realized that the man we had been walking with was Jesus himself. As soon as we became aware of who he was, Jesus disappeared from our sight. We were so elated that we made the seven-mile journey back here to tell you the good news."

At that moment Jesus appeared in the middle of the room. Everyone gasped in astonishment. Even though they had just heard eyewitness testimony of his resurrection, it was difficult to grasp the reality that Jesus was actually alive and standing among them.

"Don't be afraid," Jesus said. "I'm not a ghost as some of you might think. Does a ghost have flesh and blood and bones? You can see the prints of the nails on my hands and feet. You can even touch me since I've already returned from my Father."

For the next hour, Jesus spoke to them plainly about the present and future. He explained that his suffering and death were necessary to pay for the sins of the world. Now that his mission on earth was complete, he would leave them soon and go to prepare a place for them in heaven. God's Spirit would give them the power and courage to spread the good news of God's saving grace everywhere. He warned that they would endure persecution and even death for proclaiming the truth, but because of their faith in him, they would live with God forever. After he had finished speaking, Jesus vanished from their sight.

Following Jesus' departure, the excitement in the room nearly drowned out the sound of another knock on the door. It was Thomas. Earlier that morning he had volunteered to go into the city to buy supplies. Peter explained to Thomas all that had happened that day, including Jesus' appearance a few minutes before. Instead of being overjoyed by the news, Thomas struggled with what he heard. "When I left this morning, everyone was despondent over Jesus' death. We had lost all hope of seeing him again. That's all I could think about all day. Now you're telling me that he's alive."

"I'm not making this up," said Peter. "We all saw him with our own eyes. He even let us touch him." The others in the room concurred.

"I'm sorry," said Thomas. "But I can't just take your word on this without proof. I really want to believe what you are telling me, but I will need to see Jesus in person first. That means touching the nail marks in his hands and feet and feeling the spear wound in his side."

The following Sunday evening the disciples and other followers of Jesus, including Lazarus, were again gathered in John Mark's home. During the week, rumors had circulated that the Jewish leaders were planning to arrest them. In spite of the potential danger, they continued meeting for worship, giving thanks to God for sending Jesus into their lives.

While they were praying Jesus appeared suddenly, startling everyone in the room. He walked over to Thomas and stood facing him, eye to eye. Seemingly unfazed, Thomas backed up a step and examined Jesus from head to toe. "Thomas, I love you and want you to believe I am risen," Jesus assured him. "Here, put your finger into the nail prints in my palms. See the imprint of the nails on my feet."

Thomas did what Jesus asked, but the look on his face showed that he wasn't totally convinced. Jesus then opened his cloak and showed Thomas the place where the soldier's spear had cut into his side. "Perhaps this will finally persuade you," Jesus said. He pressed Thomas' fingers into the wound.

At this point Thomas' doubts evaporated. "You are truly my God and Lord!" Thomas exclaimed as he fell to his knees on the floor. Jesus lifted him to his feet. "I'm pleased that you now believe I have risen. Future generations will have faith even though they haven't seen or touched me as you have."

Jesus then addressed all the disciples. "The last time I was with you, I said I would soon return to my Father in heaven. But before I leave you, I want you to return to Capernaum. I will meet you there and give you further instructions."

After saying these words, Jesus disappeared just as suddenly as he had appeared. Everyone rejoiced that he had shown himself to Thomas and that he now believed in the risen Jesus. The next day, the disciples made plans to travel to Capernaum.

"If you don't mind, I'd like to go with you," implored Lazarus. "Although I have no claim to being a disciple, I feel a special bond with all of you."

Peter assured him, "We've all seen the close relationship you have with Jesus. We consider you to be one of our brothers. We'd be pleased to have you accompany us."

A week after the disciples and Lazarus arrived in Capernaum, Jesus still had not made contact with them. One evening, with time on their hands and with good weather predicted, Peter suggested they try their luck at fishing. Peter, his brother Andrew, James, John, and three other disciples left shore just after sunset and rowed out onto the Sea of Galilee. The moon was full that night, making it easy to monitor the position of the nets in the water. The sea was calm, and they fully expected to have a good catch of fish.

Hour after hour passed without any success. The men were frustrated and growing tired. Each time they moved the boat to another fishing spot, they had to pull in the nets and then cast them out again. Finally the sun began peeking over the eastern horizon. A thin layer of morning fog settled over the water. This wasn't the first time they had failed to catch even a single fish, but that didn't make their current experience any less irritating.

As they neared shore, the disciples saw several men standing there in the distance. One of them called out, "Were you able to catch many fish last night?" The disciples answered in unison, "No!"

"Then I have a suggestion," continued the man on shore. "You will have better success if you throw your net into the water on the right side of the boat."

Peter raised his eyebrows and addressed the others on the boat. "This man must not know much about fishing. The reason we have the net on the left side is because it's closer to the shore where the fish normally feed. But given our lack of success at this point, I don't see any reason not to try what he said."

The men pulled in the empty net and cast it over the right side of the boat. Almost before the net had time to sink in the water, it began filling with fish. The surface of the water fumed as dozens of fish jumped into the expanding net. The ropes connecting the net to the boat strained with the weight of the thrashing fish. The overloaded net was in danger of splitting wide open.

"Close the net and pull it toward the boat!" Peter yelled. "Then start rowing to shore. We need to get to land before we lose all these fish."

John took his eyes off the net and glanced back toward the shore. He had been so engrossed in bringing in the big haul that he forgot about the man who had made the catch possible. The man on shore looked familiar as did the other men standing with him. John took another look and shouted, "It's Jesus, and he's there with Lazarus and the other disciples!"

As soon as he heard John's exclamation, Peter put on the cloak he had worn earlier, jumped into the water, and swam as fast as he could toward the shore. Once on dry land, Peter ran to Jesus and hugged him. "Teacher, it's so good to see you again! We weren't sure when you would get here." Jesus returned Peter's embrace, drenching the front of his cloak in the process.

After the rest of the crew pulled the boat onto the shore, Jesus called out to them, "We built a fire to warm ourselves while we waited for you. We even started to cook breakfast. You must be hungry after a long night. Bring some of the fish you caught over here, and I'll prepare them for you."

Peter, with the assistance of the others, dragged the net onto the shore. They cut open the net and the fish flopped onto the sand. Peter took a quick count. "There must be over one hundred fifty fish here!" Peter exclaimed. "We've never caught that many without the net breaking. Just minutes before, we had caught nothing at all." James and John carried a few fish to the fire and cleaned them. Jesus cooked the fish on a metal grating placed over the flames. Meanwhile, Andrew retrieved some leftover bread that they had taken with them on the boat.

As they ate, Jesus gave them further instructions. "It's been ten days since I was raised from the dead. In another thirty days I will meet you at noon on the summit of the Mount of Olives. After saying farewell to you there, I will return to my Father in heaven. Between now and then, I want you to settle your personal affairs here in Galilee and relocate to Jerusalem. The city will be the home base for the church that you will establish in my name. Starting in Jerusalem you will reach out to the rest of the world and share what I have taught you."

When everyone was done eating, Jesus sat down next to Peter. Lazarus and the others watched with interest. Jesus put his arm around Peter's shoulder and asked him, "Peter, do you love me more than your fellow disciples do?"

Peter was taken aback by the question but quickly answered, "Lord, you know I love you."

"Make sure my lambs are fed."

Jesus paused and asked again, "Peter, do you love me?"

Once again Peter answered, "Of course, I love you."

"Make sure my sheep are fed."

For a third time Jesus asked Peter, "Do you really love me?"

Peter, with a hurt look on his face, replied, "Jesus, you know everything. You know I love you."

"Make sure my sheep are fed."

Lazarus could see that Peter was uncomfortable. He remembered Peter's three denials of Jesus in Caiaphas' courtyard. Was Jesus reminding Peter of his misconduct by questioning him three times?

As if reading Lazarus' mind, Jesus clarified his remarks. "Peter, you are a headstrong man who often speaks before you think. You have usually gotten away with it, but in the future things will not always go your way. You are going to be persecuted and even die for my sake. I need you to stay strong even in times of persecution. In the past I have called you my rock. From now on you also need to be my voice to those who have not yet heard my message. They are the lambs and sheep I am talking about."

"You know I will, Lord," said Peter. Lazarus imagined that Peter felt a sense of relief that Jesus still counted on him even after he had failed so miserably.

Lazarus left Capernaum the next day and returned home to Bethany. He had put his job as a scribe on hold for a few weeks and needed to get back to his clients. Meanwhile, the disciples did as Jesus requested. Peter and John and their brothers sold the boats and fishing equipment they owned. Disciples who owned houses in Capernaum and its environs sold them and moved their families to Jerusalem.

On the day that Jesus had appointed, forty days after his resurrection, the disciples assembled on the summit of the Mount of Olives. Lazarus traveled from Bethany to join them. At noon, just as he promised, Jesus appeared. He spent the next few hours reiterating what his mission on earth had accomplished and what their roles would be going forward. They would receive the Spirit and be equipped to spread the good news of salvation. Jesus also reminded them that they would be persecuted unfairly. Many of them would die for proclaiming him as the Savior. But their efforts would not be in vain. The message that they preached would endure. When the entire world heard that message, he would come again.

When Jesus finished speaking, Simon inquired, "Lord, I understand now that you came to save us from our sins and not, as I had mistakenly thought, to restore independence to

Israel. But since you know all things, will the Jews someday be free of Rome?"

Jesus answered, "Simon, Rome will continue to be a thorn in the side of the Jews throughout your lifetime. However, they will continue to thrive as a people long after the Roman empire is gone. It is your responsibility, and that of your fellow believers, to reach out to the Jews and the Gentiles to make them all my disciples. Baptize them in the name of the Father, Son, and Holy Spirit for the forgiveness of sins which was earned by me on the cross. And remember, I am always with you."

After he said this, Jesus was lifted off the ground and up into the air. He continued to ascend until he disappeared into a cloud. The men craned their necks upward, straining for one last glimpse of their teacher and friend.

To their amazement, two angels dressed in white appeared next to them. One of the angels asked, "Why are you looking up into the sky? Jesus told you that he was leaving you to go to his Father in heaven. But be assured you that he will come again one day to take you into his kingdom. Now go to Jerusalem and wait for the Holy Spirit, as Jesus told you to do."

The angels disappeared, leaving the men speechless. Peter finally broke the silence. "We have our marching orders. It's time for us to begin the work that Jesus commanded us to do. Let's listen to the angel and get back to Jerusalem to await the coming of the Spirit."

Chapter Ten

THE SPIRIT

LAZARUS DIDN'T RETURN to Bethany after Jesus' ascension. Instead, he went with the disciples to Jerusalem, where he stayed with Nicodemus. No one knew when the Holy Spirit would appear, and Lazarus wanted to be there when it happened. In order to prepare for the Spirit's arrival, the disciples gathered regularly with over one hundred fellow believers to pray, sing hymns, and share their recollections of Jesus. They met in the building where Jesus and his disciples had eaten the Passover meal. Demetrius, the owner, had become a believer.

During this time, the disciples took care of an important administrative matter. Jesus had recruited twelve disciples, a significant number in Jewish tradition. Seventeen centuries before, the patriarch Jacob had twelve sons whose ancestors formed twelve tribes that divided the promised land into twelve distinct regions. For Jews the number twelve also denoted the power and authority of God. When Judas betrayed Jesus and later hanged himself, the disciples were one short of this important number. They decided to fix this omission.

The eleven disciples determined that a candidate must have been an eyewitness to Jesus' teachings and miracles throughout his three-year ministry. Further, he must have been an eyewitness of Jesus' death and his resurrected body.

Simon proposed that Lazarus be chosen to fill the vacancy. Lazarus thanked his friend for the nomination but reminded the group that he didn't fit the first criterion. He hadn't met Jesus until a year before his crucifixion, which was already two years into his ministry.

Two men were discovered who met both requirements. Their names were Justus and Matthias. The eleven disciples prayed for guidance in making the correct choice. Each man's name was written on a separate stone. The two stones were placed in a clay jar, which was shaken until one of them fell out. The name on the stone that emerged from the jar was Matthias. The disciples praised God for giving them another faithful worker for Jesus.

Ten days after Jesus ascended into heaven, over one hundred of his followers including Lazarus assembled at Demetrius' warehouse to celebrate Shavuot, also known to the Jews as the Feast of Weeks. The Greek name for this special day was Pentecost. It marked the end of the spring barley harvest and the beginning of the wheat harvest and happened to be one of the three special days requiring yearly pilgrimage to Jerusalem. Jews from all over the world were in Jerusalem that morning.

All at once, everyone in the building heard a loud noise coming from above them. It sounded like a powerful wind swirling through the room. All eyes looked up to see what was causing the commotion. They saw tongues of flame floating through the air like burning embers carried by a strong breeze. As the believers stood watching, their mouths wide open in surprise, the flames settled on each person's head. "It is the Spirit of God that Jesus promised us!" exclaimed Peter.

The sound of the wind was so pronounced that it was heard throughout Jerusalem. Soon the street in front of the building was filled by curious onlookers trying to pinpoint the source of the sound. Inside the building, Lazarus was experiencing a spiritual transformation. It was as if his eyes had been opened. Jesus had promised that someday he would understand everything Jesus told him. That day had come. Lazarus no longer had to fear God's anger. God did love him enough to send Jesus to pay the price for his sins. Jesus was the one and only sacrifice necessary for forgiveness. A broad smile stretched across Lazarus' face.

The realization that he was acceptable to God by relying only on Jesus was so overwhelming that Lazarus couldn't keep it to himself. The others in the room were obviously affected in a similar way. Prompted by the Spirit, Lazarus and the other believers exited the building and mixed with the crowd that had gathered there. Without hesitation or fear, they witnessed to everyone they saw about the crucified and risen Jesus.

The number of bystanders grew larger by the minute, filling the street to capacity. It became impossible for the believers to individually address every member of the crowd. Seeing the need to coordinate their efforts, Peter went back into the building to a second-floor balcony and addressed the crowd below. "Fellow Jews, listen to me. I have something important to tell you. Please hear me out."

Peter gestured for quiet, and soon the entire crowd grew silent. "The loud sound you heard earlier was the Spirit of God. The Spirit descended on the followers of Jesus who were praying and praising God inside. We want to share with you what God's Spirit has revealed to us."

Someone in the crowd shouted, "I'm a Jew visiting from Syria. Our country borders on Galilee. I can tell by your accent that you are Galilean just as some of the others with you are. How are you able to communicate with me in my Syrian tongue?"

Another man jeered, "I think all of these Galileans have been drinking too much wine this morning. They're slurring their words, and we only think we understand them." The crowd laughed for a moment but became silent again as Peter resumed speaking.

"Friends and fellow Jews, the men and women you see before you are not drunk. They are filled with the Holy Spirit. Many of us who are speaking to you are Galileans. Few of us know any languages other than Hebrew, Aramaic, and Greek. The fact that you hear us in your own country's tongue is not something for which we can take credit. Rather, we have received the Holy Spirit who God promised through the Prophet Joel when he said:

> *'In the last days, God says, I will pour out my Spirit on all people. Your sons and daughters will prophesy, your young men will see visions, your old men will dream dreams. Even on my servants, both men and women, I will pour out my Spirit in those days, and they will prophesy. I will show wonders in the heavens above and signs on the earth below, blood and fire and billows of smoke. The sun will be turned to darkness and the moon to blood before the coming of the great and glorious day of the Lord. And everyone who calls on the name of the Lord will be saved.'*[8]

The crowd strained to listen as Peter continued. "The same Spirit of God who allows you to hear us in your own language has given us the courage and ability to tell you about Jesus of Nazareth. He was a teacher and miracle worker sent by God. Only a few weeks ago, the Sanhedrin sentenced Jesus to death on a cross even though he was completely innocent of any wrongdoing. You, the Jewish people, approved this

---

8   Acts 2:17–21(NIV)

travesty of justice. Jesus willingly went to the cross so that sinners like you and I could be forgiven. God, his Father, raised Jesus from the dead three days later. Jesus showed his risen self to many of us before ascending bodily to heaven. Now he is reigning in his kingdom in heaven much like King David did here on earth many years ago. Jesus is the Messiah promised to our forefathers."

Many in the crowd believed what Peter had told them. One of them shouted, "What can we do to be part of Jesus' kingdom?"

"You need to confess your sins, turn away from them, and be baptized," replied Peter. "You will receive the Spirit, and your sins will be forgiven."

"What is keeping us from being baptized?" shouted several people in the crowd.

"Nothing, if you believe that Jesus is the Messiah whom God raised from the dead," replied Peter.

"But there are so many of us," shouted another. "Where will you find enough water to baptize everyone?

"God will provide," Peter replied. "If Jesus was able to feed five thousand men and their families with only five fish and two loaves of bread, he can provide a way to baptize all who request it. Baptism is more essential to your well-being than food."

Peter paused, bowed his head, and prayed for guidance. A moment later, he looked back at the crowd below. "All those who believe, come with me to the Pool of Siloam to be baptized."

After hearing Peter's invitation, many in the crowd made their way to the southernmost corner of the city. The Pool of Siloam was a huge man-made rectangular basin of water used for ritual washing prior to going to the temple. It had been built eight hundred years earlier by King Hezekiah to make Jerusalem less vulnerable to siege by potential attackers. The pool collected water through an underground tunnel from a spring outside the city.

Upon arriving at the pool, the disciples walked down several rows of stone stairs leading to the water. Those wishing to be baptized were organized into several lines. They took turns being baptized by the disciples in the name of the Father, Son, and Holy Spirit, just as Jesus had told them to do.

Word spread throughout the city that something special was happening at the Pool of Siloam. All afternoon and into the early evening, the disciples baptized everyone who requested it. By the end of the day, it was estimated that about three thousand new believers had been baptized.

That night Jesus' followers returned to Demetrius' warehouse. They gave thanks to God for the spiritual enlightenment they had been given and for the number of new believers that the Spirit had brought to faith.

Lazarus recalled Jesus' command to teach and baptize throughout the entire world. Many of the new converts had come to Jerusalem from distant corners of the Roman Empire to observe the Feast of Weeks. Undoubtedly, they would return to their homes with the good news of the Messiah's coming. All in all, Pentecost had been an excellent start toward fulfilling what Jesus had told them to do.

Although he continued to live and work in Bethany, Lazarus remained heavily involved in the Jerusalem community of believers. He frequently made the two-mile trip to Jerusalem to worship and participate in fellowship with them. Each time he returned to Jerusalem, Lazarus met believers he had not known before. The increase in numbers was boosted by miracles the disciples performed in Jesus' name. Word of these extraordinary acts spread throughout Jerusalem and the surrounding countryside. People from all over the region came to the disciples to be healed.

The disciples taught at the temple every day, just as Jesus had done when he was in Jerusalem. The crowds grew so large that they spilled over from Solomon's Portico into the Court of Gentiles. In the evenings, believers met together in each other's homes, where they praised God and ate together while remembering the sacrifice made for them by Jesus of his body and blood.

During his visits to Jerusalem, Lazarus noticed a favorable change in behavior taking place among his fellow believers. Almost without exception, they were sharing what they had with each other without regard to wealth or social status. The faithful sold their possessions and used the proceeds to help support those in need. Their enthusiasm was genuine and contagious.

But in spite of the unity and goodwill exhibited by the believers, Satan was still working to divide them. Inequities in distribution of food and other necessities began to surface. Some welfare recipients were favored over others, particularly on the basis of nationality. Greek-speaking believers complained that they were being shortchanged of their share of food supplies in favor of those who spoke the local Aramaic language.

In order to eliminate these inequities, the disciples chose seven men to administer food distribution and other assistance to those in need. The administrators were commissioned by the disciples and encouraged to do their work in the name of the Lord. Soon the complaints were addressed, and the welfare process became fairer and more efficient.

One morning Lazarus traveled from Bethany to meet with his friend Simon. They had arranged to meet at John Mark's house. Lazarus was anxious to learn what had taken place since the last time he was in Jerusalem. Peter answered the door. "Good morning, Lazarus," he greeted. "I was expecting someone else, but I'm happy to see you. Come in. We were just getting ready to address an issue with one of our fellow believers. You're welcome to stay if you like."

Lazarus was puzzled by Peter's comment. As he entered the room, he saw the rest of the disciples standing there. Lazarus joined Simon at the back of the room. "What's happening?" whispered Lazarus. "I thought we were going to meet alone."

"I'm sorry I didn't have time to let you know. We found out earlier today that a man and his wife sold some property and kept some of the proceeds for themselves instead of donating it all to our cause," replied Simon.

"What's the problem with that? Maybe they needed some of the funds to live on. Or maybe they had debts to pay."

"That isn't the problem. The couple has been telling everyone that they gave everything they made on the sale to God."

At that moment a knock was heard at the door. Once again, Peter answered it. "Good morning, Ananias. We were expecting you. Come in."

Ananias walked into the room and looked around. He smiled timidly as if unsure why he had been invited. The other men in the room nodded to him without expression.

"Ananias," Peter began, "on behalf of all of Jesus' followers, I want to personally thank you for your generous donation. It was a significant gift and will certainly help the less fortunate among us to be fed and have a place to sleep."

Ananias relaxed a bit and smiled broadly. "Yes, my wife and I were glad to sell the property she inherited in order to do the Lord's work."

"Not everyone would have donated all the proceeds. Most of us would have kept some of it back to help support ourselves."

"Well, it wasn't an easy decision. My wife Sapphira and I have material needs too. We prayed about this quite a bit. In the end, we knew it was the right decision to share everything we made from the sale. She should be here soon, so you can thank her in person as well."

Peter looked at him sternly. "Ananias, you have lied not only to us, but you have also lied to God. We already know that you kept a portion of the sale proceeds for yourself. Yet you have been going around boasting about your generosity. Satan has entered your heart, and you need to repent and ask for forgiveness. What do you have to say for yourself?"

Ananias' eyes widened. He opened his mouth as if to speak and then grasped his chest. He fell to the floor in a heap. Peter knelt down and turned him over on his back. He looked for signs of life but found none. "I think he's dead. God bless his soul." Lazarus and the other disciples looked on in disbelief. They hadn't expected Ananias to die in front of them.

A few minutes later there was another knock on the door. "Who is it?" Peter asked.

"My name is Sapphira, wife of Ananias. We were asked to come here and talk to Jesus' disciples."

Peter opened the door and stood in the opening. "Before you come in, I have some sad news for you. Your husband is dead. We asked him to admit that you both had lied to God. We told him that we knew about your scheme to withhold proceeds from the sale of your property and then brag about giving it all to the Lord. We hoped that the two of you would confess your sin, repent, and ask for forgiveness. But Ananias was so shocked by our accusation that he collapsed and died. His body is being buried right now."

Peter moved aside as Sapphira rushed into the house. Her husband wasn't there, but his cloak was lying on the floor. Sapphira turned to Peter and screamed at the top of her lungs, "You killed him!" The veins on her neck were bulging and her face had turned crimson red. Sapphira collapsed on top of her husband's cloak. Peter knelt down and checked for signs of life. There were none. "God has spoken. May he bless her soul," Peter said. Later, the men who had buried Ananias buried his wife's body next to his.

Lazarus was stunned by this example of God's righteous anger. Word of what had happened to Ananias and Saphira spread quickly among the residents of Jerusalem. Some followers of Jesus decided to leave the fellowship. The vast majority remained committed to active participation in the community of believers.

A year after Jesus ascended into heaven, the disciples were teaching and healing in Solomon's Portico. Lazarus was with them. The approach of several Sadducees, accompanied by the captain of the temple guard, was not a cause for concern. Since Jesus' ascension, an informal truce had been observed between his followers and the Sanhedrin. The disciples didn't go out of their way to expose the hypocrisy and self-dealing of the Jewish leaders as Jesus often had done. Instead, they focused on increasing the number of believers. Because they didn't stir up trouble or cause major controversy, the Sanhedrin allowed the new sect to operate with little interference.

This day, however, the captain declared that Peter and John were under arrest. One of the Sadducees explained the charges against them. "We were here earlier today and heard you spreading falsehoods that we can no longer tolerate. First of all, there is no life after death. Therefore, Jesus did not rise from the dead. His body was stolen from the grave by you and your friends. Secondly, Jewish leadership did not kill Jesus. The Romans did. Because of the lies you are telling, we received orders from the high priest to bring you before the Sanhedrin. Since it is late, you are going to spend the night in jail and can plead your case in the morning."

The next day around noon, Lazarus and the remaining disciples could be found teaching at the temple in spite of the arrest of Peter and John the day before. Since receiving the Spirit at Pentecost, they had become fearless witnesses for Jesus. Lazarus looked up and saw Peter and John walking toward them, smiling broadly.

"God is good," exclaimed Peter. "We were released by the Sanhedrin a few minutes ago."

"We have been praying for your safety and quick release from jail. Thank God that our prayers were answered," Peter's brother Andrew said with a sigh of relief. "What happened to you after your arrest?"

"John and I spent a quiet night in jail," replied Peter. "It was uneventful. We prayed for God's will to be done and fell asleep. This morning we were taken to the Sanhedrin meeting hall in the temple. Caiaphas repeated the accusations made by the Sadducees yesterday and asked us to explain ourselves."

John continued, "Peter did most of the talking. He gave personal testimony that Jesus was raised from the dead. He also held the Jewish leaders accountable for crucifying Jesus. This was exactly what we had been accused of doing, so I thought the worst at that point. However, we were sent out of the room so the Sanhedrin could talk privately. I'm not sure what they discussed, but after we were brought back in to the room, Caiaphas simply warned us never to speak of Jesus again. Peter told Caiaphas that we couldn't keep quiet because we were teaching the truth. They let us go anyway. I think they were afraid of the public's reaction if they harmed us or put us in prison."

The believers gave thanks that Peter and John were safe. The Spirit continued to strengthen their faith and confidence as they shared the good news with all who would listen to their message.

In spite of the warning from Caiaphas, the disciples continued to boldly teach and perform miracles in Jesus' name. Peter had become the predominant spokesman within the group of disciples. Moved by the Spirit, he spoke passionately to his Jewish audiences. "Jesus is the promised Messiah who came to save all people, both Jews and Gentiles, from their sins through his suffering and death. Your leaders crucified him but God raised him from the dead. He has gone to his Father in heaven but will return to take all who believe in him to live with him eternally." The same group of Sadducees who instigated the arrest of Peter and John two weeks earlier were in attendance. After hearing him preach, they left immediately to complain to the high priest.

"This is the last straw!" Caiaphas shouted in a rage. "I told them not to speak of Jesus' resurrection or our involvement in his death and they continued to do so. They are discrediting us with the people, just like Jesus did. Not only that, but they persist in claiming that Jesus rose from the dead after we went to great lengths to convince everyone that his body was stolen. Find the captain of the temple guard and have him arrest all of the men who call themselves disciples of Jesus. Jail them overnight, and we will have the full Sanhedrin deal with them tomorrow."

One of the Sadducees spoke up. "Caiaphas, there is someone else who is actively teaching the same message as the disciples. His name is Lazarus. He is the one that Jesus allegedly raised from the dead."

"Didn't we issue a warrant for his arrest?" asked Caiaphas. "If Lazarus is with them, throw him in jail as well."

The next morning the Sanhedrin assembled at their meeting hall in the temple. They ordered the captain of the guard to bring in the prisoners to be interrogated. After a lengthy wait, the captain returned to the meeting room alone. "I went to the jail and found the guards in a state of panic," he confessed. "When they checked on the prisoners earlier this morning, the cell doors were locked but the cells were empty. I came back here immediately to let you know. My men are looking for them right now. So far no one can figure out how they escaped."

At that moment, one of the guards on duty at the Temple Mount entered the room through the open door. "High priest and members of the Sanhedrin, I am sorry to interrupt. But there is something I need to tell the captain in private."

"What is it?" asked Caiaphas. "You can tell all of us."

The guard replied cautiously, "I was making my rounds at the temple a few minutes ago and observed the usual group of Jesus' followers congregating at Solomon's Portico. I noticed that the men speaking to the crowd were the same ones we arrested and jailed yesterday. I came here to inform the captain."

"Bring them to us," demanded Caiaphas. "We need to teach these men a lesson."

On the way to Solomon's Portico, the captain enlisted several other temple guards to assist him. They placed Lazarus and the disciples under arrest and brought them back to the meeting hall. The high priest was sitting at the head of a large table in the middle of the room. Lazarus and the disciples were ordered to stand facing the high priest.

"Aren't you concerned for your own well-being?" asked Caiaphas. "In spite of my warning not long ago, you continue to disparage me and the entire Sanhedrin. Your rhetoric is filled with falsehoods. The most egregious lie was that Jesus became alive after being crucified. Speaking for all of the Sadducees here, there is no resurrection. Neither Jesus nor anyone else can come back to life. There is nothing in the Torah that says there is life after death. How can you contradict the Torah?"

The disciples stood silent for a moment until Simon pointed to his friend Lazarus and said, "With all due respect to your office as high priest, there is nothing in the Torah that rules out life after death either. All I can say is that we witnessed Jesus resurrect this man, Lazarus, after he was dead in the grave four days. As you can see, he is standing here alive and well."

The high priest responded, "The Sanhedrin heard the rumors concerning Lazarus. However, we believe they are a complete fabrication. You have no proof that he was ever dead. It would be easy for you and your friends to stage a burial so that Jesus could appear to resurrect him."

Peter interjected, "Whatever you think about Lazarus, you can't possibly deny that Jesus rose from the dead. Several members of the Sanhedrin saw him dying on the cross. The Roman soldiers who took him down declared him dead. After he was raised from the dead, all of us saw him alive. Before he ascended to heaven, Jesus appeared to more than five hundred people at the same time. They and many others are eyewitnesses that Jesus is risen."

Caiaphas responded angrily, "You are lying! We know that you and the rest of the disciples took Jesus' body and buried it elsewhere. The soldiers guarding his tomb have sworn under oath that you stole the body while they were asleep. Everyone in Jerusalem has heard their testimony. No one wants to listen to your lies any more. I don't know how you escaped from jail last night, but since you insist on spouting this blasphemy, and we can't convince you to stop, I recommend that you meet the same fate as your dead rabbi Jesus."

After hearing this threat to the lives of the disciples and his friend Lazarus, Nicodemus rose to speak to his Sanhedrin colleagues. "With all due respect to the office of high priest, before we take drastic action based solely on emotion, why don't we discuss this among ourselves before deciding what to do? You might remember how difficult it was to get Pilate to authorize the crucifixion of Jesus. We need to approach this matter with logic and not just anger."

Numerous heads nodded in agreement. Caiaphas, seeing that the majority of the Sanhedrin agreed with Nicodemus, ordered the captain to take Lazarus and the disciples out of the room. It quickly became apparent that the Sanhedrin members were divided into two factions, neither of which supported the death sentence. The Sadducees, who did not accept the concept of life after death, wanted to see Lazarus and the disciples punished severely and jailed for an extended period. The Pharisees, believers in resurrection of the body and the afterlife, wanted them reprimanded and released.

A number of passionate arguments were presented by both sides. Finally, the well-respected Pharisee Gamaliel rose to speak. "Gentlemen, you might recall that one year ago we had a similar discussion. At that time, soon after Jesus was crucified, we decided not to persecute his supporters. We felt that his small band of followers would simply disappear without their leader. We reasoned that they would return to their homes in Galilee and not bother us again. Obviously, this didn't turn out as we hoped. The disciples remained in Jerusalem and now there are thousands who call themselves believers.

"Our esteemed high priest now suggests that we adopt the same strategy that we followed with Jesus. In that case, we eliminated the leader, but it only served to make his supporters bolder. We need to learn a lesson from our previous mistake. We can't fight God and win. If Jesus was truly sent by God, there is nothing we can do to stop this movement.

If it isn't of God, it will fail. We need to let God's will run its course even if it takes longer than we expected. Killing his disciples will solve nothing and create more problems than we can imagine. Therefore, I propose that we continue the same hands-off strategy with Jesus' followers that we have followed over the past year."

By the time Gamaliel finished speaking, Caiaphas had calmed down. "Even though I seldom agree with Pharisees, your argument has persuaded me not to pursue a death sentence for these men. Do you agree? If so, indicate by a show of hands." A sigh of relief could be heard throughout the room. Seventy members raised their hands in agreement.

When Lazarus and the disciples returned to the meeting room, Caiaphas ordered them to refrain from teaching that Jesus is the Messiah. They were told not to promote their baseless theories regarding resurrection and life after death. To reinforce the gravity of his orders, the high priest commanded the guards to return the men to jail, where they would be whipped and then released.

After recovering from their wounds, Lazarus and the disciples returned to the Temple Mount praising God for allowing them to be beaten for their faith. Every day they continued to teach at Solomon's Portico, and new believers were regularly brought into the fold.

The second year after Jesus' ascension started peaceably between Jesus' followers and the Sanhedrin. However, not everyone was willing to honor the decision that the Sanhedrin had reached. A core group of ultraconservative Jews emerged who were fanatical about preserving Jewish law and tradition. They had no tolerance for any viewpoint that would conflict with the teachings of the Torah. In their opinion, the actions and words of Jesus' followers were a direct threat to their Jewish heritage. They concluded that the growing horde of believers should be crushed and eliminated. In the toxic atmosphere of increasing intolerance and hatred, a small spark could ignite a raging fire of persecution.

A young man named Stephen had been chosen to be one of several welfare administrators in the Jerusalem congregation. In that role, he was responsible for feeding and clothing the poor and caring for the sick and elderly. In addition to his duties as an administrator, Stephen was an effective evangelist. A number of Jewish priests came to faith because of him. Stephen was the only man outside of the twelve disciples given the power by God to heal and do other miracles.

Lazarus was impressed with the spiritual gifts that God had given Stephen. He made it a point to befriend the younger man and treated him like a younger brother. However, Stephen's increasing notoriety as an effective witness for Christ made him a target for persecution. One day while he was teaching on a street corner in Jerusalem, a group of extremist Jews confronted him. They accused Stephen of lying in order to subvert the Jewish religion. In his defense, Stephen used the words of Jewish prophets to show that Jesus was indeed the Messiah. Realizing that they were failing in their efforts to discredit Stephen in front of the crowd, the radical Jews walked away in frustration, vowing to get even with him.

At this time, Lazarus was in Jerusalem staying at Nicodemus' house. The evening after Stephen's confrontation on the street corner, Lazarus and Nicodemus were having dinner. "I need to tell you about something that happened at the Sanhedrin meeting this morning," said Nicodemus. "A delegation of reactionary Jews asked to be recognized, and Caiaphas allowed them to speak. Their spokesman was a man named Saul. He identified himself as a former student of Gamaliel, one of our fellow Pharisees. He works as a tentmaker in Tarsus."

"I've never heard of him," said Lazarus. "I wonder what he's doing here all the way from Tarsus."

"I think this group of extremists originated there," remarked Nicodemus. "Saul told us that he represents Jewish patriots who are extremely concerned about the false teachings of Jesus' followers. In particular, they accused a man named Stephen of perverting Judaism. I believe you told me earlier that you have taken a special interest in Stephen."

"Yes. He is a fine young man who has been a great contributor to our cause. Why have they chosen to single him out?"

"I'm not exactly sure. Maybe they want to make an example of one of the believers, and Stephen caught their eye because of his success in converting new believers."

"What is this man Saul proposing to do?"

"The extremists want the Sanhedrin to try Stephen for crimes against the Jewish religion. They want the authority to kill him."

"That's outrageous. He hasn't done anything wrong. Didn't you tell me after we were all arrested that Gamaliel convinced Caiaphas to leave us alone? Things have been going well since then. What's happened to change that decision?"

"Unfortunately, the Sanhedrin has been influenced by the increasing fanaticism of Saul and his cohorts. Saul argues that Jesus couldn't have been the Messiah because he died without restoring Jewish independence. He claims that followers of Jesus are servants of the devil and need to be stopped, beginning with the death of Stephen."

"If Saul was a student of Gamaliel at one time, didn't Gamaliel have anything to say about this?"

"Yes. He disagreed with his former student. Gamaliel repeated the argument he made in the past. If the Jesus movement is from God, it will succeed no matter what anyone does to stop it. Gamaliel advised restraint once again."

"What was the decision?"

"Caiaphas wants Stephen to appear before the Sanhedrin tomorrow morning at our regular meeting. He is going to send the captain of the temple guard to escort Stephen to the meeting hall. I don't believe Caiaphas supports the death sentence, but he might be intimidated by pressure from Saul and his group."

"I need to represent Stephen at the meeting," said Lazarus. "As a scribe, I've been legal counsel for many people who were falsely accused. I know Stephen is innocent of any crime. I have to help my friend in any way I can."

After dinner, Lazarus paid a visit to Stephen's home. He listened intently while Lazarus told him about the Sanhedrin's plans to question him and gratefully agreed to have Lazarus represent him.

Early the next morning, the captain of the guard and his men went to Stephen's home and brought him to the Sanhedrin meeting hall where all the members had gathered. He was directed to stand in front of Caiaphas. A contingent of Jewish extremists led by Saul stood on one side of the room and Lazarus stood on the other, ready to step in if circumstances required his legal expertise. The scene reminded Lazarus of Jesus' trial the night before he was crucified.

Caiaphas spoke first. "Yesterday we heard from a group of Jews who claim that the followers of Jesus are corrupting Jewish law and tradition by deceiving Jews with their lies. Stephen, who stands before us now, is accused of committing these crimes, which his accusers say are deserving of death."

Caiaphas looked directly at Stephen. "You have heard the accusations against you. What do you have to say on your behalf? Why shouldn't the Sanhedrin believe the claims of your accusers?"

All eyes in the room focused on Stephen. He acknowledged the members of the Sanhedrin and then turned to face the high priest. Stephen stood erect and appeared calm and fearless. Lazarus watched his protégé with pride. The Sanhedrin would not have expected such composure from a young man whose fate was in their hands.

Stephen began speaking, and the room grew silent. He began by recounting Jewish history from Abraham to King Solomon. He emphasized the social, political, and religious progress made by the Jews over the years even though there had been several setbacks. Lazarus approved of Stephen's strategy. His young friend was identifying with his Jewish heritage.

Suddenly, without giving Lazarus any time to react, Stephen changed tactics, switching from defense to offense. His facial expression changed from calmness to anger. "You are just like your ancestors. They killed the prophets who told them to repent. You have ears but do not hear. You think more of yourselves than the God you claim to obey. God sent his Son, Jesus, who made himself known to you by his teaching and his miracles. But you were too stubborn to listen. Instead, you killed him. You are guilty in the eyes of God."

Shocked by this sudden tirade, the high priest pointed his finger at Stephen and shouted, "Enough from you! We don't need any other testimony! You have shown yourself to be an enemy of the Jewish nation and deserving of capital punishment. You are a danger to every Jew in Jerusalem. We don't have time to wait for permission from Pilate as we did for Jesus. If we get into trouble for this, so be it. Saul, I give you and your men authority to take this man and put him to death."

The room erupted in chaos. Everyone was shouting. Seeing an opportunity to intervene, Lazarus ran to Stephen's side, waved his arms, and shouted at the top of his lungs, "Stop this illegal process! You can't do this under Jewish law." The bedlam gradually subsided as Lazarus continued to wave his arms and ask for quiet.

"Who are you and why are you here?" asked Caiaphas.

"My name is Lazarus," he answered. "You might remember me. A year ago I was arrested along with Jesus' disciples.

We were jailed and beaten. Peter introduced me as the man whom Jesus raised from the dead. I am here today to represent Stephen as his legal counsel."

Caiaphas glared at Lazarus. "Yes, I remember you now. I should have you arrested again, but I will give you one minute to speak."

"Members of the Sanhedrin," Lazarus began, "you have not given this man a fair hearing. He has shown you his depth of knowledge of Jewish history. No one but an educated, well-bred Jew would know those facts. Unfortunately, he has also offended you by accusing you of killing Jesus. I offer no defense for that behavior except that this young man is extremely passionate in his love for Jesus. In any case, however, you have neglected to follow proper procedure. The law requires a two-thirds vote for the Sanhedrin to sentence a man to death. Up to this point, there has been no such vote."

Caiaphas replied, "Passion is no defense for what your client said. However, you are correct concerning the law. Therefore, I will call for a vote of the Sanhedrin. All in favor of giving Saul and his men authority to execute Stephen say yes." The response was loud and immediate as the vast majority of members voted affirmatively.

Caiaphas continued, "All who are opposed, say no." A few voices were heard including that of Nicodemus, Joseph, Gamaliel, and several other Pharisees.

"The vote is nearly unanimous," said Caiaphas. "Saul, you and your men are hereby authorized to put this man to death."

Stephen realized that his life on earth was almost over. He looked upward and said, "I see the Lord Jesus, sitting at the right hand of his Father in heaven." Angered by his words, Saul and his men dragged Stephen out of the meeting room, out of the East Gate of the city, and into the Kidron Valley. While Saul watched in approval and Lazarus watched in horror, Saul's men picked up large stones and began pelting Stephen. Stephen raised his hands over his head to deflect the blows, but to no avail. As stone after stone slammed into his body, Stephen's arms dropped to his side. He fell to his knees and cried out, "Jesus, take me to be with you. Lord, forgive these men for what they have done." A few moments later he was dead. Later in the day, Lazarus, Simon, and several of the other disciples retrieved Stephen's body and buried it.

Chapter Eleven

SECOND DEATH

THE STONING OF Stephen marked the beginning of an intense period of persecution against the followers of Jesus. The Sanhedrin gave its blessing to the extremist Jews led by Saul to eradicate what they called a threat to the Jewish religion. This decision reversed the prior policy of tolerance advocated by Saul's former teacher, Gamaliel.

Initially, Saul and his men arrested and imprisoned believers by raiding worship services and other gatherings held by Jesus' followers. Undeterred, the believers went underground and conducted their activities in secret locations around Jerusalem. In response, Saul began infiltrating the community of believers with his own men. In spite of cautionary steps taken to avoid this trap, some extremist Jews were able to gain membership.

This subterfuge proved to be a useful way to identify believers. Once the infiltrators determined when and where the followers of Jesus were meeting, they notified Saul, who sent men to arrest them. The believers were put in prison and beaten until they divulged the identities and locations of fellow believers.

In a matter of months, hundreds of Jesus' followers were arrested. Fearing for their lives, many believers left Jerusalem seeking safety elsewhere. Similar to what had occurred at Pentecost, this dispersion helped spread the movement throughout Asia Minor and even as far as Rome. For believers who remained in the area, the persecution intensified as days and months passed.

Tobias heard the sound of hoofbeats outside the Bethany synagogue. It was nearly noon, and his students were preparing to go home for the day. Since horseback riders were relatively rare in Bethany, he told the children to sit quietly while he went outside to investigate. Shielding his eyes in the bright sun, Tobias could make out the figures of several men dismounting their horses and moving toward him. The man apparently in charge was short and stocky with a bowlegged gait. His face featured a prominent nose and eyebrows that met in the middle of his forehead. He was almost completely bald with only a thin hairline ringing his ears and the back of his head.

"Is your name Tobias?" the man asked.

"Yes, it is. How can I help you? Do you need feed or water for your horses?"

"Our horses are fine, but I could certainly use your help. My name is Saul. I'm looking for a man who lives here in Bethany by the name of Lazarus. My men and I have been commissioned by the Sanhedrin to arrest him for crimes against the Jewish nation. We heard that you have been the ruler of the local synagogue for many years. As a longtime resident of Bethany, you probably know everyone in the village."

"Yes, I know Lazarus. He was a student of mine a long time ago. Would you mind telling me what he has done to justify his arrest?"

"He is a leader of the movement promoting the teachings of a rabbi named Jesus, who was executed for crimes that included sedition and blasphemy. We need your help finding him. If we can locate Lazarus, we will not bother the rest of your village."

Tobias paused for a moment to think. "I can tell you where his place of business is located," he replied. "He is a scribe, and his office is in the business district. Just follow this road to the middle of town. There is a sign in front of his building that you can't miss."

"Thank you, Tobias. May God bless you for your cooperation."

As soon as Saul disappeared down the hill, Tobias hurried back into the synagogue. He motioned to one of his older students and told the boy, "I need you to run to Lazarus' house right now. This morning he told me he would be there all day. Tell him to come here immediately. Tell him that a man named Saul is in Bethany looking for him and that he needs to be careful on his way here. Go as fast as you can and don't tell anyone, even your parents, what you have done."

After the boy left, Tobias dismissed the rest of his students. He had to find a place to hide Lazarus and do it quickly. "The best place to conceal him would be the synagogue itself," Tobias thought. "This is a place of refuge. Even an overzealous reactionary like Saul wouldn't try to forcibly remove a fellow Jew from the house of God."

It wasn't long before Tobias spotted Lazarus coming up the hill toward the synagogue. Following closely behind him were his sisters. Tobias motioned for them to hurry. "You must hide immediately. That madman Saul is here to arrest you."

Lazarus replied, "Thank you for the warning. I've known for a long time that I'm in danger. But I'm more afraid of what Saul might do to my sisters, so I brought them with me. I wouldn't put it past him to use my family in order to get to me."

"I've been thinking about the best place for you to hide," said Tobias. "I believe it might be right here in the synagogue. Actually, I mean on top of the synagogue. There's a ladder at the back of the building that reaches up to the edge of the roof. Since the roof is flat with a three-foot high lip, it would be an ideal place for you to keep out of sight until Saul and his men give up looking for you. I don't think they will remain in Bethany for more than a couple of days. I'm sure Saul has more than enough believers in Jerusalem to chase down.

"Once you're on the roof, you can pull up the ladder. From that vantage point you will be able to see Saul and his men coming up the road. I'll provide you with food and blankets. You can use a pottery bowl as a chamber pot. At this time of year, the days are warm and the nights are comfortable, so weather shouldn't be a problem."

"What about my sisters?" Lazarus asked. "They shouldn't be climbing a ladder or living on the roof."

"Saul has no idea what they look like. They can stay at my house until we are sure Saul and his men have left town."

"I like your plan, Tobias. But I also need to consider what happens after Saul leaves. My best option might be to go back to Jerusalem where I can keep a low profile. It would also give me a chance to check in regularly with my friend Nicodemus. As a member of the Sanhedrin, he'll have a fairly good idea of what Saul is planning to do."

A short time after Lazarus settled in on the synagogue roof, the sound of horses' hooves was heard coming up the hill. For the second time that day, Tobias emerged from the synagogue to meet with Saul and his men. Lazarus could clearly overhear their conversation from his position on the roof. "How did your search go?" asked Tobias. "I don't see Lazarus with you. I hope no harm came to him."

"We went to his place of business," replied Saul, "but it was closed and no one was inside. We questioned other shop-keepers nearby and were told that they hadn't seen him all day. One of them gave us directions to Lazarus' house. We went there, and no one was home. His neighbors didn't know where he was, or at least that's what they told us.

"I have a feeling that Lazarus might have been warned in advance about our visit here today. I believe that insurgents have infiltrated the highest levels of Jewish leadership. I'm disappointed that we couldn't locate Lazarus, but he can't hide forever. We have spies all over the region searching for people we have identified as enemies of Israel. There are bounties for information leading to their arrest. If you or anyone in Bethany can help us locate Lazarus or any other of Jesus' followers, they will be rewarded."

"How long do you plan to stay in Bethany?" asked Tobias.

"Actually, we're leaving for Jerusalem right now," replied Saul. "There's still an hour or so of daylight. That should allow us to get back to Jerusalem before dark. I want to thank you for your assistance today. We'll return to arrest Lazarus if the opportunity arises. You can count on that."

Saul mounted his horse, and he and his men followed the road back to Jerusalem. Without looking up toward the roof of the synagogue, Tobias spoke to Lazarus. "I suggest you stay out of sight up there tonight and perhaps even tomorrow. Saul doesn't seem like the kind of man to give up quickly. I wouldn't be surprised if he camps outside Bethany until morning and returns to your house and business. He might have recruited one of our residents to keep an eye out for you. In any case, I will house your sisters here until it's safe for them to return home."

"I appreciate your sound advice and generous offer," responded Lazarus. "I'm convinced that I should leave Bethany and live in Jerusalem until this persecution is over. By staying here, I'm endangering not only myself but my family and friends, including you."

A week after the close call with Saul and his men, Lazarus relocated to Jerusalem. He and Simon shared a rented apartment in the Lower City near the Pool of Siloam. The persecution of Jesus' followers continued to escalate. Saul and his men had exhausted most of their investigative leads in and around Jerusalem. More believers fled the city and traveled north into Syria and Asia Minor. Those who remained in Jerusalem met in secret for worship and fellowship.

One evening Lazarus and Simon and a group of followers met at John Mark's house. They prayed, sang hymns, and read from the Scriptures. Later, they shared a meal in remembrance of Jesus. In spite of the subdued tone of the worship service, the joy of knowing Jesus and his love for them was still evident.

When the service was over, the worshippers left John Mark's house one by one, exiting from the back door in order to avoid attracting attention. Lazarus and Simon were the last to leave. As Lazarus approached the street, he saw the believer who had left before him being accosted by two men. Lazarus quickly ducked back into John Mark's house. "Simon, it appears that a couple of Saul's men have stopped one of our own. We need to help him."

The street appeared deserted except for the apparent confrontation. As they got closer, Lazarus and Simon heard the two men interrogating the believer. "What are you doing out in the street so late at night?" they asked gruffly.

"I was just going to my mother's house. She's ill, and I need to check on her tonight."

"Something tells me you're not telling the truth," said one of the men. "We've watched several other people walk past this intersection tonight. This much foot traffic in the neighborhood is unusual. If you won't tell us why you're really here, we'll have to take you to the prison and interrogate you. You can be sure that we'll get the truth out of you there. Save yourself some grief and tell us right now. Are you a follower of Jesus?"

Before their fellow believer could answer, Lazarus and Simon leaped from the shadows and pounced on the two men, knocking them both to the ground. After a brief struggle, the men surrendered. "To answer your question, we are all followers of Jesus," Lazarus said derisively. "Apparently you are members of the extremist group led by Saul. I have a message for him. He is fighting against God himself, and nothing he can do will destroy this movement. Tell Saul that you heard this from Lazarus, the one Jesus raised from the dead. He will know whom you're talking about."

Lazarus and Simon were awakened by a loud and persistent knock on their apartment door. It was the middle of the night, and they were not expecting any visitors. Imagining the worst, Lazarus assumed it must be Saul's men coming to arrest them. For a moment he regretted making himself known to the thugs he and Simon had beaten up a week earlier. The two men remained silent, waiting for the unknown interloper to go away or identify himself.

"I just arrived from Bethany and have a message for Lazarus," said a voice outside the door. "If you are in there, please answer."

Not sure whether or not to believe what they heard, Lazarus and Simon remained silent. The knocking didn't stop. "My name is Adam. I work for Caleb at the Bethany inn. I have something important to tell Lazarus."

Lazarus opened the door a crack, recognized the man, and motioned for him to come in. "Lazarus, I'm sorry to disturb you at such a late hour," said Adam breathlessly, "but I have some terrible news. Several hours ago a group of men led by a man named Saul came to the inn. They said they were there to arrest your sister Mary. Caleb argued with them for a long time until the argument escalated into violence. One of the men pulled a sword and wounded Caleb severely. They took Mary away. I heard one of them say they were going to Martha's house next. After dressing Caleb's wounds, I ran here to tell you what happened. He was in no shape to travel, so I came by myself."

Lazarus couldn't believe what he had just heard. His worst fear had materialized. Saul was using his sisters to get at him. "I appreciate you coming here right away to tell me. I also appreciate that you took care of Caleb. But I'm really worried about my sisters right now. By any chance, did you hear the men discuss where they were taking Mary and Martha?"

"When they led Mary away, I overheard them say they were taking her and her sister to the public prison in Jerusalem," Adam replied.

"That's where they take people for interrogation," said Simon. "The conditions there are poor, especially for women. We need to do something quickly to help them."

"Obviously they're using my sisters as leverage to force me to give myself up," Lazarus observed. "But before I surrender myself, I'll need some assurances that my sisters will be released. They have done nothing to deserve imprisonment. I need to talk to Nicodemus. He'll know what Saul is planning to do next. Perhaps he can help negotiate their release."

Lazarus thanked Adam for his help and invited him to stay the rest of the night at the apartment. Adam declined the invitation, citing the need to get back to Bethany. He had to make sure that Caleb was recovering from his wounds. He also needed to operate the inn the next morning.

After Adam left, Simon turned to Lazarus. "I have an idea that might free your sisters and keep you from being imprisoned or killed. Why don't we enlist the Zealots to help us break Mary and Martha out of jail?"

"I should have known you would come up with something like that," remarked Lazarus. "Ever since I've known you, even from as early as synagogue school, you've always been overly aggressive. I thought being a disciple of Jesus would have calmed you down, but I can see that didn't happen."

"Actually, I'm very serious about this," Simon responded. "We aren't talking about attacking the Roman garrison. The public prison isn't very secure. It's manned by former temple guards, most of whom would rather be doing something else for a living. The prison was hardly utilized until Saul started jailing believers. Now it's overcrowded. I don't think it would be difficult to break in and release everyone. That way Saul wouldn't know that it was done in order to free your sisters."

"You make it sound so easy," replied Lazarus. "But there are so many ways your plan could go wrong. What if we run into problems and all the prisoners, including my sisters, are killed trying to escape? Even if they do get away safely, where would they go? Saul would use every resource available to recapture them."

"Spoken like the Lazarus I know and love," said Simon. "Ever since we were children, you've been afraid of what might happen. You invent the worst scenario possible, and it always keeps you from moving forward. I admit that my plan would involve risk, but we could definitely pull it off."

Lazarus thought for a moment and said, "You're right about my inhibitions. But sometimes being cautious is a good thing. I'll consider your suggestion, but I want to talk to Nicodemus before I make up my mind on what to do next."

At noon that day, Lazarus went to see Nicodemus at his home. The Sanhedrin usually met in the morning, so Lazarus assumed that he would have the latest news on Saul's activities. Nicodemus invited Lazarus in. "I thought you might come to visit today," said Nicodemus. "This morning I found out that Saul put your sisters in jail last night. I'm so sorry for them and for you."

"That's why I'm here," replied Lazarus. "I need to find out if I can get a guarantee of their release if I turn myself in to Saul. It would also be good to know what his plans are for me and my sisters."

"Saul is required to report his activities to the Sanhedrin. However, he usually tells us after the fact. In this case he didn't tell us about your sisters until after they were jailed. But he did say what he's planning to do with them. You are correct in assuming that he's using Mary and Martha as bait to arrest you. I'm afraid that you won't get any guarantees for their release. Saul is so angry with you that he has made you his number one target. He was incensed at your defense of Stephen, but you really made him angry when you beat up two of his men and taunted him afterward. This morning he asked the Sanhedrin for approval to have you executed."

"What was their decision?"

"The Sanhedrin voted to approve your death. They aren't even going to allow you a trial. As you know, they put a bounty on your head before they crucified Jesus, so this is just a continuation of what they wanted to do earlier. I wish I had better news, but you need to know what's going on."

"Thank you for keeping me informed. I have some decisions to make. I'm more worried about my sisters than I am about myself. It sounds like none of us will emerge unscathed if Saul gets his way."

After meeting with Nicodemus, Lazarus concluded that he had no choice other than to adopt Simon's plan of action. If he turned himself in to Saul without a guarantee of his sisters' safety, he would be killed and they would remain in prison. After Lazarus notified Simon of his decision that evening, a crew of Zealots willing to assist was assembled by the next morning. The Zealots despised the high priest and the Sanhedrin almost as much as they did the Romans. In their eyes, anyone who hindered Jewish independence was an enemy.

The public prison was located near the Hippodrome, southwest of the Temple Mount. Unless chariot races or other major events were being held, the area was relatively quiet. Vaulted openings surrounding the perimeter of the Hippodrome provided Lazarus, Simon, and the Zealots plenty of cover prior to attacking the prison.

The Zealots who volunteered to help knew the layout of the prison well. Most of them had been incarcerated there before. A solitary entrance was located at the front of the one-story building. The doorframe was made of carved stone blocks topped by a large wooden lintel. The door was constructed of thick slabs of wood with a narrow slit at eye level that served as a peephole. The outside walls were built with limestone blocks, smaller versions of the ones used to build the walls of the Temple Mount. Two small windows high up on the front wall provided the only light and ventilation for the front half of the building.

Inside the entrance was a large vestibule used to process prisoners. Two wooden tables sat at the far end of the room. A door at the back wall of the vestibule led into the adjoining cell block. Overcrowded cells lined its walls. The midsection of the cell block was large enough to interrogate and, if necessary, torture prisoners. Hardcore prisoners were shackled to the cell walls. Women were not segregated from men. The entire cell block was dark, filthy, and smelled terrible.

Lazarus and Simon decided to strike that evening. The sky was cloudy, which would obscure any light from the moon. No activities were planned in the Hippodrome that day or the next, so the area around the prison would be deserted.

Before storming the prison, Lazarus needed to make sure that his sisters were actually being held there. For all he knew, Saul might have lied to the Sanhedrin or moved them to another location. In order to make sure, Lazarus asked Mary, John Mark's mother, for help.

Prisons in the Roman Empire were generally not used to house convicted criminals for a long time. Instead, prisons were usually short-term holding areas for the accused awaiting trial. Relatives or friends of the prisoners were expected to provide most of their food and other necessities. Prisoners with no outside help received only basic, inadequate essentials.

That afternoon, Mary took a basket of food to the prison. She asked the guards on duty to give the food to two women named Mary and Martha. When the guards accepted the basket and promised to deliver the food, it confirmed that the sisters were being held there. Mary reported that only three guards were on duty that day.

Just before midnight, Lazarus, Simon and the band of Zealots gathered under the portico that circled the Hippodrome. Light from oil lamps inside the prison leaked out of the two windows and the peephole in the front door. Clouds covered the moon, leaving the ground between the Hippodrome and the prison in complete darkness.

All of the men were armed with swords and daggers. Lazarus hoped they wouldn't have to use any weapons. He said a silent prayer, asking God for a successful rescue of his sisters. At Simon's signal, the men moved forward toward the front of the prison.

One of the Zealots swung a large sledgehammer at the door handle. Lazarus gasped as the door remained firmly in place. He could hear the guards yelling inside, now aware they were under attack. Two more swings shattered the handle and the lock, and the door swung open.

The three guards on duty that night were at the door with swords in hand. The entrance was wide enough for only one attacker at a time, giving the initial advantage to the guards. One of the Zealots charged through the door. His sword fended off the initial blow from one of the guards, but he was cut down by the blade of another. The odds changed quickly as the rest of the attackers ran into the prison. They quickly subdued the guards, killing all three of them. The Zealots had sustained only one casualty.

"Where are the keys?" yelled Simon.

One of the Zealots spotted a key chain strapped to the belt of one of the guards. Turning the dead guard over, he removed the belt and threw the keys to Simon. He tried several keys and finally found the one that opened the door into the cellblock. Simon flung the door open and stopped before entering. It was too dark inside to see anything clearly.

"Bring me one of the oil lamps," ordered Simon. The darkness evaporated and a spontaneous cheer arose from the prisoners as he came through the door. Lazarus followed into the cell block and heard his name called out. He turned to see Mary and Martha, their faces beaming, hugging the bars of their cell.

Simon unlocked the door to their cell, and the sisters raced to embrace their brother. "Lazarus, have you heard any news about Caleb?" asked Mary. "He was trying to protect me when one of Saul's men slashed him with a sword. They dragged me away before I could see if he was still alive."

"The night you were arrested, Adam came from Bethany to tell me what happened. Caleb was hurt badly, but he survived. Adam dressed and bound his wounds before coming to Jerusalem. He returned to Bethany that evening to look after Caleb."

"Thank God he's all right. I've been praying for him constantly since we were separated."

Lazarus reassured his sisters. "You'll be fine. Simon and I will take you to John Mark's home tonight. You will be safe there for a few days. After that, some of our friends will take you to Capernaum in Galilee. Peter has relatives there who will care for you until this persecution dies down. When the time is right, you can return to Bethany."

"Aren't you going with us to Capernaum?" asked Mary. "You're the one in the most danger. I heard Saul say that he put us in prison in order to capture you."

"I can't leave Jerusalem right now," replied Lazarus. "I can be of help to Simon and the others if I stay here. What matters right now is that you both remain safe."

While Lazarus and his sisters were talking, Simon unlocked the other cells and released the remaining prisoners, twenty men in all. Some had been severely beaten during earlier interrogations, but all were able to walk out of their cells without help.

"We need to get out of here before we're discovered," Simon advised the freed men as they all moved into the vestibule. "Tonight you'll need to seek shelter with friends and family. I suggest that you leave Jerusalem as soon as possible. There is an established group of believers in Antioch in Syria who will help you with housing and food if you decide to go there. God be with you all."

At that moment, the front door swung open, and the Zealot who had been standing watch outside the prison burst in. "You need to stay inside," he ordered. "A group of men has surrounded the prison. Because of the darkness, I didn't see them approaching until it was too late. They must have known we were here because they didn't make a sound."

"I was afraid something like this might happen when I proposed rescuing your sisters," said Simon apologetically. "But I thought if we acted quickly, we would have the element of surprise on our side. Unfortunately, it appears that Saul was either watching the prison day and night or had inside information about our plans. We walked right into his trap."

"It isn't your fault," Lazarus replied. "Yours was the only option that might have worked to get my sisters released. We took a chance, but our wager doesn't appear to have paid off."

Just then they heard a shout coming from outside the prison. Lazarus recognized Saul's voice. "Lazarus, I know you're in there. I also know your sisters are with you. Instead of starving you out, which would take a long time, and instead of storming the prison, which would kill many on both sides, I have a proposition for you. If you step outside and give yourself up, I will allow everyone in there with you, including your sisters, to walk away unhurt."

Inside the jail, Lazarus turned to his sisters and then to Simon. "I'm going to do what he says. I need to give myself up. Saul just guaranteed the safety of everyone other than me."

One of the Zealots spoke up. "I'm willing to fight to the death to defend every person in this room. Saul is working with the Sanhedrin, who are nothing more than disloyal Jews who collaborate with the Romans at our expense. Now they're attempting to destroy innocent people whose only crime is to honor the memory of their rabbi." The other Zealots voiced their agreement.

"I appreciate your willingness to give up your lives for us," replied Lazarus. "That's what Jesus did when he died on the cross. But I won't allow you or anyone else to die on my behalf. I'm going out there and give myself up to Saul."

Simon put his hand on Lazarus' shoulder. "As much as I hate to say it, that decision might be the best way to get your sisters out of here safely. Normally, I would have agreed with our Zealot friends to fight our way out of here. But your sisters are your main concern as they are mine. Since you're convinced you need to surrender yourself to Saul, I suggest you go about it a bit differently."

"How could it be done differently?"

"You can't hand yourself over to Saul and hope he'll keep his promise after he arrests you. He needs to allow safe passage for everyone before you give yourself up. I don't trust him a bit. But if we're allowed to go free, I'll take your sisters to John Mark's home and see that they get to Capernaum safely. I will make sure they return to Bethany when it becomes safe again."

"You're a true friend, Simon. But what happens if Saul doesn't keep his word?"

"If he tries to stop us when we leave the prison, the Zealots and I will turn on Saul and his men. Hopefully, in the melee you and your sisters can run away along with the rest of the former prisoners."

One of the men who had been imprisoned spoke up. "I don't know about the others, but I'll fight as well if necessary. Even though I'm unarmed, I can help to keep Saul's men occupied until Lazarus' sisters escape. If every one of us is willing to fight, there will be about thirty of us altogether. I don't know how many men Saul has, but it can't be many more than that." The other former prisoners agreed to fight as well.

"All right, then," said Simon. "Lazarus, you can give Saul your demands. When we walk out the door, the Zealots and I will go out first, followed by the other men. Your sisters will go out last. You stay inside until all of us are safely away or until a fight breaks out. If there is a fight, rush out to your sisters and take them to the home of John Mark."

"Your strategy is fine except for one thing," replied Lazarus. "If it comes to a fight, I'll be there alongside the rest of you. Mary and Martha know the way to John Mark's house. If I attempt to escape with them, I'm sure Saul will send some men to chase me down. That would put my sisters in more jeopardy than if they ran off by themselves."

Lazarus turned to his sisters and embraced them. Mary and Martha were both crying. "I love you both," he said. "You heard what you need to do. Stay with John Mark tonight. Get to Capernaum as soon as you can. If it is God's will, we will see each other there. If God wants to take me to him sooner, then we'll see each other in heaven. Jesus has made sure of that."

Saul's voice boomed from outside the prison. "Lazarus, I've given you enough time to consider my offer. What's your answer? If you fail to respond in the next five minutes, my men and I will come into the prison and take you out forcibly."

Lazarus stepped outside and addressed Saul. "I accept your offer under one condition. Before I surrender myself to you, you must first let everyone else walk away safely and not pursue them. I will give myself up to you after they are all out of sight."

"You have my word," said Saul. "Stay in front of the building so I can see you. Then your sisters and the others can walk away."

Lazarus looked back into the open door and motioned for Simon to lead the procession out of the prison. He and the Zealots left the prison first. Simon embraced Lazarus and offered words of encouragement. "God be with you, my friend. No matter what happens, we will see each other someday. I pledge to take care of your sisters. They have nothing to worry about."

The believers who had been in prison followed next. Mary and Martha were the last ones out the prison door. The sisters cried as they hugged Lazarus. "We love you very much, brother," said Mary. "I pray that Jesus will protect you. We will be together again because of him. God bless you and keep you safe."

Surprisingly, Saul kept his word. His men opened their ranks, creating a gap through which to pass. Simon and the Zealots kept their weapons at the ready, making sure to keep themselves between the sisters and Saul's men. Lazarus breathed a sigh of relief as the entire procession walked through the opening without incident. After getting past Saul's men, they all continued toward the city in the direction of John Mark's home.

Lazarus watched until he couldn't see them any longer. Then he walked toward Saul, who was dismounting from his horse. "Thank you for keeping your word," said Lazarus.

"You were more cooperative than I expected," replied Saul. "This could have gotten very messy. Now it will be easy for me to accomplish what I have been trying to do for a long time. The Sanhedrin has given me authority to execute you, which I plan to do. However, before you die, I want to hear you deny that Jesus is the Messiah. I also want you to admit that Jesus never raised you from the dead and that he didn't rise from the dead either. If you do, I will make sure you die a quick and relatively painless death."

"Then I'm afraid you're going to have to kill me slowly and painfully. I won't lie about what I know is true. I'm not afraid to die because I know I will live forever with Jesus in heaven. He did, in fact, raise me from the dead, and I am one of many witnesses to his resurrection. I saw him ascend into heaven where he sits at the right hand of his Father. Jesus is the Messiah. Nothing you can say or do would make me deny him."

"I'm impressed," said Saul. "I don't hear one ounce of fear in your voice. But then again, you haven't felt any pain yet."

Saul ordered his men to take Lazarus back into the prison. Before he entered the door, Saul gave orders for the majority of his men to remain outside and stand guard in case anyone returned to help Lazarus escape.

Once inside the prison, Saul took Lazarus into the cell block. "This is where we interrogate the prisoners. Invariably, we get them to tell us what we want to know. Now it's your turn to feel the pain inflicted by a few well-placed blows from the whip."

Saul ordered his men to strip off Lazarus' cloak and the tunic beneath it. His back was now bare. One of Saul's men kicked the back of Lazarus' legs, causing him to drop to his knees. Another retrieved a whip that was hanging on the wall. The whip, also called a scourge, had multiple thongs with hard leather tips intended to tear flesh. It slashed across Lazarus' back and buttocks. He screamed in pain. After ten lashes, he could no longer hold himself up in a kneeling position and fell face down onto the floor. Saul ordered the beating to stop.

"Lazarus, are you now ready to deny Jesus? He doesn't seem to be helping you at this point. Will he send down his angels to save you? I don't think so."

Lazarus gasped in pain, "I will never deny him. Even if I die here today, I will be resurrected to live with him forever in heaven. As for you, someday you will regret what you're doing."

"Flog him again," ordered Saul. "Beat him until he's unconscious."

The man with the whip struck Lazarus with another ten lashes. By this time, Lazarus' eyes were closed and he was no longer screaming in pain. Blood was oozing out of his wounds and running off his back. One of Saul's men reached down to check for a pulse. "He's still alive, sir."

"Good. We'll revive him and see if he comes to his senses."

A bucket of water was poured over Lazarus' head. His body shook, and he gasped for breath. He was conscious but barely coherent. Two of the men turned him over onto his back.

"One last time, Lazarus," said Saul. "Will you tell the truth about Jesus? Will you admit that he was a fraud and that you and the rest of his followers fabricated everything about his resurrection and his claims to be God?"

Lazarus narrowly opened one eye and looked up at Saul. "I am telling the truth. Jesus suffered and died so that I could be forgiven. Because of his sacrifice, I am blameless in the sight of God. I pray that someday you'll see the truth so that God can forgive you as well."

"I have nothing to be forgiven for. I'm doing God's will by stopping the lies that you and the others are spreading," countered Saul. "Now you will get your wish to join your precious Jesus in death."

At Saul's signal, another of his men approached Lazarus. He unsheathed his sword and raised it above Lazarus' chest. As the swordsman prepared to complete his task, Lazarus looked at up him and prayed aloud, "Lord, forgive these men who have harmed me." The man stopped his weapon in midair, stunned by the unexpected comment. Before proceeding, the swordsman looked toward Saul as if to provide him a chance to reconsider.

"Go ahead and finish the job," snarled Saul. "If anyone needs forgiveness, it's Lazarus and the other followers of Jesus who have tried to deceive the Jewish people." The swordsman raised his weapon again. Lazarus' body convulsed reflexively as the point of the sword sliced through his chest. The tip of the blade lodged in the dirt floor beneath him.

Barely clinging to life, Lazarus felt as if he were hovering in the air. Below him he watched his attacker step on his chest, pull out the sword, and wipe off the blood with the tunic he had been wearing. He saw Saul, expressionless, turn and walk out of the room as if nothing had happened. Lazarus' heart stopped beating, his lungs expelled their last breath, and darkness enveloped him. Lazarus died for the second and final time.

Lazarus was able to visually identify his surroundings and hear sounds even though he was no longer in his body. What he was experiencing seemed vaguely familiar. He felt indescribable joy and peace. He saw angels and heard them singing and praising God. It seemed as if he had been there before.

"Welcome to your new home, Lazarus," greeted Jesus. "Your soul is now in heaven for eternity." Lazarus hardly recognized the man he had watched ascend into the sky years before. Jesus was dressed in a dazzling white robe. His face shone with a radiance that rivaled that of the sun. Any question about Jesus' identity disappeared when Lazarus saw the wide and welcoming smile that he remembered.

"Jesus, it's wonderful to be here with you. Your divine presence is beyond anything that I could ever have imagined. It was difficult to picture you as the Son of God when we walked and talked with you, even after you rose from the dead. Now there is no doubt."

"I have good news for you, Lazarus. The Day of Judgment is approaching. At that time, your earthly body will be resurrected and be transformed into a glorified body that won't be subject to sickness, pain, aging, or death. Your soul will be united with your body, and you will live eternally in the presence of God."

"That sounds fantastic. But if I'm going to be judged a later time, how can I be sure that I will be allowed to remain in heaven?"

"You haven't brought along a touch of anxiety, have you? It isn't allowed to exist in heaven."

"I wasn't worried, just curious."

"To answer your question, you have already been judged. You have been declared innocent. That is why your soul is here in heaven. There is no waiting period to determine a final verdict. There is no temporary middle ground between heaven and hell in which to await the judgment. Only those who are alive when I return will discover their fate at that time. The Day of Judgment will be a marvelous confirmation of your innocence before God."

"Somehow I don't feel very innocent."

Jesus sighed and continued lovingly. "Do you remember when we first met? I came to your office and offered to help you. What did I tell you then?"

"You told me God loved me more than I knew."

"That's correct, but there was more. Do you remember what else I told you?"

"You told me that my sins wouldn't condemn me because you would be condemned on my behalf. Then you said that when I died I would live again."

"Lazarus, on the day we met did you believe what I told you?"

"You know I didn't. I couldn't wait to get you out of my office. I thought you were deranged. But you also said that someday I would understand who you were and what you wanted to accomplish."

"It took you a long time for you to trust me, didn't it?"

"Yes, it did. But you were very patient. In spite of my reluctance to believe, you held nothing back. You told me multiple times that you were sent to be the perfect sacrifice for the sins of all people. It didn't sink in until I saw you on the cross. Even then I probably didn't fully understand what you had done. It took the Holy Spirit at Pentecost to make everything clear. At that point, I couldn't help telling everyone I met about you. I knew then that you would always be with me, even to the point of death."

"Now, after what we just discussed, do you have any doubts that God has declared you innocent?"

"No, I don't. Just as you said, my sins will not condemn me because you were condemned in my place. I can say with complete confidence that God does love me more than I ever could imagine and much more than I deserve to be loved."

Jesus smiled. "You do understand. I am pleased. Now go and enjoy the place I have prepared for you and all believers."

At that moment, Lazarus recognized the souls of his parents, his wife, and his son approaching. As they reunited in indescribable joy, he thought about his sisters who would someday join them. Soon they would all be together eternally in the presence of their loving God.

DAVID G. FISCHER

DAVID G. FISCHER is a first-time book author and life-long Christian. Thanks to parents who understood the value of Christian education, he attended a Lutheran school from grades K – 8 forming the foundation for a relationship with God that continues to grow to this day. Whatever success he has achieved in life is due to the grace and love that God has shown to him.

After receiving a BA in Psychology from the University of Arizona, David served in the U.S. Air Force during the final years of the Vietnam War. He returned to the UofA to earn a Master of Accounting degree after which he obtained a CPA certification and began a career in banking which lasted over forty years. He is now retired, living in Las Vegas where he serves as treasurer of his church and plays golf several days a week. He is currently working on a sequel to *Lazarus*.